# GUNMETAL LILY

MAFIA WARS

REBECCA ROYCE

# WARNING

**TRIGGER WARNING—This book contains scenes that some readers may find disturbing. This is a dark book and awful things have happened to some of the characters. Although these things are told in a recounting and handled as gently as possible, some readers will want to avoid this book.**

# COPYRIGHT



Gunmetal Lily



Ebook: 978-1-951349-73-8

Print: 978-1-951349-74-5

Cover Art: Maria Spada

Content Editing: Virginia Nelson

Copy Editing: Jennifer Jones at Bookends Editing

Final Proof Editing: Meghan Leigh Daigle of Bookish Dreams Editing

Formatting: Michelle Duke



Published by Rebecca Royce

www.rebeccaroyce.com

Created with Vellum

*For Loxley Savage. Thank you for asking me to be a part of this.*

Dearest Reader,

Thank you for picking up *Gunmetal Lily*. This is a contemporary, dark reverse harem novel that falls within the shared world called *Mafia Wars*. Every book in this series is a stand-alone story written by a different author. This one is mine. Technically, it is the second book in the series. I hope that you've had a chance to read Ivy Fox's amazing book *Binding Rose*, but if you didn't yet, you can still read this one and then go back and read hers!

When you're done with me, check out all the upcoming authors who have contributed to making this amazing series. They are: Ivy Fox, CR Jane, Loxley Savage, Katie Knight, Susanne Valenti, and Caroline Peckham, all so talented, and I'm lucky to be writing with them. We all have different families to write about and you don't need to worry about any backstory from other books. Some characters appear in multiple books, but we have you covered. I promise.

Enjoy this story of men who walk the dark side of life and the women walking with them.

All my best,

RR

# AUTHOR'S NOTE

Hello! I have been to Mexico but not to the places where the action in this book takes place. I hope to visit them someday and have spent a lot of time online reading about them, examining pictures, and reading travel guides. I even read about real estate. In the end, I made up my own places within these locations. Please forgive me if I have gotten any facts or things wrong. It is always my intention to be as true to a place as I can be.

All my best
Rebecca Royce

# PREFACE

Since the dawn of time, waging war on those who have wronged us has been embedded in the very fiber of mankind's true nature. The thirst for vengeance and retribution has always prevailed over turning the other cheek to one's enemies. Creating chaos and bloodshed is preferable to being subjected to vapid dialogues of peaceful negotiation.

None hold this way of life more sacred than made men.

Honor.

Loyalty.

Courage.

These are the codes of conduct of every mafia family.

However, the same cannot be said when dealing with their enemies.

Through recent decades, in the midst of civil evolution, an ancient war was being fought. From both sides of the globe, blood was spilled in the name of honor, while the brutal carnage each family bestowed upon the other was anything but noble. Soldiers, kin, and innocent lives were lost on all sides, and the inevitable extinction of the Mafioso way of life was fast approaching.

In the most unlikely scenarios, six families came together in an undisclosed location to negotiate a peace treaty. As the leaders of the most influential crime families in the world, they recognized that a cease-fire was the only way to guarantee their endurance. Should this attempt fail, then their annihilation was all but inevitable.

The treaty was effectively simple.

Each family would offer up one of their daughters as sacrifice to their enemies. Marriage was the only way to ensure that the families wouldn't retaliate against one another. It would also guarantee that the following successor's bloodline would be forever changed, creating an alliance that would continue through generations to come.

Not all in attendance were happy with the arrangement.

The deep scars gained from years of plight and hatred can't be so easily healed or erased. However, even the cynical and leery knew that this pact was their best chance of survival. Although the uncertainty of the treaty's success was felt by every mob boss there, one by one swore an oath that would bind them to it forever.

And as the words spilled from their lips and the scent of blood hanged in the air, they made sure innocent lives would yet again be deemed collateral damage to their mafia wars—one last time.

Their daughters would have to pay the price for peace.

Whether they wanted to or not.

# PROLOGUE

*Miguel Hernandez*—ten years ago

I looked around the room. A lesser man would be intimidated. In front of me were the heads of every strong mafia family that I'd ever done business with. But they didn't make me nervous. In the end, they needed me more than I needed them. I sent them the product that they used to keep their customers in line, their government in this pockets, and their wallets fat with money.

Without me they had nothing to sell.

Still, I was tired of the bullshit so I'd come here to see if we could put a stop to the in fighting and get back to what mattered—earning money.

"So you want my daughter to go to Boston and marry there and for his daughter," I pointed at Giovanni Moretti. "to come to my home and marries my son Alejandro. That is what I'm understanding?"

Heads nodded and I digested the news around me. There were other deals. Lots of swapping going on. I only cared about this as far as it pertained to me. Daughters were nothing. I had one and I hardly ever thought about her. Who cared what happened to her? Sons were currency, sons made business better. And I had three of them. This would be better if it was a deal for Javier or Francisco to marry the girl but if it had to be Alejandro than it had to be Alejandro. The point was that the money kept flowing.

"And if I do this, then my product doesn't get stopped by any of your men. You don't do business with anyone else. You stop sending people to try to assassinate me or my brother. It stops. We get back to what we do and leave the rest of it alone."

Next to me, my brother shifted in his seat. He always found this sort of thing boring but I wouldn't have anyone else with me. No one could be trusted like family and I hadn't become who I was by trusting the wrong people.

When nods and affirmatives were made around the room I added my own. Alejandro wouldn't like it but his feelings on this didn't matter.

Only the product mattered.

Daughters. Sons. Who cared. "Yes, fine. I'll do it. Send your daughter to me in ten years. Screw me over and the last thing you'll see is the wrong end of my gun."

No one would fuck with me and I wouldn't screw with their deals either. Fine. What was next?

# 1

*Lily*

I had to assume the priest marrying us conducted a legitimate religious service and wasn't just pretending to as some kind of guise which I'd find out was a big joke later. Even though I was familiar with the ceremony, having seen it many times growing up, I couldn't understand a word of the Spanish he spoke right then. He could have been promising me great fortune or insisting that I would produce three chickens and a pig for breakfast every morning. As I stood under the watchful eyes of my family and my future family, I did my best to look serene at the farce that was my wedding.

Unfortunately, there was no laughing at this. It was really happening. Despite the fact it was all happening in Spanish, in a lavish cathedral in the heart of Mexico City, a place I'd arrived only that morning, it was legitimate. At the end of this mess, I would be Mrs. Alejandro Hernandez. I had no choice. I'd been sold ten years ago in the most ridiculous attempt to link together families that I'd ever heard of.

No one had asked any of the women being thrown into this mess if we wanted it. Then again, misogyny was king in our families, filled with bad men and poor decisions. I always knew about our lives—none of it had ever been hidden from me—although I hadn't been told until yesterday that I would be getting married today. I swallowed. I'd been working on one of my grad school classes. *What a joke. Why had my brothers let me apply?*

I blinked and tried to force my attention back to the present. To my fucking wedding. I stared at my groom, Alejandro Hernandez. He wasn't gorgeous. I tended to prefer men who looked like they'd stepped off the runway, and that was why I was constantly getting my heart broken. I didn't look like I'd stepped off one myself most of the time, so it meant that they were really only after me for the wrong reasons.

Alejandro—who would be my husband any moment now—wasn't the type that anyone would put on the cover of a fashion magazine. He was hard looking. His dark hair was combed and neat—which was more than I could say for one of his younger brothers, who was downright haggard looking at the moment—but I imagined it wasn't hard to keep Alejandro's hair that way since it was so short. His eyebrows were big, prominent, and his nose was a little bit too long for his face. Still, he had amazing cheekbones and a chin that could have been sculpted around his full lips.

I'd never have given him a second look before, because he would have been just too much for me. And now—because I was pretty sure they'd just said husband and wife in Spanish—I was married to him. He leaned over and kissed me. I closed my eyes, and the jolt that passed between us made me gasp and open my lids almost as soon as I'd closed them.

*What was that?*

I blinked. For one long second, Alejandro, in his Tom Ford navy tuxedo, looked just as flummoxed as I did. Then the moment passed, and his cool countenance returned. That was okay, I'd seen it. Somewhere inside this man I didn't know, had never met before I walked down the aisle toward him, there were real emotions. He could get caught unaware too. Now, the trouble was that I knew my family, knew my brothers—they could all be great sometimes and absolute nightmares at other times. They were bad men, hands down. They did shitty, unspeakable things. Ruined lives and destroyed people's existences. They were born to do it, and I'd never seen a sign yet to indicate they were changing at all.

This man I'd just married—he and his entire family—they were cut from the same cloth as my own. Maybe worse, even. Or maybe I'd just built a tolerance for what my family did and hadn't yet for my new one.

I'd certainly read about Mexican drug cartels. They were always on the news, the issue of the week sometimes. Drugs. Violence. Sex trafficking. Coyotes bringing people over the border, sometimes literally dropping children from great heights to do so. I shuddered, and Alejandro shot me a look. It was time to walk down the aisle. I'd come down this way a single woman forced to wed and was leaving married to a stranger the same way. I stared at his brothers as we passed them—Francisco, who had barely brushed his hair, and Javier, who kept his head shaved, probably so everyone could see the snake-slash-dragon tattoo that covered half of his left cheek, then continued past his eye and onto his scalp.

If I'd known I was going to be married to this man and become part of his family, I would have studied Spanish. I spoke four languages, so why hadn't anyone insisted that Spanish be one of them? I laughed at my thought, which made my oldest brother, Salvatore, and Miguel Hernandez, Alejandro's father, both throw me looks. My brother's expression seemed full of retribution if I didn't behave, and my father-in-law's spoke of concern that I might be out of my mind.

"Something amusing?" Alejandro asked in a low whisper.

I'd been told he could speak English, and they hadn't lied to me…at least not about that.

"No, nothing is amusing." Nothing likely would be *amusing* ever again. All laughter had fled from the world. I stared down at my dress. It was so ugly. I didn't even know who'd picked it out. It fit perfectly, so someone had my measurements, but they clearly had no idea of my style.

The dress went all the way up to my neck like a turtleneck, even though my wedding day had to be at least a hundred degrees. It was long-sleeved, covered in lace, and went down to the floor with a cathedral length train. I'm sure whoever bought this thing believed it would look pretty in the church, since it had such a long center aisle. In fact, someone was taking pictures of us now. I winced. I should look the glowing bride, but I couldn't help but wonder if that was the CIA, the FBI, or border patrol agents posing as the photographer. Maybe I was too much like my mother. Paranoia did run in my family, even if it was justified.

We stepped outside, and our guests finally caught up with us, not that I had too many of those. Just my family. I actually had a ton of friends from college and graduate school back home, but they weren't there. They were part of my old life, the one they'd let me have temporarily, like it was some kind of gift—all while they'd known I would eventually have to live like this.

I swallowed. I hadn't cried—truthfully, I wasn't much of a crier —but I felt the tears at the back of my eyes, and it was everything I could do to keep them from falling.

Alejandro stared at me for a long moment. "Time to go. Francisco," he spoke over his shoulder, and a quick glance told me his brother was indeed right there. *How had he known he would be?* "Take my bride back to the house so that she can rest. I have to deal with everyone here."

I blinked. "You're staying, but you want me to leave?"

Wasn't this *our* wedding? Arranged and ridiculous as it was, I was now his wife. Shouldn't we be staying together at our wedding? Doing wedding things?

"Yes." He nodded. "You'll go home and wait there." With another nod to his brother, he turned his back on me.

Evidently, we were done with our very first conversation. I opened and closed my mouth. *Well, that was that, I guess.*

"Lily." Armani, my brother, called my name, but I didn't turn to look at him or otherwise respond. Armani and I had always been close, but he'd helped perpetrate this. He'd done this to me, or at the very least let it happen and not said a word to warn me.

Francisco took my arm and headed for a waiting limousine. My brother shouted, louder this time. That was too bad. Apparently, I was going home, in my ugly dress, to wherever I would be living from now on.

Before I had any champagne or even a bite of cake.

Francisco practically pushed me inside the car and then got in next to me. The door was hardly closed before we zoomed away into traffic. That was one thing I'd noticed about Mexico City—there was a lot of traffic, but that was true of a lot of places. Most of the big cities I'd visited were the same, since infrastructure never kept up with population anywhere. I chewed on my lower lip. Of course, Salvatore said that Mexico City had the worst traffic in the world. I would have to see if that proved true or if it was just the grumblings of an old man who wanted to marry his only daughter off as fast as possible, so he didn't have to think about how he'd ruined her chances of happiness.

"You want something to drink?" Francisco leaned over and opened a small fridge under the bar. He pulled out a bottle of whisky and poured some into one of the glasses on top of the bar. It was a generous pour.

I'd been thinking of champagne, but being alone with the wild haired Francisco made me pretty sure I should keep my head on my shoulders. Alejandro had married me. I didn't know what happened after that. Did he have an obligation to keep me safe, or was I in this limo with his younger brother because I was about to be offed?

The thought made me swallow fast. Didn't the drug cartels behead people regularly? Was there some kind of ax in the trunk ready to do the job?

My hands burned with anxiety.

"You look nervous." He leaned back in his seat. "Do you speak Spanish? That would be easier."

I slowly shook my head. "No, I'm sorry. No one ever even suggested I learn it. I speak four languages, though."

"Which ones?" He looked bored, not like he was about to murder anyone. His dark eyes were striking, even though it was hard to see anything else past how disheveled he looked. What had he been doing before his brother's wedding that made him such a mess?

"English, obviously. German, Arabic, and some Russian. I guess I should say I'm really proficient in three and passable in the fourth."

He blinked. "Not one romance language in that group. If you spoke French, I'd think you could probably transition pretty easily to Spanish, but not one."

"Not one," I agreed.

"So you'll learn it now." If it was possible, he looked even more bored.

I shrugged. "Maybe."

In a million years, I would never be able to explain exactly why I had done that. I knew better than to push at dangerous men. I'd spent most of my life saying *yes, sir* to my father, until he died—exploding in a boating accident, or whatever it was—and then I moved to pacifying my brothers. Well, except Armani. Until yesterday, we'd been close. Then he'd been the one to finally push me onto the airplane when, for the first time in my life, I'd actually resisted something that they told me to do. I didn't want to marry a drug lord in Mexico. He hadn't cared, not even a little bit.

"Maybe?" He sat forward. "Why maybe? It would only make sense for you to do so. You're living in Mexico now. Do you expect everyone to speak to you in English all the time?"

I pointed at him. "Am I going to be *living* here? Or are you going to take that gun out of where you have it sort of jammed in your back belt—probably the only reason you're wearing the belt, considering you barely tucked in your shirt—and shoot me through the head? If you do, I don't suppose it'll matter one bit if I speak Spanish or not, since I'll be dead. Or I'll spend the rest of my life living on machines, if you execute people as sloppily as you dressed for your brother's wedding, and don't manage to get the job done with your first attempt."

*Fuck.* It had to be the stress of the day that made me blurt that. I'd never spoken to a dangerous man like that in my life. I'd barely raised my voice to my mild-mannered graduate advisor when he'd suggested that he'd see to it that I got the best classes if I gave him a blow job. I hadn't taken him up on his "generous" offer, and instead, made sure he knew what family I was a part of.

This was karma. Or something. Was it my punishment for all the times I'd used my family's ill-begotten strength to my own advantage? *Fuck.* I had just thought the word ill-begotten. I was in *that* frame of mind. This wasn't going to go well.

Francisco smirked at me before he downright grinned. He pulled the gun out from his belt. Salvatore had made sure I knew my weapons. From the time I was a little girl, it had been etiquette tutoring, the best schools, and weaponry to go with the cereal I ate for breakfast every day. This one was a Desert Eagle, favored by the Israelis, maybe because they manufactured it. Or maybe it was just that good of a gun. I'd never held one, but now I itched to. One thing was for certain—if he fired that at my head, I was done. There wouldn't be any whoops with that, and I didn't know how I should feel about it.

Relieved, mostly.

What did it say about me that my husband's youngest brother looked so fucking hot holding that gun?

"This gun?" He stared at it and then me. "Do you think I came in the car with you to blow off your head?"

"Maybe." I held his eye contact. I very rarely spoke to Salvatore like this, but on the occasions that I did, this was how I did it. When one spoke to a predator, one had to be careful not to be too submissive, because they might decide you weren't worth having around anymore. A predator's main objective in life, whether they knew it or not, was to hunt and kill prey. I couldn't start out my married life with my head down, waiting for one of them to do something to me.

Or perhaps that was just the story I was telling myself and would stick to in order to explain the strange way I had suddenly decided to act in Francisco's presence.

He leaned forward. This time, his smile was huge. "There would be blood, skull, and brains all over the upholstery. Not my problem to deal with, but Alejandro so hates when we make a mess."

*Good to know*. "Little type A?"

"To say the least." He put his gun back in his belt. Fuck me, he was sexy. That couldn't be good. I'd already decided Alejandro was handsome, despite his not fitting into fashionable standards. Why was I thinking about his brother like that?

He sipped his whisky and then, despite the fact that I'd said no, poured me a drink just the same as his and passed it to me. "Here."

I took it. Truth was, I always preferred the smell of whisky to the actual taste of it. Still, I sipped a little bit, whether it was a good idea or not. I was a lightweight.

"You're prettier than I thought you would be."

I almost spit out my drink. "What?"

"You're prettier than I thought you would be. We looked you up last year when we realized the noose around Alejandro's neck was growing tighter. We thought we might take a look at who would be bearing his children."

Hell… I knew where this was going. I took a bigger sip. It burned my tongue, but I ignored the sensation. There was exactly one searchable photo of me on the internet. My family was careful with publicity. It would be hard for my brothers to do what they did if everyone knew who they were. In the same spirit, they didn't want me to become a kidnap risk if I became too easily spotted in a crowd.

But there was one photo snapped of me when I was twelve at a birthday party and had promptly been posted online. Ten years ago, I'd posed with the daughter of a district attorney of the southern district of Chicago. Ironic, that the daughter of the most notorious—now dead—man in the city got to be schooled with the children of the people whose job it was to uphold the law.

Of course, that was funny. Politicians—I made no mistake of not understanding that was what the district attorney was. But the company that my brothers employed to keep us off the internet hadn't wanted to touch that mess. So there I was, my red hair frizzy beyond control, wearing braces and forty pounds that shouldn't have been there. Oh, and the picture featured my old nose.

My brothers had loved me but not known how to raise me after my father died. I had what I needed, mostly. Kids got braces, and one of them, I couldn't remember which of my brothers, had thought to do that for me. Nannies took me back and forth to my dental appointments. It wasn't, however, until a friend's mother taught me how to groom myself that I'd learned how to keep my frizzy hair under control. It took daily maintenance, and if I got caught in a random thunderstorm, it was all over. If it poured on me, my hair still looked just like that picture.

The girls at school had taught me the truth about the rest of me. My weight. My nose. One could always count on other women to point out, either overtly or with subterfuge that the CIA could only hope to ever have, just what was wrong with other women. The nose worked on my brothers. It made them look strong. On my face? It'd been downright ugly.

Maybe that wouldn't have mattered in a different world. Maybe it should have only been important that my IQ was off the charts and that, before I'd learned to cloak my sensitivity behind a shield of indifference for the world to see, I'd been kind.

Only it hadn't.

Anorexia had taken care of my weight problem. I wasn't proud of that. I'd needed therapy and medical intervention to pull out of that. To this day, I struggled with it. My love of fashion did nothing to help me, either. Couture continued to be made for the very thin, and fashion was my vice. It had taken begging to get my nose done, but they'd relented, and now I finally understood why.

Maybe they hadn't wanted to deliver an ugly bride to the Hernandez family. Better I look the part of sacrificial lamb and not the ugly duckling.

"Well, maybe you just didn't have the right imagination." It had taken me too long to answer Francisco's jab. He'd know I was lying. Probably he knew I'd been under the knife. I wasn't ashamed of it.

"No one is going to kill you." He did like to jump around his conversation. With a long pull on his drink, he regarded me for a long moment of silence before he spoke again. "No, you have never been so safe as you are right now. We're going to San Ángel. Do you know where that is?"

I didn't. "I only found out this was happening yesterday. I had no time whatsoever to learn anything about Mexico City."

He nodded like that made sense. If it did for him, I was shocked. I hadn't made sense of any of this. Not at all. "We don't live here full-time. We keep a place here, but our lives are spent elsewhere. Still, we own this place, a penthouse in a gated community, and that's where you'll stay for the next three days before we make our way to Culiacán, which is where we live most of the time."

Well, that was more than I'd known coming into this crazy day. My wedding day, that I was spending with Francisco in a car that kept stopping and starting so much, I didn't know if we were still in the parking lot of the church. I looked out the window. "Traffic is bad."

"Always bad." He agreed with me. "You know how to shoot a gun? Like the one I showed you."

The whiplash of the conversation was going to give me a headache. "That's quite a gun. I've never shot a Desert Eagle, but I have shot many guns, so if you wanted to teach me, I'm sure I could learn."

He blinked. "I could do that."

"When you have the time." When he wasn't beheading people who betrayed them and arranging to have drugs brought over other countries' borders so they could reach people like my brothers, who would then arrange their sales. And other things. But I wasn't going to bring any of that up. It wasn't polite to remind bad men that they did bad things. I still had some manners, and he'd said I was safe, so that was something.

Maybe.

It seemed as good a time as any to make my appeal. "I want to finish my master's degree and get a PhD afterward. That's what I always planned. I can do some of it virtually. Or you can let me go back to Chicago. You've fulfilled your obligation. Well, Alejandro did. There's no rule that says we have to live together, right? I could go back to Chicago and finish, and you could all go about your lives."

He quirked his mouth in that smirky way of his before he scooted closer to me. He was so close, we practically touched. One inch more, and we would. "You'll have to discuss that with your husband. I'm just the guy who gets things done for him, but I doubt he'd let you go." He tugged on my hair. "I wouldn't."

# 2

"Oh." I pointed my finger at Francisco. "You're one of *those* guys. You flirt with someone, and then you expect to get whatever you want. I know your kind."

He threw his head back and laughed, his eyes actually jovial for a moment. "I may actually like having you around." The car came to a stop, and he nodded. "We're here."

We were? How did he even know? The starting and stopping seemed all the same to me. But he was right. The driver opened the door for us. Francisco got out first and then turned to offer me his hand, which I took out of habit. I'd been getting in and out of cars this way forever. I was always the last one out, and I was always offered a hand like I couldn't do it myself. That was what came with having drivers who were also security officers. Our bodyguards, in case someone wanted to gun us down entering or exiting vehicles. I suspected this driver was the same. He was certainly carrying. For years, I'd hardly noticed whether or not the people around me were armed, but then when I'd gone off to school, I'd become more acutely aware that those men at my university weren't always prepared to take down anyone who looked at them funny, as opposed to the way I used to live.

Now I noticed it everywhere. The people who were carrying, those that weren't. I paid attention. And sort of resented that I wasn't carrying a gun myself. Maybe I could have fit it under my dress. I could start a whole new trend.

We entered the building through a nondescript entrance that immediately led to an elevator. Francisco put his finger on a device that read his print, and we were then in the elevator, leaving our driver-slash-extra-guard behind.

"Can I get coded into that?"

He shrugged. "We'll ask Alejandro. I don't know how he wants to handle your life going forward. He didn't share that with me. Good, you're still holding your drink."

I stared down at it like it was a foreign object. Yes, yes I was. I somehow hadn't realized I'd done that. "Why waste good whisky?"

He scrunched up his nose. "If you think that is good whisky, I'm going to have to educate you. It's crap whisky, but it's kept in the car, so what do you want? It's not even a car we take out very much."

Francisco caught my arm and quickly led me out of the elevator when it dinged. But as soon as we crossed the threshold, which had been about two feet from the elevator door inside, he let me go. In one impressive move, he spun in a circle, kicking off his shoes.

Right in that moment, he seemed younger than he had in the car or at the church. I stared at him for a minute. "How old are you?"

He tapped his chest. "I'm the baby in the family. I'm twenty-five. How old are you? Twenty-two, right?"

I nodded. With my ugly dress trailing behind me, I took in my new surroundings. The place was covered in windows. My brothers tended to avoid them, so we had very dark homes. This place was bathed in light. I walked toward the windows, seeing one was actually a door as I got closer to it.

"You're not worried about being gunned down?" I touched the door handle as it dawned on me that I might just want to stay inside. But Francisco came around me and opened it for me, stepping out in front of me like he might shield me from the bullets I was preoccupied with today.

"You worry too much, Lily." He winked at me. "Beautiful girls shouldn't spend so much time worrying. It's a beautiful day."

I shook my head. "You don't worry?"

The way that we lived—and, yes, I had to include myself in that, since I'd married a drug lord, removing any chance of escaping my brothers' lifestyle—meant we had to be careful. People wanted to kill us.

But Francisco was obviously not concerned. "I don't worry. I'd worry more in Chicago. Here, we take steps to be careful. If someone did kill me, Javier would come after them with the force of God and Alejandro would have them hung from their toenails before he slit their throats. No, I'm not worried right now. There may be times that I am. I'm actually smarter than I look, beautiful."

I poked him in the side. "Stop flirting with me. I'm your brother's wife."

"Do you feel like his wife? What's his middle name? How does he take his coffee?" He winked at me. "Yes, you're legally his wife, but you're really not, right? You're just a girl who lives with us now. You are allowed to be flirted with, and I'm going to flirt with you."

I looked away from him. He was right—Alejandro was a guy who had sent me away to hang out with his brother on our wedding day. I didn't know one thing about him. Maybe I didn't need to be so concerned with my behavior at the moment. I sipped my drink. It was getting tastier, or maybe I was just starting to feel it. With nothing to say, I stared at the view.

It was gorgeous.

I could see green trees surrounded on all sides by tall, white buildings and smaller red roofs. In the distance, mountains seemed bathed in shadows. What secrets did they hold?

"Hey." He nudged me. "What are you studying in school?"

I lifted an eyebrow. "I'm getting a master's degree in anthropology. My interest is mostly in cultural anthropology, but I haven't specialized. I'm just getting the MA in anthropology, and I'll specialize in my PhD." I took another drink. "Well, at least, that's what I planned. Who knows what will happen to me now?"

He pointed at me, and as the wind picked up slightly, I got a whiff of his clean scent. He might have been bored and hungover at my wedding, but he wasn't dirty. He'd showered before he let himself look so terrible at what should have been the most important day of my life. I imagined if I pushed my nose into his chest right then, I'd get a good dose of that aroma. The soap. The hair product. His natural maleness that couldn't be hidden behind perfumes or masked with scented products.

I blinked. *Whoa.* My mind had really flown away with that one.

"You'll be fine." He looked away from me, and a muscle ticked in his jaw. "My sister liked her life here. You will, too."

"Because all women are the same?" I spat back at him. I didn't know their sister at all. She'd been another victim of this arrangement none of us had agreed to. Still, I felt like she'd gotten the better end of the deal. According to Armani, she was twenty-seven. That meant she'd gotten five more years than me to live her actual life.

He stroked a finger down the side of my face. "I like how you strike back when you're upset. I like how you aren't afraid, even when I pulled out my gun. I like how you talk." He frowned. "I'm not stupid. I have a degree too."

"I didn't think you were stupid."

He nodded, once, as though that settled something for him. What? I wasn't sure. But it settled *something.* I pulled my gaze from him to look at this place that would be my home for three days. Four patio chairs pushed back against the wall spaced nicely the length of the porch. In between them, midsized green plants—maybe small trees?—sat in pots that matched the same brown color as the chairs.

"Who decorated this place?" I asked.

Francisco shrugged. "Some decorator. I don't know. Come." He crooked his finger, and I followed him inside. I had to get out of the dress. It was making it impossible to be comfortable. Then again, I had nothing to change into. I'd had suitcases packed for me, but I had no idea where they currently were.

I kicked off my shoes and pushed them aside. My feet could at least be comfortable.

Having paid no attention when I'd first come in, I took the chance to admire the entryway. The apartment's modern, loft-style layout offered no division between the rooms whatsoever. *Talk about an open floor plan.* I smiled, hearing years of *House Hunters* playing in my head. My college roommate had been a big fan, and I'd gotten addicted to it too. The brown wall unit, which matched the color of the potted plants and chairs outside, held the television and a collection of books I would have to poke through later. But the couches, which were legless and on the floor, were gray.

The decorator had known she was dealing with men. The whole apartment, except for the light wood floors, screamed masculine to me. The rug, a lighter shade of gray than the couches, gave a finished look, while the coffee table, also gray, matched everything else. The walls were white, and I looked away from them. I'd never been a huge fan of purely white walls.

But I was a guest—even if I was lady of the house in name only—and I wouldn't dream of criticizing. Well, I *would*, but in my head. I was allowed to do that.

I followed Francisco through the dining area, which was really close to the living area, and made note of the modern design. The colors were all relatively the same, and the decorator clearly favored marble. Even the table was marble. I touched it, feeling the cool smoothness as we passed. Eventually, he flung open a door. The bedrooms had doors that could close, at least.

"This is where you'll stay."

It was as untouched of a bedroom as I'd ever seen. Behind the gray topped bed, wood paneling covered the wall like a headboard. It matched the flooring. Two brown night tables framed the crisply made bed, and a bigger version of the tables sat under the window.

It was huge, but there was nothing on the walls. Not a picture to be seen anywhere.

"Thank you." I did have manners. "This is lovely."

He did his shrug thing again. "It's fine, but Alejandro likes it."

"Oh." I shouldn't have been surprised, but I was. "This is his room?"

"You are his wife. We have staff that come and go. It wouldn't do for the heir to the throne, so to speak, to be seen sleeping separately from his wife like he's living in the proverbial doghouse. Don't worry, beautiful, you'll be nothing more than roommates. I can promise you that."

So abruptly, it took me right out of what I was going to ask him, he whirled me around. "You need help getting out of this dress."

He wasn't wrong, but I caught my breath while pressed against his chest and lost the ability to think for three seconds. "Yes… I do." Forcing my brain to turn back on was easier said than done. "But I have nothing to change into. I have tons of clothes, none of them here."

Francisco tapped his foot. "I bet they're being sent straight home and bypassing here. Hmm. Okay. Well, you'll have to borrow something for a little bit from one of us. Javier is the shortest, you can wear his clothes." That was true, he was the smallest, but not by much, and all of them were significantly bigger than me. I was going to look like a child wearing my father's clothing. That was fine. For now.

"Okay. Thank you."

He spun me around again. I really should have been objecting to the way that he was manhandling me, but I couldn't bring myself to do so. There was something very powerful about Francisco, and it had nothing to do with the big gun that he carried around. It probably had more to do with the gun inside his pants, if his big dick energy was any indication.

With quick hands, he released the buttons that it had taken two silent women minutes to button up this morning. I caught my breath. Francisco was, unsurprisingly, clearly adept at handling women's clothing. Just how many had he taken out of their clothes?

It didn't matter. I wasn't virginal. *Better a man know what he is doing.*

*Wait.* What was I doing? I wasn't about to sleep with Francisco. He was my husband's brother. My dress fell down to my ankles, and he picked me up out of it, leaving it a mess on the floor.

Setting me down, he didn't hide the fact that his gaze roamed my body, taking my nearly naked figure in as he did so. I shivered, and not in a bad way. No, that shake was anticipation. Maybe I *was* going to sleep with my husband's brother. But really, what did I care? I'd spoken to Alejandro once. He wasn't even there.

He made no move toward me, but his eyes darkened, and for just a moment, we both breathed.

"Can you feel what is between us? This energy. It's so palpable, I could cut it." His Ts had suddenly become more pronounced. It was like he might actually be able to cut me with the word itself. I might let him. I might roll around in the wound, in the blood of it.

I breathed heavily. "I can feel it. I should be covering up. Backing away from this mess."

"Mess is the only way I know how to be. There's attraction in chaos. There's truth in it." He cupped my cheek. "And although we barely know more than each other's names, I already know you are a woman who has long tried to swim away from darkness, even if you should be embracing that nature in yourself. Don't you yet understand the power?"

I kissed him. Right there, on his mouth. Seduction came in many forms, and he had wooed me right into it. I had no illusions. This was going to be a big fucking problem. Later. But here I was, in Mexico City, married to a stranger, and his very hot brother wanted me as much as I did him. I owed Alejandro nothing. I'd lived up to the bargain my family had made without my consent. If Alejandro didn't like it, he could send me back home to Chicago tomorrow and I'd be better off for it.

He kissed me back, but not with the frantic energy I wanted. Instead, it was slow, meticulous, like he was drinking me in as he kissed me. With his tongue, he licked my bottom lip. Then, just as abruptly as he'd spun me around, he laid me down on the bed. Francisco certainly had no problem moving my body whenever he saw fit to do so.

He pulled his gun out of his back belt and placed it down on the dull, matching everything brown table by the window.

"Take my clothes off." He didn't ask. He was clearly instructing me on what he wanted.

I'd actually never been with a man who really knew what he wanted in bed before. We mostly seemed to muddle through until we got off. Or didn't, mostly in my case, until I took care of myself later. But I clearly liked his ordering me about, because I creamed my panties from his voice alone.

And they were thin, barely there, white string bikini undies that had to be so small because otherwise, the dress would sort of clung to them. I hated bikini underwear. I'd rather wear none than have it up the crack of my ass. Only that wouldn't have worked particularly well with the team of women I hadn't known who had dressed me this morning.

In a moment, I'd be dripping through them.

I sat up onto my knees so that I could get close enough to Francisco to take off his clothes. I started with his blazer. It was of really good quality, so I was gentle with it, folding it nicely and setting it to the other side of the bed.

My soon-to-be-lover watched me intently. He wanted this, and if this was a sexual need of some kind—to be undressed by me—then he was going to get a good show. Maybe it had something to do with being taken care of? Or perhaps he simply liked to dominate. I was game, either way.

I sat up further on my knees. His shirt, which had been badly tucked in and was partially undone, was soft cotton. It had a V-neck, showing me the top of his chest. He wasn't hairy, at least not there. I ran my hands over his skin before I took the shirt off him, and his breath caught. Yes, this was a ritual, and so far, it looked like I was getting it right.

I hadn't been graceful in how I'd removed his shirt. I didn't take the care with the shirt that I had with his jacket. Instead, I just sort of plopped it down in that general area of the bed.

His belt was next, but first, I had to admire his abs. Most of the men I knew were inked somewhere. It was the thing to do lately, a way to express themselves about things that were important to them.

For some, it was just trendy. In any case, Francisco didn't have any. I ran my hands over his exposed skin. A dusting of hair showed up on his lower abs, like when I took his pants off, I'd be able to see the trail from his groin upward. It was one of those beautiful things on the male body that I wished they wouldn't wax off.

It looked like Francisco didn't. Not that I could imagine him in a skin salon letting someone do that.

Running my hands over his bare chest, I got to feel the muscles jump lightly under my fingertips. That told me he was tuned into this, primed, wanting more. He might be controlling the interaction, but I wasn't without my own power.

I tugged at his belt, undoing it and setting it aside. Like most men who carried hidden weapons, he wore a thick belt to hold the additional weight. It wouldn't do to have a gun flailing around every time he walked. Did he only have one gun? It surprised me. He must be confident he could handle things in nine rounds or less.

His dark pants didn't need the belt, they stayed up just fine as I undressed him. After I unzipped him, I had to really tug them to get them down. He did me the favor of stepping out of them, which was good because I wasn't sure how I was going to get them off his feet in any kind of way that wasn't terribly awkward and completely unsexy.

Maybe sex shouldn't be a show. For couples who had been together since kingdom come, I imagined it could be that way. Just two people joining. But first times? It was always about showing the other person just how incredible you were in bed, just how much they should feel really lucky to have ended up naked with you.

I'd never been in a relationship long enough to know the difference.

His cock pushed against his boxers, revealing just how hard he was, and we hadn't really done anything yet.

"Can I?" I wanted to touch him.

He shook his head. "After you take them off."

*Fair enough.* This was his show, and I was good at taking directions. I pulled off his boxers, slipping them down his legs until he stepped out of them as he had done with his pants. I looked up to meet his gaze, and he nodded. "Yes, now you can."

I stroked him, one long pull from his balls to the tip of his cock. He was long, hard, thick, and warm in my hand. He audibly sucked in his breath, which might have been the best sound I'd ever heard. I wanted this. My nipples ached, begging for him to touch them.

The more I stroked him, the more I wanted to touch. In fact, my mouth watered. Some women didn't like blow jobs. I actually did. I loved to get a man off like that.

"Can I?" I repeated my earlier question, but I hardly had words at the moment. Besides, he seemed to understand me.

"No." He pressed me backward until I was flat on my back on the bed. "That's not how I want to get off tonight. I'm going to come in your pussy."

I smiled. He spoke perfect English. It would seem he even knew the dirty words. Hell, maybe he'd known those words before any others.

He stared down at my bra. It was white, like my panties, and lacey. It also itched, but that was neither here nor there at the moment, other than the fact that I wanted it off fast. Francisco reached between us and undid the front clasp. "Up a bit," he commanded.

I arched my back, and he took my bra off, throwing it aside. "White is supposed to be virginal. You all wear it at your weddings like it's a symbol of something. It's so much bullshit. You're no virgin, and I'm grateful for you."

It would absolutely not be sexy for me to start discussing the historical context of how it had come to be, in post-World War II, that women wore white to their weddings. What it had meant in pagan religions and the whole dang story. I bit my lower lip to stop myself from speaking. Sometimes there was no filter between my brain and my mouth, like all I wanted to do was tell everyone everything I knew so they'd know it too.

He lifted an eyebrow. "You can talk. I don't want you silent. Say all the things to me."

I shook my head. "You really don't want to hear about the history of white dresses."

"No, at the moment, I don't. But I do want to hear it later. All of it." He flipped me over. "Hold onto the headboard."

That wasn't going to be so easy. It was mostly wood on the wall. There weren't really handles to hang onto. I stared at it for a second. "I don't…"

"Palms flat against it, then," he said, interrupting me. It would seem in bed, we were good with shorthand speaking.

I did as he said, although I wasn't sure that I wasn't about to take a header into the wood.

"I won't let anything hurt you. Not even that mean wall."

I laughed. "That obvious?"

"Your whole body got tense. You should never play poker. You'd be bad at it."

He might be surprised.

# 3

Francisco grabbed my breasts. He wasn't gentle, and he quickly found my nipples with his thumbs. With a swirl, he pressed down on them. I cried out. They ached, and what he was doing, it really was just what I needed. I pushed back at him.

"Good, you're a woman who knows how to claim her orgasm. I can tell already."

I did love to orgasm—who didn't?—and I did demand to come with my lovers. If they couldn't get me there, I got myself. So far as I could tell, it was simple. If I set out to have one, I was going to have one. Period. End of sentence. But I didn't think that I was going to have that problem right then. Francisco acted like a man who knew how to give one to a woman.

From where I gripped the wall, that was a very, *very* good thing.

He kissed my shoulder blade and then my back, taking his time while he massaged my breasts. It didn't take long before I panted for him. All of a sudden, he stopped and pulled my undies off. It was a relief. I might not put them back on when it was over. Fashion was often painful, but I hated those fucking undies.

Francisco slipped a finger inside of me. "You are so wet. So lovely and so wet. I knew that you wanted me like this. I was sure of it."

I leaned my head back against him. "I'm not usually quite this, ah…easy."

"Good. You want me. I'll feel special." He kissed my neck again, this time leaving his mouth there while he found my clit and began a slow, rhythmic circular motion that was exactly what I needed. I moaned, wishing I could let go of the wall. Only that would be wrong, and I wanted to be right. Doing as Francisco said this way would get me there faster. I understood that in my deepest, darkest places. I needed him to do this for me, and that meant that I would listen to him.

Intently.

"The next time we do this, I'll make you come with my mouth. Right now, I'm too worked up."

I smirked at him over my shoulder. "You're so sure we'll do this again?"

"Very fucking sure." He pushed into me with those words, and he wasn't gentle about it.

A thought dawned on me. "Condom?"

"You're right." He pulled out. "Got a little carried away there. Hold on. Do not move."

I did as he said and stayed put, my hands on the wall as my arms shook from excitement. Behind me, he grabbed his pants off the floor and must have found the condom there. I could hear the whole thing, not see it. Then he was back, and with his cock sheathed, he pushed back inside of me again. "Thank you for the reminder."

Francisco wasn't gentle, and I wouldn't have expected him to be. But oh, did he know how to move. In and out of me, each pass hitting the spot I needed, he didn't slow down or falter at all. His hips jerked. In and out. Again and again. I cried out but hadn't come yet. The pressure was so good and also awful, but I wanted release. I didn't want it to stop, and yet I so did.

Over and over again, he pleasured me with his body until I couldn't stand to hold on anymore. One second, I wasn't coming, and the next, I was. Hard. My hands fell off the wall because I couldn't hold on anymore. He grabbed me before I'd have fallen and yanked me hard against his chest. Inside of me, he pulsed and then came. I almost wished he weren't wearing a condom so I could feel him dripping inside of me.

I shook my head. I'd never had sex without protection. I wouldn't even know what that felt like. We were both breathing hard, his forehead on my shoulder.

*Wow.* My head cleared slowly, pleasure continuing to rage through me like a machine that wasn't quite ready to turn off.

Francisco said something I couldn't understand in Spanish, and then he kissed my shoulder. "Wow."

I grinned. "Wow, yes."

With a grunt that sounded an awful lot like his moans, he pulled out of me, and with a hand steady on my hip, let me go. I righted myself so I wouldn't fall over and then rolled onto my stomach to watch him. He pulled the condom off and discarded it in the wastebasket in the corner. Done, he leaned over to kiss me. "Thank you for that."

"I should be thanking you." I winked at him. That need I'd had to do everything he wanted had fled. It must've just been a sex thing between us. Or maybe a one-time deal. We'd have to have sex again to see how that went.

His smile was huge. "So thank me."

Rolling my eyes, I stretched out further. "Thank you, Francisco."

"There. Now we're both thanked." He lay down next to me. We both had our feet where our heads should be. "Are you hungry?"

"No." I was very rarely hungry, and feeding for me was more like a job. I did it at certain times just to make sure it got done. My therapists had all hoped that would change in time, and I'd eventually get pleasure out of food. So far, that hadn't happened. Every once in a while, I found something I couldn't get enough of, like strawberry ice cream. In that case, I avoided it. Too many calories, too hard to get them off. I didn't have to lose weight, but I did have to maintain.

He pulled me against him. "It's lunch time."

Was it? I was off-kilter with my timing. I had eaten breakfast. "Still not hungry, but if you want to eat…"

"No." He sighed. "We can eat later. I didn't sleep last night, and it's hitting me now. Tell me about white wedding dresses."

I smiled. "So you can knock right out?"

"Knock right out?" He took a second. "Oh, fall asleep? No. I'm interested."

I leaned on my elbow to look at him. "Really?"

His eyes were already closed, and in a second, he let out a low snore. I grinned. Yep, that was pretty standard. There were others like me who cared about that sort of thing. We went to school together, we had text chats about all things related to cultural variants. Well, I used to have that. I didn't have my phone anymore. It had been taken from me by Salvatore, and I didn't know if I'd get it back.

I sighed and lay down. Maybe that was something I could recover. There were people who cared about me. They'd want to know where I was. Francisco's breathing was audible but not obnoxious. I closed my eyes.

* * *

"Good, you two got along." A voice that seemed to boom in the room woke me, and I screeched. The sun was going down on the horizon, and my husband stood in the doorway, staring at the scene that was Francisco and myself in front of him.

I was totally naked. With another screech, I grabbed the top of the blanket by where my feet were and tried to drag it over my body. Fuck. No. This wasn't how I intended to greet Alejandro.

Francisco groaned. "You're back early. I didn't know if you'd come home tonight."

Alejandro strode farther into the room. He opened the closet and took off his coat, which he hung up. "I got things wound down and the Chicago contingency on their way home."

I assumed he meant my family. "Are they okay?"

"Disappointed you wouldn't converse with them but otherwise fine." He stared at us for a long moment, which made Francisco roll over and pull himself out of bed. He grabbed his underwear and seemed not at all bothered that we were naked in front of my husband, his brother.

I sat up, the blanket still pulled up to my neck, and rearranged myself so I was a little bit more presentable. "Hello."

Francisco shook his head. "Don't be frightened. He's not upset, and even if he were, he wouldn't kill you. He'd have Javier or me do it, so you're pretty safe right now."

That did not fill me with a great deal of comfort. I was okay until he decided to have Javier kill me? Maybe I should have thought things through more clearly. I didn't really want to be one of those people that was considered too stupid to live. But Francisco had been incredibly sexy, and obviously, I'd needed the release.

He hadn't put his shirt on and was yawning like he had no cares in the world. Obviously, he wasn't at risk of dying.

"No one is going to be having anyone killed." Alejandro shook his head and then asked Francisco something in Spanish, to which Francisco shook his head no.

What had that been about? I did really need to learn enough of the language to be able to understand what was said around me. It was rude that they didn't speak English around me, if they could, but it was also completely unreasonable for me to expect them to constantly speak English, considering this was their home and I was basically going to be living as a visitor in it.

This was going to be complicated.

Alejandro clapped his hands out in front of him. "It's late. Have you eaten?"

"No, she wasn't hungry." Francisco answered for me. With that statement, he exited the room, his shirt in hand, still not on his body. Did he just walk around like that normally? We'd been pretty formal at home about things like that. Everyone was fully dressed all the time. Although now that I was gone, maybe that would stop? Maybe they'd be messy and half-dressed without me in the house?

That was a funny thought, but it didn't help my current situation.

"Then you'll eat now. We all should eat. I didn't get anything at the reception. Come. There is food left for us in the kitchen."

I looked down at myself. "I don't have any clothes. Just the wedding dress, and I'm not putting that thing back on."

He stared at it on the floor for a second before he picked it up, grabbed a hanger, and hung it up, placing it on the side of the closet that was, presumably, mine. It was empty, unlike his, which had a few items hanging on display. This wasn't their regular home. They must just have a few things here and there throughout it.

Still, without saying a word, Alejandro pulled open a drawer and brought out a T-shirt that was going to be huge on me. It looked like some sports team logo on the front.

"Put this on and the white bathrobe from the bathroom. You'll be fine like that. It's just us here right now." He grabbed his phone and started texting. "By morning, there will be something for you to wear out so you can go shopping. What size are you?"

I perked up at the S word. *Shopping*. Yes, it was cliché, but I did love it. I found very few activities Zen-like in my life, but shopping did it for me. Always had, regardless of my clothing size. I just loved it. Sometimes I didn't even buy anything, I just liked to look.

"A two in US sizing. Is it the same here?"

He shrugged. "I don't know, but the person I'm sending the information to will. She's the wife of one of my lieutenants. She owes me a favor. It'll be done." He put the phone back in his pocket. Alejandro wore only his tuxedo shirt, pants, and shoes. He rolled up his sleeves as he spoke to me and undid his top button. I swallowed. I'd just had incredible sex with another man, but once again, I was turned on.

This time, I was going to ignore the warmth starting inside of me.

I wasn't a sex addict. I didn't think so, anyway.

"You must have many questions. I can imagine some of your concerns, but it is getting late. I'm going to be honest and admit I can't deal with any of that right now after the long day I've had."

I nodded. "Our wedding reception was hard?"

"Yes. Everyone, of course, sends their regards...even those you will never meet. I'm glad it's over. It wasn't a party, Lily. I don't have those in my life. It was a reception filled with those who wanted to kiss ass, pacify me, or vaguely threaten my life. If you had been there, it would have been your life they'd have been threatening." He walked to the window and knocked on it. "This is three sheets of the best bulletproof glass made in the world. You are as safe here as anyone could be. I'd avoid the balconies."

I lifted my eyebrows. "Francisco took me outside."

He paused on that. "That was foolish. Although, any who might wish us dead were likely in attendance at our wedding. I'll speak to him. Sometimes he forgets he is mortal. If he wants to risk his own life, we will mourn and miss him always, but he isn't going to do that with you."

"Alejandro—"

He interrupted me. "We will have dinner tomorrow night, just you and me. We'll hash out the truths of our arrangement and what you should expect. I will answer all of your questions then. In the meantime, you will eat, and then we will go to bed. As uncomfortable as it will be for you, you must sleep in here with me. There is staff that comes and goes from our life. It would not do for me to be seen sleeping away from your side. It would be risky for both our lives. In the morning, you will shop and have dinner with me. In two nights, we will eat with my father."

*Well, wow...* He had spit out a lot of information right there.

"Get dressed, and I will see you in the kitchen."

Turning fast, he exited the bedroom. I put my head in my hands. What the fuck had just happened? Alejandro had come in, seen me naked with his brother on my wedding day to him, and then treated the whole thing like a business arrangement. Of course, it sort of was. Francisco hadn't cared about sleeping with his brother's wife, and Alejandro didn't give a shit I'd slept with his brother. Why was I getting worked up when no one in this whole penthouse floor seemed to care at all?

I took a deep breath. If I ever saw Salvatore again, I wouldn't ignore him. I'd break his fucking nose.

I got out of bed and quickly did what he said to do. I put on the T-shirt and, with no other choice, I had to stay panty-less under it. The good news was that the T-shirt went down to my knees. I'd really, really love a shower, but that would have to wait.

Grabbing the bathrobe meant I got to see the bathroom for the first time. It was gray, huge, and the tile was cold on my feet. Still, the bathtub looked inviting, but all bathtubs did to me. A glass of red wine and a good hot soak cleared my head from stress better than anything else. I finished up, washed my hands, and grabbed the bathrobe hanging behind the door. It was clean and warm. For just a second, I pressed my nose against it to breathe in the smell of the fabric softener. Fresh laundry was one of those scents that always spoke of comfort.

But I couldn't stand there just breathing it in.

There was food in the kitchen, and I'd been given instructions of what to expect for the next two days, including who I'd be sleeping next to in order to save appearances. All right. There might come a time I'd fight against orders, but first I had to see exactly what the circumstances were here. It might even make sense for me to convince Alejandro that he wanted to send me back to Chicago. His wife who lived out of the country could be convenient for him. He could easily go back to sleeping with whomever he shared his bed with in a committed manner, because there was no way a man who looked and moved like Alejandro was not having regular sex.

The question was with whom, and if they were going to come at me with a machete while I slept because I had the bad fortune to be sold into marriage with Alejandro.

I padded into the kitchen, which was as untouched as the rest of the house. Javier stood in it, his back to me, but the other two weren't anywhere to be found.

He looked over his shoulder. "I hear I'm taking you shopping tomorrow."

There was no question that the ink on his face was designed to intimidate. *I mean…ouch.* You had to mean business doing something like that. The question was what did the dragon-snake thing on his face represent to him and others that he wanted them to understand immediately upon meeting him? It couldn't be anything gentle, that was for sure. It wasn't like he wore a flower or a butterfly.

"I didn't know you were in charge of that. I'm Lily, by the way." I put out my hand, and he turned around, staring at my outstretched offering like it was a bomb about to go off. Then, just as I was going to retract my hand, he took it, giving it a quick shake.

"Did you think I didn't know who you were?" He smirked. Francisco had that same look. If Alejandro did it too, I'd think it was a family thing. "Go sit down at the counter. I'll warm up the food. My brothers are having a discussion about acceptable risk. You may hear yelling. I hope you don't intimidate easily, or this is going to be a long fucking life for you. It might be anyway. You don't speak Spanish?"

I did as he told me because that dragon-snake ink told me I'd better. I hurried over and sat down at the counter. "You know, if anyone had even hinted it was going to be important, I'd have learned it. No, not currently. I think I'll have to get on that fast. Presuming I'm staying."

He blinked rapidly. "Where else would you be going?"

"I could go back to Chicago. Then you could all be done with me. I could go to school, study, live a separate life, and you'd never have to deal with me again. Alejandro and I don't have to divorce. We'll just be husband and wife from afar."

He laughed, which startled me, and then grabbed what looked like a pasta dish out of the refrigerator. "That's not going to happen. I can predict that right now. How could we secure you like that?"

"You wouldn't have to. My brothers could." It made perfect sense to me.

"No. You aren't theirs. You're ours. Someone would have to live there with you. The FBI would never leave you alone, and you'd become a constant risk of security, both physically and of the information kind. You'd be under constant assault one way or another.

No, I guarantee it. You're staying where we are. Welcome to your life."

I cleared my throat. "It was just a thought."

He warmed up the pasta in the microwave and then started dishing it out. "We're not so bad. We're even interesting, once you get to know us."

Javier set out four plates, four sets of forks and knives, and then hopped on the stool next to me. He looked up. "Drinks." With that word, he jumped off the stool again and grabbed two seltzers from the fridge before coming back over. He handed me the drink.

"Thanks. For all of it." I opened the can and took a sip. It tasted nice on my mouth, which I thought became dry when he laughed at my idea of leaving. "I've always lived with the threat of the FBI, by the way. I'm not a snitch, and I'd never tell them anything."

Javier patted my arm. "I know, but things have changed for you since you became Alejandro's wife. Being Salvatore's sister is different than being Alejandro's wife. Now someday, Salvatore's wife? That will be a different story, too. But that is for another one of you girls to deal with."

I hadn't let myself think about that. Someone would be showing up soon to marry my brother. How would that go? I took a bite of the pasta, it was hot and delicious. "So good."

"Yes, our cook is exceptional. You'll like everything she makes. It's not fair that the whole world doesn't get to eat her food."

Because I had to and I was past politeness, I pointed at his face. "Why the dragon-snake?"

He rubbed his face, letting his fingers trail over it. "It is the family crest. It represents us. You haven't seen Alejandro's back yet."

I'd seen Francisco's. "Your younger brother doesn't have one."

"No, he's being a dick about it. Francisco likes to cause problems just to cause them sometimes. We babied him, Rosa particularly." He smirked. "Someday, he'll be inked too."

I pointed again. "Did it hurt? Getting it on your face?"

"I'm sure it did." Francisco laughed as he followed Alejandro into the room. There hadn't been any yelling that I'd heard. "But he'll never tell you. He's the tattooed doctor. It would ruin his reputation to admit it hurt."

My mouth fell open. "You're a doctor?" The things I didn't know about these men could fill the ocean.

"That reaction you just made? That was what I was going for." He took another bite. "Eat. It'll get cold. I love to be underestimated. Makes things so much easier. I only work for the family and our associates. I can look however I like, so I don't give a shit."

Alejandro sat on my other side, while Francisco took a seat by Javier.

It was my husband who spoke. "Did Javier tell you he's taking you shopping?"

"He did." I nodded. "I'd like to finish school."

There were probably better ways to have handled that, but it was on my mind. So far, both Francisco and Javier had thrown the gauntlet onto Alejandro. He was going to say no. I was going to let him.

"What are you studying?" He didn't look at me, just his food as he ate quickly.

Francisco and Javier made eye contact. I had no idea why, and I wasn't particularly interested in finding out. My morning-slash-afternoon with Francisco felt far away, even though it had just happened, like my brain had reset. *Control. Alt. Delete.*

"I'm getting a masters in anthropology," I supplied for him.

"She likes cultural anthropology best." Francisco smiled as he spoke.

Alejandro looked up at his brother. "I think she can talk for herself."

"What? Why should she have to repeat herself about things I already discovered? We had whole conversations you're never going to know anything about."

The oldest held up his hand, effectively dismissing Francisco, who went back to eating. "Can you take these classes virtually?"

"I can this semester. Next semester has to be in person."

He sighed and set down his fork. "Your brother should never have let you start this track."

"Salvatore had almost nothing to do with me the last few years. I lived my life. He lived his. Armani was different."

Alejandro rubbed his eyes. "That is unfortunate. Yes, do your virtual classes. After that, no. So if you want to quit now to make that easier, do that. Otherwise, find a different program you can do virtually or find no classes at all."

I opened my eyes. He had essentially just gotten rid of everything I wanted to do with my life. I set down my fork. I'd had enough. My stomach clenched. "Thank you, this was delicious."

Javier stared at my plate. "You can't possibly be done."

"Oh, but I am." *Very, very done with this.*

# 4

The rest of the pasta eating dinner had been awkward. I almost wished they'd all just started speaking Spanish, because then I could have zoned out. But Javier and Francisco kept making an effort to change the subject to pleasant things like horses—a subject Javier loved. And race cars—Francisco's preference. Alejandro was just coolly silent. My husband. I supposed I could feel badly for him if I were in a generous sort of mood. As Shakespeare said, uneasy is the head that wears a crown. But I wasn't feeling like I cared that maybe his having to make that decision hours after meeting and marrying me was tough.

All I knew was that I was going to have to figure out what to do with my life, since the plans I made didn't fit into his idea of how our lives should be.

"Are you tired?" He interrupted his brother's talking to address me directly.

I shook my head. "No."

That was going to be a problem. It was a long night ahead of me, and I had nothing with me. Not even a toothbrush. Well, I had my wedding dress. At that moment, I'd have liked to have burned it.

"Javier will give you a pill. You need to sleep tonight. We have long days ahead and no time for you to adjust to the time change."

The time change? "It's one hour. It's not like I went to Australia. That had been an adjustment. And actually, I don't suffer that badly from jet lag."

"Are you a nighttime person?" Javier asked me. "Or an early riser?"

Maybe I just felt like being difficult. "More of an afternoon person. I like cocktails at four."

Francisco laughed, but the other two didn't. Maybe he was amused by just how childish I could behave? Truth was, I got up early for school but still partied on weekends with no problem. Or I used to. Now, I was here doing neither of those things.

"I don't take sleeping pills. I've had two friends end up dead in bathtubs after taking them." Both had been devastating losses. *Their poor families.* I'd been sixteen the first time that happened, twenty the second. I didn't like to think of those lost souls. Then again, there was death every day. I had no living parents. And one of them had actually gotten me in my current situation when he'd agreed to this mess.

Maybe it was better he was dead.

I both loved and hated my brutal temper.

"That's tragic," Javier whispered. "I'm sorry to hear that. Truly. Your brother sent your medical report, and I've seen it, so unless you have taken something today that I'm unaware of, you'd be fine to take what I'd give you."

I couldn't believe what I was hearing, so much so that my mouth fell open out of pure shock. "You read *what*?"

"Your brothers sent a medical report, compiled from the last five years. You're in excellent health right now. Did you take anything today I need to know about?"

I shook my head. This was fucking unbelievable. "I had some whisky earlier."

"Not very much." Francisco got up and grabbed my plate when he took his own to the sink. He started washing them both.

"That has to have been hours ago." Javier rose and grabbed his plate and Alejandro's. "You're fine."

"Great, then it's settled." Alejandro sighed. "You'll take a pill and be ready for tomorrow. No one will let you in any bathtubs after you have taken it." He put out his hand. "Come."

I could have refused it. But that wasn't a small rebellion, like saying I preferred afternoons. No, it was a big one. A big fuck you. He'd given me a strong hit to my happiness. How much worse did I want to make things between us? I didn't know if he was a hitter or how his anger would show. So far, he'd found me naked with his brother and hadn't said a word about it except to express his pleasure because we were getting along.

How was I to make sense of Alejandro Hernandez, heir to the drug lord empire that ran most of South America? He was strong, educated. Willful. Clearly in charge. And he had secrets, which any man in his position would. I didn't want to be a body he buried because he couldn't deal with my attitude, but I also didn't want him to think he could walk all over me.

This was too complicated for knowing each other for so little time.

I put my hand in his and let him lead me to the bedroom, where I knew we wouldn't be having sex. I just didn't know why. He'd told me he didn't want to talk about it tonight, and I decided to leave it alone. We were going to have dinner tomorrow. I'd wait until then to inquire about the physical side of our relationship.

Still, there were some things to settle between us. He closed the door, and I stopped on the side of the bed. "Which side is yours?"

"I tend to prefer the right." He shrugged. "But I don't suppose I'll really care. I've never shared a bed before. I can probably adjust."

I shook my head. Okay. That had gone fine. "Left is my side. Can I have my cell phone back? I have friends who will be wondering what's happened to me."

He sighed. "Believe it or not, I don't relish having to deny you things. You didn't know this was happening, I did. I've known you'd be mine, even with little information about you before yesterday. I want you to be happy, not pissed, surly, and mad—all things you are entitled to feel, since you were planning for a life you were never going to have. No, you can't have your cell phone back. But tomorrow, Javier will give you a new one. It's better secured. If you want to contact your friends, I'll have my security team vet all of your friends and give you the numbers of those I deem acceptable so you can enter them into your phone."

I breathed through my nose. "You're going to vet my friends? What does that mean?"

"Surely you must know by now that no one is to be trusted. Almost everyone is not who they say they are in our lives."

That was sad he felt that way, but it certainly led to my next point. "Really? You don't trust anyone?"

"I can count on one hand whom I trust. My brothers, without fail. My father and my uncle Ricardo. Those are the only people I will ever trust."

It was like a wall of misery settled on my shoulders. "Then let me ask you a question. If that is all true, if the fact that we were all born into this life and you clearly chose to continue pursuing it" —he lifted his eyebrows at that, but didn't argue my point— "then would you want your sister to take a sleeping pill the first night that she had to spend the night with a complete stranger? Just take the pill that would completely knock her out and go to bed?"

"My sister is actually very happy with her unconventional relationship." He looked away from me. "But your point is taken. Still, I have to ask, you slept quite soundly next to Francisco, even had sex with him. Is he more trustworthy than me? Somehow, you were safer in his presence than my own?"

I put my hands over my heart in mock hurt. "Are you…slut shaming me?"

"Not even the least. We're talking about trust. I'm glad you slept with Francisco." He held up his hand. "Don't interrupt me and hold off your questions. We're getting off the point. If you don't want the pill, don't take it. That is entirely up to you. I'll even give you something you can bludgeon me with in my sleep if I do something you don't like. Warning, you'd better not miss. I won't like it. And if you do manage to kill me, you'd better get my brothers too. Plus be prepared to run the rest of your life."

I was done. I sank to the bed. "Alejandro, I'm not really the kind to kill anyone. I'm…just done."

Deflated. That was how I felt. I didn't know that I'd ever felt this way before. Even grief, the cruel mistress that she was, hadn't hit me like this.

I put my hands over my face and just tried to not cry. It was all I could do right then, concentrate on not crying. The bed dipped, and a strong hand rubbed my back. "Lily, please look at me."

I didn't comply. I simply couldn't. Not crying was all I could do. *Breathe and not cry.* I couldn't even move my hands right then.

"Lily," he said again. "I am terrible to argue with. The worst. Of course I was not slut shaming you. I've never heard that expression before, by the way." He tugged my arm until I was pressed up against his side before he brought both of us up the bed toward the wood wall.

"Alejandro, I can't…"

He put my head down on his chest. "It's been a long day. Let's both lie here. Just lie here for a minute and leave it be. You found out this was happening yesterday, and the buildup of this has haunted me a good portion of my life. Too much for today."

My voice was low. It was all I could manage, practically a whisper. "Trying not to cry."

"You can cry." He matched my tone. "Soak me if you want."

I shook my head. "Remember the trust thing?"

"Yes." He ran his hands over my hair. "We are going to do this a long time. Some day, you will trust me, and I will add you to that list of people in my life. We will both wait for that."

The night was quiet. So quiet that, as the minutes passed, all I could hear was the occasional shuffling of feet outside the doors as Javier and Francisco did whatever they were doing in the apartment. I hadn't made note of how many bedrooms there were, but I'd guess they each had their own room.

Alejandro continued stroking my hair. It was nice. The need to weep passed with each second until it was just a dull ache in the center of my chest that I could ignore as I had many times before. "Your English is perfect. I will learn Spanish."

"It had to be. We started traveling over the border back and forth to America when we were twelve years old. Not speaking fluent English would have been a disgrace to our father. We went to boarding school in Switzerland when we turned fourteen. There, we learned many languages as part of the curriculum. It's necessary in our…line of work."

I swallowed. "Then what?"

It was nice when he talked. "Then we went to college in Mexico City. Francisco and I studied business and Javier medicine. Here we all are now. Francisco just finished his education recently."

They'd all gotten to have advanced degrees, so they could live their lives, and I was not going to be allowed to do the same. I pushed away the thought. It wasn't helpful right then. There was tomorrow to fight for what I wanted. No one said all the battles had to be won tonight.

He was tired, he'd said so, but instead of going to sleep, he was comforting me. We didn't know each other, but he'd done me this courtesy.

"I need to get ready for bed. I don't have a toothbrush. Or a hairbrush. Or anything."

Alejandro nodded. "Do that. Drawer next to the sink, you'll find what you need. Let me know of anything else you want. I am going to change the sheet. Not judging, just thinking I'd rather not sleep where my brother has been."

I snorted, a totally ridiculous sound. "Sorry, that just struck me as funny. I don't usually make that noise. And…"

His smile was what interrupted me this time. It was huge, genuine, and the biggest one I'd seen so far from my husband. Yes, it was probably a good idea for him to change the sheets. Also, I was impressed he knew how to do that. So far, they'd seemed very competent with household chores—the dishes, now this—for drug lords. Someone had taught them to take care of themselves.

*Bad men on the streets, but they know how to change the sheets*, I thought in amusement.

I found toiletries where he said they'd be. Getting ready was easy. Routine, even, and doing so, despite the fact I wasn't using my normal stuff, allowed me to calm further. *One thing at a time*. Next on the list was seeing if I could get through tonight and handle tomorrow. I'd gotten married to a stranger because I didn't have a choice. That had happened. Railing against things right this second solved nothing.

Still, despite my near-emotional turmoil, I was wide awake. Maybe a shower would help? I got into it, careful to not get my hair wet, since that would be a disaster without my own stuff, and cleaned myself off, fast. The tiredness I hoped for didn't come, and by the time I'd toweled off, I'd made a decision.

Putting the T-shirt back on, because I didn't have another and I'd barely worn it, I went back out. Alejandro lay on the bed, which he'd covered with white sheets and a matching comforter, staring at the TV, which was on low. He shut it off when I entered.

"Hair dryer," I said in a low voice.

He grabbed his phone and texted, presumably the woman purchasing me clothes who owed him a favor. "What else?"

"I need undergarments and shoes. 32 B in the US and a size 7 shoe."

He texted that and then set it aside. I didn't need specific product for my hair right away. I'd have that when I got to their other home and my bags arrived—assuming he could trust them after they were vetted. That was a ridiculous thought. *Or* maybe it wasn't? How paranoid was he? I supposed I would find out.

He was shirtless and gorgeous, built like he could be in a men's fitness magazine, yet somehow, he wasn't bulky looking.

"And, ah, I'll take the sleeping pill."

He sat up straight. "Nothing will happen to you in my care. I promise to wake up if I hear any water at all."

That was a legitimate concern for me. "Thank you. I don't think they filled the tubs in their sleep, but yes, anxiety doesn't always give in to reason."

He stared at me for a long moment. "Oh, trust me. I know."

Alejandro got out of bed and left the room. What did that mean? I didn't get the chance to wonder about it, mostly because I could finally see his tattoo, which distracted me. Yes, it matched the one on Javier's face, only bigger and broader. The brightly colored design took up his whole back. *The family crest.* I sat on the edge of the bed. All questions would wait until tomorrow. How was it possible to be so bone-weary and also so fucking awake? I'd never felt quite this way before.

Javier came back into the room with Alejandro. "This is an easy one. It will simply allow you to rest. People take this on airplanes for long trips. Gentle. If you have any problems, I'm just next door." As he spoke, Alejandro slipped into the bathroom and came back with a cup of water for me. I took it and swallowed the pill. Javier put his hand on my cheek. "Tomorrow, you will teach me all things about shopping for women's fashion."

I doubted we'd have time for that. "Don't you have a sister? Surely you've done some before."

"Rosa didn't want us anywhere near her clothes." Javier grinned at Alejandro. "And she'd have brought Francisco if she wanted company. Blame her if you ever find him spoiled and difficult."

Alejandro patted him on the back, and Javier left. With that, he pulled the curtains closed and rejoined me in bed. He turned off the lights with a remote. "Is the dark okay with you?"

"Things are scary regardless of whether they're in the dark or the light. It's the same either way."

I scooted over until I was on my left side and under the covers. This was awkward. I was under the covers with a gorgeous, dangerous stranger who happened to be my husband. How strange was life?

Eventually, the pill must have worked.

"Back to bed, *belleza*," a soft voice said in my ear. "You can yell at me in the morning. You are apparently the type to sleepwalk. I don't know if it's regular or just because of the sleeping pill."

I was so confused. What was happening? It didn't matter. There were warm covers and someone to tug me close in the darkness.

The light creeping through the cracks of the curtain woke me. I blinked awake, at first with no idea where I was. Then it rushed back. *Mexico City. Married to Alejandro. Sleeping with Francisco. Shopping with Javier today*. All of it.

But I had slept well, and I was wrapped up in Alejandro. My body was practically on top of his, his heartbeat steady and slow beneath my ear. He breathed deeply, evidently unbothered by the fact that I'd sprawled on top of him.

*Wow*. I'd shared beds with lovers but never done that before. What was the matter with me? I rolled off him, trying to give him back his space, but he just turned with me, wrapping his arm around my waist and tugging me toward him so that my back was against his chest.

What was the protocol in this kind of situation?

I lay still, but eventually, I had to pee. It was very early, but I really had no choice. I slipped away and made my way to the bathroom where I quickly took care of business. However, as soon as I'd finished washing my hands, the door swung open and a wide-eyed Alejandro stared at me in the doorway.

"Hi," I whispered. It was very early. "Are you okay?"

"Are you?" He tugged me into a hug. "No more sleeping pills for you. Forget it. I'll never suggest it again."

My head pressed into his shoulder was kind of nice. "Did something happen?" I couldn't remember a thing. It felt like I'd had a long, eight-hour knockout where I'd hardly moved at all.

"You sleepwalked and scared the shit out of me, because for a moment, I couldn't find you. When I did, I found you by the backdoor, which makes me terrified you could go on the balcony. Unless you do that? Do you sleepwalk regularly?"

I shook my head. "No. Not at all."

"Then it was the pill. Javier says it happens to a very small percentage of people. He offered to sit with you, since he gave you the pill, but no, you are my wife. I'll stay with you. Anyway, I heard the water, and I thought, fuck, the tub."

I took a deep breath. "Thanks for taking care of me. I'm sorry I disrupted your sleep and made you worry."

He caressed my cheeks, his eyes intent. "This is not your responsibility. It's mine. I made you take that pill, thinking to help you, and it bit me in the ass. You're okay. That is what matters this morning. Come, Guadalupe is here. She will have made us breakfast. I should warn you, there is something unusual about her. You have to understand..." A knock sounded on the door to the room, and he sighed. "Hold that thought."

I followed him back into the bedroom, and he let Javier inside.

Javier smiled at me. "See? No worse for wear. I told you she'd be fine."

"Only because I caught her before she hurt herself. Lightweight pill? I blame you for this." Alejandro walked into his closet. "Take her to breakfast."

Javier extended his hand. "This way, Lily. I'm glad you're feeling well. No residual hangover feeling? Or exhaustion?"

I shook my head as I followed him to breakfast. "I'm wide awake."

"Good," he smiled at me, which didn't look like a natural state for him. The severe man from church seemed more natural. "Clothes have been delivered for you to wear today. Also, Josefina sent a note saying she'd like to get together when we all get back home. Like you, she's not from here. Maybe she could also use a friend? They're a nice couple, and David is a good lieutenant. Big earner. He gets his job done. They'll be around for a long while."

*That is nice to hear, but he isn't on Alejandro's list of trusted people*, I found myself thinking.

I wore a T-shirt and it wasn't ideal to meet Guadalupe, but I had no choice. Wherever these clothes were, I needed to find them and get dressed soon. Still, when I came into the kitchen I stopped, abruptly catching my breath. The other woman was there, and nothing was overtly wrong with her at first glance. She was a little taller than me, brown hair, and brown eyed. Lovely long hair. Long face. She wore black pants and a gray shirt. But that wasn't the problem.

I caught my breath. Francisco looked at his phone, drinking coffee as if nothing were amiss, while the woman made eggs in the kitchen. Her lips were sewn together with big, zigzagged strokes that crossed from her upper lip to her bottom one. She lifted her eyes, and our gazes met for a long second. I covered my mouth. I should have been more polite but—although I thought myself worldly, that I'd seen things that would scare others…like the night I saw Salvatore covered in blood coming home dead-eyed—I'd never seen anything like the woman's face before.

Javier put his hand on my lower back. "Apologies, I would have thought that Alejandro would have told you."

I ignored him. The woman was there. Lips sewn closed or not, I knew better than to stare. Forcing my brain to react, I pulled my hand off my lips like I wrenched it down with weights and walked toward her. "My name is Lily. I'm…Alejandro's wife. And…and…what happened to you?"

She couldn't talk. Why was I asking her? I rounded on Javier. "You have to help her." He was a doctor. Wasn't that what they did?

Unless…he was the one who'd done this to her.

He held up his hands. "Lily. Take a breath. I know. It's disconcerting if you don't know. Guadalupe understands that too. I would help her, if she'd let me." He looked over my head at the other woman, who had returned to the eggs. "But she did this to herself. Anytime someone fixes her, she does it again. So for now, this is how she'll stay."

I swallowed. "Why would someone do this to themselves?"

"To make the point that they'll never tell something they know. To make that point to someone who might kill them otherwise. In a dramatic fashion. We don't know what that is. But her point is made."

Yes, yes, it was.

# 5

Okay. This was real. Something had happened to this woman—I didn't know how long ago, nor was it actually my business to know—that made her sew her own mouth shut. Not once, but anytime it was undone. This was some kind of illness. Or just absolute terror I couldn't possibly understand. It wasn't my job to judge it, just understand that she was so utterly afraid that she did this to herself. Mutilated her body. And I was just a spoiled girl in my husband's T-shirt who had just been terribly rude.

I walked over to her. "My apologies. I know better than to stare, and we certainly shouldn't be talking about you as you stand right here. Let me try again. My name is Lily. I guess my last name is Hernandez now. Alejandro and I just got married, and I'm so grateful you made eggs."

Francisco didn't look up from his phone. "Morning, Lily. Guadalupe only speaks Spanish, so she has no idea what you're saying anyway."

The woman cooking us breakfast patted me on the arm. She might not understand me, but if the kind look in her eyes said anything to me, it was that she was grateful I'd taken the time to make the effort. I nodded at her and backed up to take a seat while she spooned eggs onto my plate and placed them in front of me.

Francisco reached over and rubbed my arm, then stopped. He made a face and looked back at his phone. "I'd love to show you a better morning than this, but I have an incredible amount of bullshit to handle today, and we have company. Guadalupe isn't the only one here. The staff is here most days, so we are going to behave like everything is normal, because that is what we do."

Javier sighed. "He wakes up in a terrible mood every morning."

"That would presume I slept." Francisco sipped his coffee. "But yes, bad mood today. Although it's better because of the view this morning." He grinned at me.

Javier sat down next to me. "Don't you need to leave?" He talked to his brother. "Like five minutes ago?"

Francisco pushed his chair back. "The good news about being me is that people wait. My showing up at all is a gift to their fucking lives."

Having delivered that line, he winked at me and left the room. His gun was on full display tucked into his belt. Presumably, he'd grab a jacket on the way out. Or maybe he wouldn't? I didn't know the rules here. I'd have to learn how people behaved, how they pretended they were normal when their lives never would be.

But first, I needed food. I spooned what I thought was a reasonable amount of eggs into my mouth and set down my fork. Guadalupe had made them, so I thanked her. I knew *gracias*, and so I said that. She smiled with her eyes at me and patted me once again on my shoulder.

Javier pointed at the chair behind him where there was a wardrobe bag I'd missed when I'd come in because I had been so preoccupied with other, more disturbing things. Grabbing it, I almost collided with Alejandro, who spoke rapidly on his cell phone. He darted out of my way at the last second and hurried toward the exit.

If Javier found that weird, he made no indication, continuing to eat his eggs. "Is that all you're going to eat?" he said, not looking up at me.

"Yes," I answered. "You've seen my history. You know that I struggle with anorexia, but that isn't this. I don't have a huge appetite most of the time. That is my normal."

He spun around in his chair. "I have seen it, yes. I'm the only one, by the way. I'm going to be your doctor. It's complicated, because I might be other things for you too. If it doesn't work for me to take care of you the way I do the rest of the family, then we'll find you a different doctor. All of this is to say, neither of my brothers know about your medical history. It isn't their business to know unless you tell them or unless I think you're in some kind of danger. I'm not going to watch every morsel you do or don't consume. That would be invasive, and I have no interest in that. I am going to point it out if I see a trend I don't like, and we can get you help." He rubbed his eyes. "I'm rambling. I need more coffee. But you get the gist of what I'm saying?"

I nodded. "You're here for me, you're aware of it, and you will intervene if you see a problem."

"That's it. Yes. And you can come to me."

He was a little bit flustered and sort of adorable at the same time. I shook my head. I shouldn't be thinking that way about Javier. We were in this strange situation, but I knew nothing about him. And I'd already had sex with a person who was basically a stranger yesterday. Today, I didn't intend to make the same decisions. Not until I had all of the information I needed, anyway.

Not to mention, Francisco was either flirting with me or ignoring me. I had enough awkwardness in the house right then. I was going to keep my legs closed this morning, that was for sure.

I took the garment bag and fled the kitchen with as much dignity as I could muster, hoping he didn't see it as the fleeing that it was. Alone in the bedroom, I took a look at what Josefina had brought me. All in all, it wasn't bad. The black, V-neck, one-piece, sleeveless pants romper would do nicely for a trip to the stores. She'd paired it with a pair of black slip-ons I wouldn't have picked myself but were comfortable on my feet when I put them on. Underwear and bra were all black. I got dressed quickly and tried to run a brush through my hair. This was going to get ugly with my hair soon. When we were out, I'd get product. I needed to wash it and be able to take care of it. There was a hairdryer in the bag, which was hugely helpful.

I didn't want to be the grownup version of that little girl they'd looked at in the picture online, and if that made me shallow, then so be it. I wasn't cruel or even mean. That would have to be enough for now. Maybe I'd have years to work on my character. Right then, all I could deal with was putting one foot in front of the other.

A long glance in the mirror told me that I was put together but that the outfit did very little for me, figure wise. I didn't have huge breasts, but they were perfectly fine for my frame. In this outfit, however, I looked completely flat chested. It wasn't a look I would have chosen for myself. But I was dressed, and it would have to do. I had more than enough clothes, I just didn't have them with me. I needed two days' worth of outfits before I could get back to the ones that made me feel good about myself.

I wished I had something to really take care of my hair.

Still, I had long since stopped trying to impress store clerks, and Javier probably didn't care what I looked like. I headed back to the kitchen to find him waiting, staring out through the windows at Mexico City in front of us.

He turned when I entered. "Ready?"

I nodded. "Where are we going?"

Javier blinked. "Shopping."

Well, that much I knew. "Yes, specifically where?"

"You don't know? I thought you'd tell me." He shook his head. "Fuck. Alejandro says *take her shopping*, like I have any idea where and how to do that. I've never taken a woman shopping."

I lifted an eyebrow. "Never?"

"Well, not for what I'm going to buy you. I mean…unless you want me to go buy you dirty lingerie and sex toys."

My mouth quirked. Javier was really such an interesting mix of scary, serious, and funny. He was probably a million other things too. But if he thought to shock me, he had the wrong girl. "Well, how about we look for that stuff *after* we get me four to five outfits? That way I can be prepared for whatever happens over the next two days, so I don't have to walk around in your brother's T-shirt?"

He opened and closed his mouth. "Sure. We'll swing by for the vibrators if we still have energy after buying pants."

"That'll work." I patted him on the arm. "Now, those women you buy those things for? Do any of them dress nicely? Like you could eat with them in a fancy restaurant kind of a place?"

He stayed so silent that I almost laughed. It struck me as ridiculously funny that he didn't know any women that he would do that with. Sex, yes. Food, no. That was interesting. Or maybe he just didn't eat fancy food. He finally nodded.

"Not any of them, but my friend married a very nice woman. I could ask her where she shops."

"That sounds perfect. Could you explain what I need to do over the next few days and see where she would suggest?"

He started texting, and my hands actually itched from the lack of having my own phone. I hadn't considered it before, but I might go into some kind of withdrawal if someone didn't give me access to the outside world via cellular data and Wi-Fi soon. It was like I was going to need a fix.

Quickly, he looked up. "Okay. I know where we can go."

*Great. Problem solved.*

"Where are we headed?"

He motioned toward the door. "Out."

I rolled my eyes. I had brothers. When men wanted to be tools, it was just better to let them do it. Kill the game before they got really invested in it. If he didn't want to tell me, I wouldn't ask again. Either way, I'd end up buying clothes.

He was quiet until we got in the car, the same one I'd been in the day before. Unlike Francisco, Javier didn't immediately start drinking whisky. Instead, he scooted close to me and scowled. "I can't make sense of you."

"Maybe I'm senseless." I was sort of proud of my response. I wasn't always clever.

It made him smile. "Why aren't you demanding to know where we're going?"

"Well, I figure I'll get there either way. If you don't bring me, it won't be me who has to explain to Alejandro why I'm eating dinner in his T-shirt. I have nothing to be ashamed about. I have great legs."

I kicked one up to draw attention to it, and he smiled wider. "Fair enough."

"Did you always want to be a doctor?" There, I'd changed the subject. He might even tell me now.

He shook his head. "I thought I'd be a baseball player or a superhero. Then I found out that we kill people for a living. This seemed like the closest I could get to being a decent human being, considering I'm actually an asshole and also bathed in blood."

I understood him perfectly. "I am also bathed in blood. It doesn't matter what I do from here on in, does it? Every piece of food I've eaten, every book I've read, every piece of clothing I have ever owned is bathed in blood." I took his expression because I really liked it. "And now I'm married and continuing the tradition."

"Well, I'm sure we could cut you off and let you starve so that you wouldn't have that problem."

I pointed at him. "And I'm sure you could run away, practice medicine elsewhere, and never have anything to do with the family business again."

He snorted. "Sure. We'll both just give it all up."

I liked talking to him like this. "Totally start over."

"We're going to a place in Antara Fashion Hall. It's located in Polanco. I think you'll be able to find whatever you need there."

I had no idea where that was or what that meant. But so long as I didn't embarrass myself at dinner tonight, I was going to consider today a win.

A thought dawned on me. The woman in their kitchen with her lips sewn together. An image of that floated through my mind. I had a feeling that was going to be happening a lot.

"You really have no idea what prompted Guadalupe to do that to herself?" I shuddered at the thought. Had she been able to numb her mouth before she took the needle to it, or did she just go for it and damn the pain?

He shook his head. "If I did, the person who was responsible would be dead. It's possible Alejandro knows, but he keeps his counsel to himself, doesn't trust often. I imagine if he does know, then it's taken care of. He's not shy about doling out justice. Or revenge. But I don't think so. I think Guadalupe's story remains her own, and much as it breaks our hearts, she pretty much raised us after our mother died a year after Francisco was born. None of us have heard her voice in two decades."

I swallowed. That was…a lot to process. I pushed the image of her pain out of my head. It would haunt me when I wasn't careful to not think about, that much I already knew. Women were disposable in our world. I was sitting in this car for just that reason.

"Alejandro told me he trusts four people. So he *does* trust. Just very few." I looked out the window. That was four more people than I trusted. I had literally no one whose intentions I could count on. No one who would be there for me if I needed them, not that I could count on, anyway. Every person I met was new, and those I'd thought I had, turned out to be unreal.

I was glad my head was turned from Javier. The tears I'd managed to not spill with Alejandro the night before threatened again. I blinked them back. I was good at that. I could thank my previous life for giving me those tools.

Javier squeezed my knee. "You okay?"

I smiled at him, and I was sure I did a good job of pulling off happy. I always did. "Sure. Just taking in the sights outside."

He lifted an eyebrow, which raised the snake slightly on his face. "Of all the traffic? Really exciting out the window?"

"Well," I said, even more brightly. "They're new cars to me."

I wasn't sure he bought my bullshit, but at least I had distracted him. "Who were the other two that my brother said he trusted? Me. Francisco. Who else?"

I had to think on that answer. "Oh, your father and uncle."

Anger crossed his gaze before it vanished as quickly as it showed up. "That's a mistake. I'm not saying anything to you I haven't said to him by the way. He has no business trusting my father and my uncle. They're only out for what they want, what they think this family needs, even if it goes directly against everyone else's best interest. Don't assume you can trust them. When we have dinner at Dad's house tomorrow night, be on your guard every second, or you might find yourself in a pit full of trouble you never saw coming."

That was good advice. Still, it begged a question. "Thank you. I will. Why are you warning me?"

He tugged on the end of my hair. "Because I've decided I like you, and I'd like you to stick around in this life and not die."

Just then, the car moved again, and we were on our way to buy me some clothes. He liked me and wanted me to stick around. That was…nice. It wasn't conclusive of anything really. I liked people and wanted them to stick around, and then I didn't anymore. I might be more like a plaything he'd eventually grow tired of. And then he wouldn't care if I were alive or dead. I needed to be on my guard all the time, because I couldn't count on others to do so.

Javier moved closer. "You and I, we're going to know each other very, very well."

The temperature in the car had just risen a lot, and it was all because Javier looked at me like he wanted me wrapped around him that very second. "Will we?"

"Yes. You saw how Alejandro was actually pleased that you and Francisco got to know each other?" That was an interesting way to put it, but I nodded my head just the same. I understood what he meant. "He wouldn't be upset if we got to know each other that way either. We can know each other very, very well. Anytime you want to." He held my gaze. "Or not, if you don't want to."

I squirmed. "This is really strange for me. I'm not complaining, but I need answers from your brother about some things. Otherwise, this just feels like some kind of game, and I don't know the rules." Even as I spoke, my nipples hardened. "You're gorgeous. And honestly, a little scary. Yes, I'm very attracted to you, but I promised myself I wouldn't have sex this morning."

He smirked at me. "Then I guess we'll have to discuss this again after lunch." Javier leaned over and kissed my neck, which made me jolt because of how unexpected it was. "I think you might be a little scary too."

*Me?* I was the least frightening person ever born. I opened my mouth to tell him that, but we arrived at our destination. The car pulled over, and Javier's mood immediately changed. Charming would-be seducer was gone, replaced by the serious hard-eyed man who I'd seen in the church.

"Let me get out first, then you."

I nodded. "Are we at particular risk here?"

"No, but I'm never off my guard unless I'm at home, and by home, I mean our actual home, not the place we keep here."

*Fair enough.* I could see feeling that way. "I think you're probably more at risk than me."

"You're Alejandro's wife. There are a lot of people who want to cause him pain. They don't know the deal that brought you here, and he's allowed people to believe that he fell in love with the daughter of a wealthy family he does business with in Chicago. They think you're a love story. Couldn't resist each other anymore and had to wed fast. Some people probably think he knocked you up. In any case, you'd be a target they think he'll pay for."

I supposed that made sense. "Do me a favor? If there are any more pretend games I should know that I'm playing a role in, please make sure I know. I can do a great job being whoever you think I need to be, but I can't lie if I'm not in on it."

He shot me a look. "Good point. And I sort of love that you are so easily able to go with this stuff. If you were squeamish, this would be harder."

I doubted there was much that could make me squeamish. Well, no, I knew what could make me squeamish, actually. A woman so terrified that she might be forced to talk, she sewed her own lips together made me absolutely uncomfortable. Nope, wasn't thinking about that anymore.

Getting out of the car, I took Javier's offered hand and squinted at the sun that assaulted my eyes. Sunglasses would be a plus too. Our driver was the same person from the day before. Once we were out of the car, he stepped to the left to let us pass him before he followed behind us.

"Okay to walk right next to you?" I asked Javier, hoping the answer would be yes. The three of us in a line was bound to draw more attention, like we were on a little parade or something. We might as well start humming or break out in song.

He nodded. "Sure. Which store do you want to go in first?"

That was a good question. This was an open-air market. Some of the stores were chains I recognized, and some were brand new to me. As we passed, I looked in the window to see what they displayed inside.

"Where is he taking me to dinner tonight?" It was strange to talk to Javier about his brother just moments after Javier had propositioned me for sex. But it wasn't as strange as it should have been, and I didn't even want to delve into the parts of my mind that were going to have to make sense of that.

He shrugged. "No idea, but this is Alejandro, so it'll be really good food."

That told me nothing. Okay, I needed a little black dress. Those tended to be good in many situations, and maybe I needed two that weren't quite the same. One for dinner with Alejandro, and one for his father's house.

I pointed at a boutique. "Let's go there. Wait." I grabbed his arm. "What is my spending limit?" I could do a lot with a little or splurge. I'd always been good at either, depending on how much Salvatore allotted me at the time. I liked really high-end clothes, but I wasn't the type that had to have them. Well, not all the time.

"You don't have a budget. Get whatever you like."

I blinked. "Really?"

"You're Alejandro Hernandez's treasured wife. Being kept on a budget would bring up all kinds of questions about his ability to manage the business after our father is out. It wouldn't do for someone to think we had a cash flow problem. Buy whatever you want. Buy the store if you want it."

I really didn't want that much, but it was good to know I could have it if I so chose.

"You do know your brothers could buy and sell Chicago if they wanted to? You could have had what you wanted with them too."

I shook my head. "No, we can't be seen overspending. No one wants to go to jail for flagging the IRS' attention by spending more than the income you show."

He pointed at the boutique. "That one?"

Javier strode ahead of me. I guessed, like the car, he was going in first. Or maybe he was just done discussing the money issue. That was fine. I'd been forced into a marriage I'd known nothing about, stuck in a relationship with a man who didn't want me but didn't mind if his brothers did. I decided I wouldn't have a problem using his credit card. Not even a little bit.

# 6

I stared at myself in the mirror. Well, no, I actually didn't. I was pretending to stare. Instead, I watched the saleswoman behind me hit on Javier. Despite the scary tattoo, or maybe because of it, women seemed drawn to him. At least five had hit on him since we'd entered the store. I knew that without being able to understand a word that they said. Body language said a lot. The trouble was I couldn't tell if he was reciprocating their interest. I also had no business caring about that one way or the other.

I'd already found a black dress and a skirt and top combination that would work well for their dad's house. Now, I was just playing around. The place had designer jeans I was going to buy and some tops that would work, so I had no business hanging out in the ivory dress that clung to me like it had been painted to my curves. I didn't look good in white, but ivory I could carry off rather well. In pure white, I was just so pale that I might as well have been the walking dead.

Maybe it was because my wedding dress had been pure white, so I was desperate to reset the image? Or maybe I was just wasting time on something I didn't need because I had liked how Javier looked at me in the clothes I'd brought out, each one catching his attention until he nodded at me, like he wanted me to wear that. So far, I hadn't had any nods for this dress.

Did he not like it? Or was the five-foot ten model-esque saleswoman with the gorgeous, long dark hair just too appealing for him to notice me at all? *Fuck.* I was such a brat.

She was chatting away, and mid-sentence, he left her, which promptly shut her up. He walked up to me, which was not something he'd done before then. "Are you trying to get someone killed?" he whispered in my ear, keeping a distance from me that I could only call appropriate. It would seem—in public, at least—he wasn't going to hit on me or act in any way like he wanted me. A good distance away, so as to not raise anyone's suspicion. It would be normal, maybe, for Alejandro to have his younger brother guarding his new bride. Something a drug lord would do.

"What?" I didn't understand his question. "Something you and the saleswoman were discussing? I can't understand, so I have no idea."

I hoped I didn't sound as put out about that as I thought I did. *Fuck.* I had to get it together.

He smirked for one second, but then I saw it. "No, she was discussing wanting me to take her out, and I was ignoring that and sticking to things like the weather. But before you launch into another adorable attempt to not seem jealous when I could see that you were, and I sort of liked it, let me ask you… Are you trying to get someone killed?"

My cheeks were red. I didn't have to look in the mirror to see them to know because they burned. I could feel it as the heat rose. I must be beet red. I swallowed. "Why would I be trying to get someone killed?"

"Because if you walk around in that, I am going to have to kill any man who looks at you for too long. It will get messy. So buy this if you want, but only wear that at home for me and only when my brothers are out of the house, unless you suddenly feel like being sociopathic."

That shouldn't have made me so hot, only it did. I swallowed. "I'll leave it. I have what I need."

"Good." He stepped back. "Finish up, and we'll go eat lunch. I've been waiting for lunchtime all day."

I went back into the small changing room and got back into my black jumper. When I came out, my order had been rung up and the driver was outside holding the bags.

I might have imagined it, but it certainly seemed like the salespeople shot me dirty looks on my way out. Whatever Javier had said or done, he'd not given the women the attention they wanted.

"We can't eat yet." Outside, the warm air greeted me again. "I need underwear and shoes."

He groaned. "Really?"

Clearly, this man was not a shopper. "I'm sure I could do it myself. You could leave me here with…" I looked at the driver, who was also our extra guard. "I'm totally rude. I don't know his name."

Javier shook his head. "You don't have to know his name."

"I do, actually, because that's polite." I walked toward the lingerie store where I fully expected Javier to leave me. Instead, he pulled it open and walked in first. Like before, everyone in the store quickly exited upon seeing us, leaving the store to us alone.

He swung around. "It's very American for you to think you have to know everyone. You don't. The man outside works for us. He is under my family's protection. We make him very rich. He will stay that way until he retires or dies. Or betrays us. If the first two things happen, his family will continue to have our protection and thanks. If the second, his children's children will wish they'd never been born. And no, you can't be left with him. We're very clear on your protection. It's Alejandro, Francisco, or me. That's it. Other people can be bought off. We can't."

I took a deep breath. "I'd like to know his name, even if it's very American of me. He's carrying my clothes."

"His name is Eduardo. Don't talk to him. He doesn't speak great English, and it will make him stressed." He gestured forward. In this store, the sales staff were less enamored with him. They looked more scared than turned on. It was the difference in the way they all kept widening their eyes.

I patted his arm. "I'll be fast, but it's going to get old for you guys to have to alternate who is with me all the time. You have lives."

"After tonight, you'll understand more. Get your stuff."

He stepped back, and I got busy purchasing four days' worth of panties and bras just to be safe. After that, we did the same thing at the shoe store. "Can we stop on the way home later to get some toiletries I need?"

Javier had gotten incredibly quiet. He probably needed to eat. On our way back to the car, I took his arm. It wasn't a weird thing for someone to do with their brother-in-law, I didn't think. "Hungry?"

"No," he answered fast. "You should have shopped with Francisco. He likes this stuff. I'm not good at it."

"You didn't have to be. I actually could tell what you liked and didn't."

He stopped walking. "Really?" I never got to answer him, because his phone lit up and he looked down at it, his face hardening. "We've got to go. You're going to have to come with me. There isn't time for me to get you home."

That was fine. "Sure. Whatever you need."

Relaxed Javier had fled sometime during our shopping trip, but this was even further. For the first time, I was seeing angry Javier. If I'd thought I'd seen him before, I'd been wrong. He practically radiated rage from his pores. His fists were clenched, and we were in the car faster than I could have imagined getting there. He said something to Eduardo before he got in the car, and we squealed out of the parking lot.

"What's happening?"

"Someone is hurt because someone else can't keep his fists to himself. I need to check on her."

That was awful. I squirmed in my seat. He was the family's doctor, so that probably meant that people like Eduardo, and the unknown hurt woman, used him when they needed help. It had to be a lot of pressure on him. Particularly because I knew that bad men did bad things. Sometimes they did them to their loved ones. Was I going to have to call him someday if I made his brother mad?

I chewed on my lip. Probably not, if last night was any indication. Alejandro and I had argued, and I hadn't ended up bruised. Still, I really didn't know what he'd do, or for that matter, what either of his brothers would do.

Maybe I should start making a list. In fact, when I had my computer back—assuming they let me have it when we got to our permanent house—I'd make a list of things to remind myself I needed to be careful about. *People. Occasions.* All the things I should constantly be on guard against.

And I'd make it like a daily affirmation.

*Don't forget you don't know these people...that you never really know anyone...because at any time they could betray you... Look what your family did.*

That sort of a thing.

We arrived quickly at an apartment building, where people were gathered outside. Eduardo popped the trunk of the car, and Javier was out of it fast, giving the other man directions in Spanish. If he said anything to me, I didn't understand it. Did he want me to wait in the car?

He and Eduardo were through the crowd fast, leaving me alone. He'd been big on me not being on my own. Did that include sitting in the car? I might have remained where I was, except I saw a little boy weeping on the steps of the building. He was alone, tiny—like he was just out of diapers—with huge sobs racking his body.

I'd never been able to stand children crying on their own. Maybe that was because I'd been left—forgotten really—in a park when I was just a little older than the child. To this day, I didn't know what happened, but I'd stood there and cried for hours. No one had helped me or even questioned why I was there alone. Eventually, someone had come back and gotten me.

That was the day I should have realized I'd always be alone—even in a crowd.

I jumped out of the car and approached the boy quietly. He stared up at me, big tears pouring down his face. I stood in front of him. Approaching him had seemed like a great idea, but I didn't speak his language, and I was a stranger. Maybe I should have thought it through better? A quick glance told me that Javier was busy. Someone had beaten up an old woman. She was tiny, wrinkled, and bleeding. My mouth fell open. When he'd said someone was hurt, it wasn't the person I'd pictured. Bad enough that anyone was injured, but seriously, who beat up a granny?

The little boy caught my attention, raising his arms. Without giving it another thought, I picked him up. "Do you need help? Who do you belong to, little one?"

He didn't answer me, but at least his tears stopped. I wasn't going to go anywhere with him, just staying where I was, while Javier dealt with helping the poor woman over there. Why was no one looking for this child? "Do you live with your granny? Is she hurt?"

In a heartbeat, he put his head on my shoulder, fully cuddling down on me. Well…I hadn't expected this exactly, and I didn't know what I was doing. But I held him, sort of rocking. Back and forth. Kids liked this, didn't they? He certainly seemed to.

I was a stranger, but at least he wasn't alone. We'd just wait together. Javier picked the woman up like she weighed nothing and brought her over to join us. I moved out of the way since he was obviously going to bring her into the apartment building. Someone stopped him. Another man. I didn't know what was happening, but Javier passed the woman over to him. He was a gray-haired gentleman but younger than the woman he now carried.

Javier blinked, seeing me for the first time. "What the hell are you doing? I told you to stay in the car."

"Did you?" I legitimately didn't know.

He frowned and then sighed. "Okay. Maybe I didn't say it in a language you'd understand. Who is this child?"

"I have no idea. He's crying by himself. I couldn't stand it." I still rocked the warm bundle of child.

"Well, now he's sleeping on you." He called out in Spanish, and people turned around, one of them running over to take the child from me. "That's his uncle. You can give him over."

I passed him, annoyance at the man making me glare. He wasn't much of an uncle if he'd just left the kid there screaming. I didn't say anything, but I thought it. That would have to do for the moment.

A car pulled up, screeching its tires, and we both turned to look. Before I could so much as turn around, Javier rushed the car. In two seconds, he had the driver out, after he practically ripped the door off the vehicle. Javier and the newcomer were the same size, but he had no chance to even blink before he had the stranger on the ground and was beating the shit out of him.

I watched in fascination. Distantly, I knew I should have been horrified, only I wasn't. Two seconds ago, he'd been bandaging an old woman, and now, he was beating the shit out of this man.

Eduardo stood watch over the fight, his gun drawn like he might take out anyone who got too close. The crowd pressed inward, but no one interfered. Javier pulled out his gun. Was he going to shoot him right here on the street? I stepped forward, not to stop him, but because it was like I couldn't stop myself. Javier yelled at the person but didn't fire. I didn't know his handgun. It didn't look like standard anything, and I'd not even considered the fact that he'd carried it all day hidden behind his jacket, like Francisco had.

Javier jumped back, shaking his head, but he never fired his gun. The man on the ground cried. It was sort of a pathetic sound, but I'd never been beaten to an inch of my life, so I couldn't judge. Okay, maybe I did a little bit. Men like these guys didn't cry. Presumably, he was one of them. Or he had been. Would he lose whatever position he had now?

With a turn of his heel, Javier returned to me and gestured toward the car. I got in. Maybe he was past the point of speaking? Eduardo drove us back out into traffic.

Javier didn't look at me. He breathed heavily for a moment, shot a look my direction, and then back out the window. We'd really only just met, but did I see remorse on his face? For what?

"He beat up that old lady." I stated the fact. That much, I'd figured out.

Javier nodded. "His grandmother."

"Who beats up their grandmother?" I slid closer to him. I'd barely known mine, but I couldn't fathom it. "I'm glad you made him pay."

He swung around to stare at me, his mouth falling open. "What?"

"I'm glad you beat him up. He deserved it. And then some." I took his hand in mine. His knuckles were red, torn. They'd hurt him soon, if they weren't already. The doctor with the face tattoo who had gone from fixing the old woman up gently to beating the shit out of someone on the street in just minutes. Who was this man? Well… other than my husband's brother and at the top ring of a drug cartel.

"I shouldn't have done that with you there. I forgot my role today, which was make sure that you were okay. I shouldn't have let you see that. The wives of high up lieutenants…they don't see that kind of thing. They're protected, taken care of. They don't have to witness people getting the shit beat out of them. Lily, I—"

I put my hand on his mouth to stop him. "I'm not the wife of a lieutenant. And whatever rules there are, I'm not sure they apply to me anyway. Despite what we may be selling the public, I'm not Alejandro's beloved new wife. I'm a business arrangement, and I get what that means. I get it perfectly. You don't have to pretend with me." I scooted closer. "You don't have to be afraid of your dark side or apologize for it. You liked doing it. I could see that. The same way you liked helping her. And, if I'm being honest, I liked watching you do it."

He moved my hand away but just so he could kiss me. We breathed hard together. I'd promised myself we wouldn't have sex that morning, and fuck if it wasn't the afternoon. I didn't know any better what my situation entailed. I still had no idea why this was okay. But if it was, I was going to do it. As much as I wanted. Pleasure was pleasure. I needed release, and so did he.

I climbed onto his lap. Thank God there was a barrier between us and Eduardo, because I wasn't sure I'd care right then if we had an audience. I craved this, and damn it, Javier and I were both going to get what we wanted.

Pulling at his clothes, I had him shirtless fast, and he did the same for me. My bra was bland, but I hardly thought he noticed. No, he unclasped it and threw it aside.

I unzipped his pants while he sucked on my nipples. It was awkward like this, his gun had to be placed aside, and I had to get him out of his pants to stroke him. He was erect in moments, practically the first time I touched him. I stroked him, and he moaned against my breast, letting go to look up at me.

"I've wanted you all day. Yesterday too. Hard like a teenager for you. Did you know? This whole time?"

I shook my head. "Not a clue."

Javier flipped me over so I lay on the seats and he was on top of me. "I'm on top."

I nodded. Okay. Whatever he needed. I had no particular preference, except that one time I'd tried being tied up and hated that. If he wanted to be in charge of this, then more power to him. I was game.

He stared at me for a second. "You're so beautiful. You walked down that aisle to my brother, and if I hadn't known there was a chance for this, I might have killed him. I love my brother, and I'd never betray him, but I thought it. That's how fucked up I am."

I kissed him. It was time we all owned our fucked up. We were dark, difficult people. "Just fuck me, and I'll forget all my questions."

"Done." He grinned and reached into his pants, pulling out a condom. He set it down and pulled my jumper all the way down before pushing my undies to the side so he didn't have to deal with them at all. When he'd done that, he pressed a finger inside of me. "You're so wet."

"Want to know when I got this way?" I sighed. "It'll help you understand just how fucked up I am."

He bent his head so that our lips were almost touching. "When you watched me beat the shit out of Lucas?"

I nodded. "Yes."

"Let's see if we can get you wetter." He pressed his finger against my clit, and I cried out. Yes, I wanted more of that. And it was like he knew how to touch me. Deep pressure, circular motion. Exactly what I wanted. Soon, I writhed against him. He jolted his hips against the seat. "You're so responsive, and it's real. You want this."

I kissed him. "Stop talking and fuck me."

"Dirty mouth. As you wish."

Javier rolled the condom onto himself and was inside me in seconds. My body stretched to fit him. For just a second, we stared at each other. There was a feeling of not being real, at least for me. How had this happened? I didn't care. I just wanted him.

His mouth met my own. I wasn't sure which one of us had actually initiated the kiss. It didn't matter. We moved together, our lips, his cock in my body. Over and over. Moment after moment. I cried out, he moaned. For long moments, it was like we were the only people on the planet. The car stopped, it moved. Who cared? We just had each other. I didn't know his middle name, and he had no idea how I took my coffee. What the fuck difference did it make?

There was just this. Just now. Pleasure. Sometimes a jolt of pain. It was real. It happened.

We were two people who the world would never understand, and that was okay because it didn't take long until I was coming. Yeah… I was that wound up. It only took minutes. He needed it too, because his body followed mine like we had always been doing this together.

I came around him, and he cried out my name.

It was beautiful. And real.

Then it was over.

He kissed my face, murmuring things I couldn't understand. I listened to the tone. He was being sweet. I touched his cheek. "I have no idea what you're saying, but I like how you're saying it."

Javier grinned at me. "I was saying…you're amazing."

I kissed him. "The car has stopped moving. Traffic or the apartment?"

He looked up and out the window. "Home."

That was good. A lot had happened this afternoon. We should

probably both process the events. Only, he was still inside of me, and when he moved his hips, I sighed. Yes, that felt nice. I could probably go again if he wanted to.

Javier ran his hand through my hair. "You're so pretty. I can't say it enough. Your skin is like porcelain and…your hair. All the colors of sunset."

I kissed him to stop him. "I know you saw the picture of me when I was young. You have to know that some of what you see, I paid to have fixed." I didn't do well with sweet. Real worked better for me. It always had.

He ran his finger down the slope of my nose, confirming my suspicion that he knew just what I was talking about. "I would have thought you beautiful whatever this was. You were a cute kid, despite what you think I thought."

I shook my head. "No, Javier. You wouldn't have."

I could promise him that. There was real and what we did to make what we wanted real. Then there were falsehoods. He and I were both seriously messed up, but we could tell each other the truth.

"Shit." A thought dawned on me. "I never got hair product."

He pulled out of me to bang on the partition between us and Eduardo. When he called out, it was in Spanish before he turned back to me. "We'll go to the store."

That was probably best. I was going to be a huge mess now. But then again, all things were a mess until we fixed them. Just the nature of the beast.

# 7

Francisco was inside when we finally made it back to their apartment. He stared out the window, sipping coffee, but turned when we entered. His smile was huge. "You're back."

That was when I saw his black eye and the fact that his knuckles were bleeding, very comparable to Javier's. They'd clearly had a similar day.

I walked straight for the refrigerator and opened the freezer. Guadalupe wasn't in the kitchen anymore, and I didn't know if her duties included taking care of these guys when they busted open their hands. I had years of experience doing this, mostly from my brothers pounding on each other. By the time they were grown, they weren't asking for my help anymore.

Grabbing two plastic bags, I filled them with ice. "You two, over here, please."

Javier set down my bags on the couch and came right over, Francisco followed him. They sat at the counter where we'd had breakfast, and I placed the bags on top of their hands. "Sit there for a few minutes."

"Thank you," Javier smiled. "That's really nice of you."

Francisco looked at his brother as he took his own bag. "What did you do to your hand, big brother?"

"I beat the shit out of Lucas." He added something in Spanish I couldn't understand, and I tried to ignore the burn of that. I'd only been here twenty-four hours, but I could already tell that the not speaking the language was going to get old fast. As soon as I had the technology, I intended to study.

Francisco winced and then looked at me. "Got to see the best of my brother, huh?"

I made eye contact with Javier. "I think I did, actually."

The youngest brother groaned. "I don't want to know, but I'm happy to show you all my best parts again too." He leaned over and kissed me. "I beat up two people today. They owed us money. Now they don't anymore. They paid. Little below my level most of the time, but it seemed my father wanted me to handle it, so I did. He seems to think my only purpose in this family is to beat the shit out of people, so that's what I do when called upon."

Javier shook his head. "It does seem to be a rather large part of his business model."

I smiled at them. "Well, have fun with that. Oh, Javier? I need a phone. I need a laptop. Something."

His nod was slow. "You'll get them, just not today. After you talk to Alejandro. I swear it'll make sense. Keep your patience."

I leaned forward, close enough I could smell his heady maleness that I'd had all over me in the car. "Is this some kind of a test?'

"Everything in life is a test. This is just another one." He winked at me. "Maybe you want to rest? Are you tired?"

I laughed. "I'm fine. But if I wore you out, you should go take a nap."

His eyes widened before he shook his head. "The mouth on you."

I'd iced their hands, and it felt like a good time to exit, so that was what I did. I closed the door to the room and leaned against it, closing my eyes. I'd had quite a few days. But I didn't know exactly what to do with Francisco and Javier, if we weren't on some kind of activity, or if I hadn't just gotten married and was in a little bit of shock. They were strangers. I'd had sex with them both, but that was what they were. Plus, they probably wanted a little bit of a break from babysitting—sorry, guarding—me. I'd been hoisted into their lives just as much as they'd been shoved into mine.

All of us could use a little space. And now that I had hair products, I was actually going to shower and relax.

Tonight, I'd get some answers, hopefully. I needed to know what was happening. Badly.

* * *

A long shower improved my mood. I washed away my insecurities. This was going to turn out to be a really simple problem. Alejandro didn't want to sleep with me, his brothers did. Why? Maybe Alejandro was gay. I put the conditioner in my hair and stood there, letting it settle into my long locks so that I wouldn't look like I'd just been zapped by electricity when I next left the house.

Or maybe he wasn't gay. Maybe he was taken. That was going to be more complicated. He'd known for a decade he had to marry me. That didn't mean he hadn't gone and fallen in love with a woman. Unable to marry her because of me, he'd made promises to her that they would live as man and wife in all ways except legally. That meant that I was basically an intruder on their love story. Showing up at his home in two days, I could expect to receive hostility as a person pushing in on her territory. My heart sped up at that thought. That could be true if he were gay, as well. He might have a husband in all ways except under the law.

I chewed on my lip. If that was the case, then I had to get out of there. Let him send me to some far-off country where I could make myself happy and out of the way. I'd find my own secret love story. And finish my fucking degree somewhere.

We didn't have to be bound to unhappiness. So far, Francisco and Javier were really wonderful, but babysitting me was going to get old for them. Soon, I wouldn't be a novelty. Then I'd be stuck in a house with an angry almost-wife or husband, living my days alone until I drank myself to death or started talking to the hundred cats I'd have to adopt for company.

I rinsed out the conditioner. Alejandro was the heir of a drug empire. When his father died, it would become his, just as my father's had become Salvatore's. He had an MBA. Surely, he could see the best thing to do to keep everyone happy and producing income would be to send me away. I just had to appeal to his sense of logic.

Unless the truth was he'd taken one look at me, seen through the façade I presented to the world, known my soul was barren, my nose was fixed, and that someday, I would be a very unattractive woman trying to wear designer outfits, and decided he was never sticking his dick in that. His brothers were happy to fuck around with me for a while, and then I'd live behind the closed doors of some compound where everyone forgot I existed.

I think I preferred the scenario where he was basically married. At least then, it wasn't about me being somehow unfit.

Truth was, I should've been grateful Alejandro didn't want me that way. We'd both been sold like chattel to each other. I was getting released from obligatory sex. The problem was he was sexy, I liked him, and I wouldn't mind fucking him, even if that were all our marriage was. Without that, I wasn't bound to be very important to him, and since men all but ruled us in this life I'd been born into, I wanted him to want me too. My chances of happiness were higher if we could be friends who were married and sometimes fucked.

I was killing feminism minute by minute with my thoughts. My problem was I was a realist. This had happened. I needed to live with it.

Turning off the water when I was done, I dried myself off, took care of my hair with the product we'd bought, and set about drying it into some semblance of normalcy so I could stand to look at myself. I'd hung up my clothes in the empty half of his closet and used the empty drawers for the things that needed to be folded. I didn't have a suitcase to pack any of this up when I left, but maybe he'd have one for me that I could borrow when we went to their other home.

At least by then, I'd know what to do—maybe I'd be heading off to hide away in New Zealand or Australia, out of his view, to let him get on with his life. His brothers would forget me, and somewhere on a blip of a screen, looked at by law enforcement forever dodging his trail, would be the question of the missing wife that eventually everyone would forget existed.

Except I'd be living a great life, doing as I wanted elsewhere.

I put on my makeup using the mirror in the bathroom and then finally donned the black dress I'd bought for dinner. It was short, spaghetti stringed, and while it hugged my curves and showed off my cleavage with a scoop front, no one would call it overly sexy. I'd bought some strappy heels, and I put those on too. If I got cold, I'd gotten a cardigan to cover myself. The outfit made my legs look longer than they were.

To my eye, I was presentable and on time to go out. If Alejandro was back, he hadn't come into the bedroom, which meant I needed to go see if he was there or if I was meeting him at the restaurant. Surely, Francisco or Javier wouldn't have to accompany me in the car? That was going to get old for them fast. I liked their company and didn't want to be their burden.

All three brothers were in the living room. Alejandro stood, his back to me, looking out at the scenery that was Mexico City beneath us. Francisco leaned against the wall. Upon seeing me, he actually started to slow clap, which made my cheeks heat up immediately. Now, I was going to be red. Truth of a redhead was that we could never own our blushes.

"I know." Javier rose from where he sat on the couch. "I've gotten to see her in it twice. As far as I'm concerned, she wins the award for hottest woman in a little black dress ever."

"Why did I put on makeup when you two are going to make me so red?" I walked closer into the room, and my dinner date finally turned around.

If I'd expected him to give me any kind of once-over or approval, I'd have been disappointed. Well, I actually sort of was. He'd rolled up his sleeves and wore the same black pants and dress shirt he'd been in this morning. His jacket was swung over one of the chairs.

"Ready?"

Well…I guessed that was it. If either of his brothers thought his behavior strange, they didn't indicate it, and that was fine. I looked the best I could, and that was all I could manage for this evening. I supposed I didn't need a wallet, and that was great because I had no idea where that was, either. Probably with all the rest of my stuff in the mysterious home we'd be going to at some point.

I nodded. "I'm ready."

He grabbed his coat, and I followed him to the elevator. I was going on a date with my husband so he could finally explain to me how my life was going to go. Of course, I was so nervous, I wasn't sure I'd be able to eat a thing. We might as well have just stayed in the apartment and talked there.

But I followed him silently to a different car than the one I'd been in earlier, but the same driver waited with the door open. To the right, three men cleaned the vehicle that Javier and I used earlier that day. I tried not to be horrified at the thought that they knew what we'd been doing in it and that was why they were scrubbing it down. Maybe they just regularly detailed all the cars.

This time, I smiled at the man who held open the door. "Thanks, Eduardo."

He blinked, a small smile spreading over his face. Maybe he didn't speak fluent English, but he'd gotten that much of what I said. Alejandro shot me a look of surprise before he held out his hand, and I followed him into the car.

This was a smaller sedan, with a separation between Eduardo and us. It wouldn't be so easy to lie down and do dirty things in this ride. Not that Alejandro would want to. He'd been very clear about that.

"Did you enjoy your day?" he asked me as we pulled out into traffic.

I smiled. "I did. Very much. Thank you."

"Good." He nodded. "I'm glad to hear that."

*Well, this is awkward as fuck.* It was worse than sitting next to an utter stranger on a subway. That person you could ignore. In this case, we were forced to make some kind of conversation.

"Did *you* have a nice day?" I asked him.

He sighed. "I don't really have nice days. I have fine days and rough days. That is just the nature of it, I suppose." He stretched out his legs a little. "Today has been fine, and the way this evening goes will determine the end result."

"Where are we going to dinner?" I hadn't asked him before. It didn't really matter. The food was secondary to whatever conversation we were going to have.

"Your brother told me that you like Italian food. He suggested that pasta tended to put you in a good mood."

My mouth twitched. That was Armani. He was the one who would know that. A pang of regret hit me, and I missed him. We'd always been so close. It didn't negate what he'd participated in, but it mattered that he'd thought to tell my new husband details about me.

"Then I suppose, to bring the topic back to your previous point, do you think that something terrible will happen tonight over pasta that will change your day from fine to awful?"

Alejandro looked out the window. "It might."

His words did nothing to alleviate my nerves

We finally arrived at the restaurant, and Alejandro took my arm. It was fancy inside, but not more so than I was used to in Chicago. What was different however, was that it seemed like all eyes in the room were on us. Alejandro said something to the host, who took us to the back of the restaurant. My brothers didn't like to talk in public, tables could always be bugged, but Alejandro didn't seem concerned.

Seated, I looked around while he spoke to a waiter and a person who was maybe the owner. I wasn't sure. He introduced me to both, who said things that I didn't follow. It didn't really matter, because I smiled and that seemed to be all that was asked of me. Menus were set down.

I wished I had my phone so I could translate some of it, but since I absolutely didn't, I was going to need some help.

"I don't know what I'm looking at. Can you order for me?"

He gave me a small smile and set down his own menu. "Yes. Absolutely."

A few more words to more people, and then wine sat in front of us. That was good. I needed a drink. A big one. Probably one stronger than that wine was going to be, but it would do. I hadn't eaten lunch. That meant that breakfast was the last time I'd really consumed food. The wine might go right to my head, so even though I wanted it, I didn't touch it.

Finally, we were alone, waiting for the food with the door closed to the outside restaurant. I expected him to speak, and he didn't. In fact, he wasn't even looking at me, but off to the side. I looked where his gaze had wandered, and there was nothing on the wall. That meant that he wasn't really with me.

"Do you have this room regularly swept for bugs?"

He blinked and stared at me directly. "Bugs?"

"Sorry, listening devices."

Alejandro nodded very fast, as though it just occurred to him what I meant. "Yes. I know bugs. Sorry. Listening devices. Yes, we do. Here and several other restaurants that we eat at regularly. They are swept. You are safe to speak here, as am I."

I took his hand across the table. Right then, I wasn't sure if I was doing it for his sake or mine. Alejandro looked lost. He visibly swallowed and then pulled his hand away from mine before he leaned forward. "Trust is interesting, isn't it? Once it's gained, it's the most precious thing in the world, but lose it, and you can't get it back. In my business, not being able to trust someone means they're dead. I don't necessarily trust everyone I work with, but if I absolutely don't trust them, they're done."

I picked up my wine and took a long drink. "So now that you've threatened me, let's get to the point of it, shall we? I get it. If I betray you in any way, tell anyone anything, I'm dead." I set down my drink. "I am sufficiently chastised to behave myself. I have no phone, which is purposeful, I imagine. Or computer, so I can't run out of here with whatever you're going to tell me and stick it on social media. The truth, however, is that I wouldn't have anyway. I grew up in this life. There are many truths I don't tell, many things I will take to my grave."

I was good at secrets—like how I was never really convinced the boating accident that had killed my parents had been an accident. Boats didn't just blow up. But I'd kept it to myself, always. Like a big secret never to be discussed.

"When I was twelve years old, I started going on runs across the border with some of my father's top lieutenants." He didn't look angry as he spoke, it was like he was just going to tell me a story about his life, not like it was the kind of thing that warranted being warned about death first before I could hear it. "I told you that was about the age we did it."

Yes, it was yesterday. I remembered that. I nodded, not wanting to interrupt by saying anything.

"One time, on the way back, I was kidnapped. The lieutenants watching me were dead. For all that I feel I have seen it all now, I hadn't yet at that time. Still, there were things that I knew. Kidnappings happened to the children of the rich, and that I would soon be home. That is what I believed. Only it didn't happen like that."

My hands started to buzz. It was like my whole body knew that whatever I was about to hear was awful. "What did happen?"

"They started to talk about wanting to break the boy. That was the line they kept saying, in English, actually. *Break the boy*. Ransom was sent out, but they were in no hurry to bring me back. Instead, it was all about breaking me. They did things. Unspeakable things that should never be done to a child. And, when it was over, I guess they felt I was sufficiently broken."

I forced myself to swallow. "Alejandro…"

"Do not pity me, Lily. Don't you *ever* pity me."

I shook my head fast. "You are the heir to one of the biggest crime families in the world. I think pity would be the wrong emotion for anyone to have for you. They obviously didn't break you. I am, however, terribly sorry that happened to you, and I'm allowed to feel that way."

My words seemed to calm him, because he sat back in his seat a little and unclenched his fists. Would he have hit me if I pitied him? I didn't think so, but how could I be sure? This was not a story he'd have told me if he had any other choice, so we hadn't really gotten to the bad part of this yet. What he'd told me so far didn't amount to anything I absolutely had to know. I could have gone my whole life without knowing it.

"With no other choice, I quickly had to force myself to get on with things. My father would not have tolerated a broken son. He already had two spares, if I didn't amount to what he wanted, so I pushed on. Went to school, and honestly, I might have believed I was okay until it came time for other things to happen." He grabbed his water.

"Other things?" I honestly wasn't sure what he meant. What *other* things? Killing someone? Was that a ritualistic thing they did?

"Sex." He set down his water. "I was a teenager very interested in sex, except my body has apparently decided it was not interested."

What he was saying finally hit me square in the head. He *couldn't* have sex. "In what way?" There were lots of ways people had sex. If it were just that he didn't like to do it one way or another, we could work around that. Lots of people had triggers that didn't work for them.

He held up his hand. "I don't get hard. I just don't. It's not lack of interest. I just don't...respond. At all. Ever. I don't wake up hard. There is no imagery that makes me that way, nor does any kind of stimulation. As privately as I could manage it, I've seen doctors and therapists. At this point, it seems a done deal. I don't let myself even think about it most of the time. Sex isn't a factor in my life, and I avoid all things that might make it one. Most of our high up lieutenants think I'm very religious. Javier and Francisco indulge in things publicly. It keeps everyone distracted from the fact that I don't. My father doesn't know. Nor my uncle, but my brothers know, and that was how we concocted this scheme. You shouldn't be forced to be married to a man who can't give you a full life. My brothers can. So I am your husband, but they'll be your lovers, which I hear has already happened, and that makes me think this might actually work."

My head was spinning. He had just said quite a lot of important things to me. "I am…I am so sorry that happened to you. I think how you have found a way to keep going when things are not all as you'd have liked them is amazing."

Really, fuck his father and uncle. No one had thought to get him actual help when he got home? They had a woman in the kitchen with her lips sewed together. It hadn't occurred to me to ask how she ate. Somehow, she was getting nutrition, and Alejandro had been through a living hell.

He let out an audible breath. "Thank you. That is…very nice for you to say."

"It's just true." I cleared my throat. There wasn't going to be enough wine in that bottle tonight, so I just wasn't going to touch it at all. In fact, I sort of wished he hadn't ordered any food. I wasn't going to be able to eat it. "Would it be okay if I asked some questions about our situation? Not about what happened to you. I understand that you aren't going to talk about it, and I'd never ask."

He nodded, a lot of the tension in his back visibly relaxing. "Ask. This is your life too."

Yes, it was. Now I understood it a little better.

# 8

"You told your brothers to sleep with me." He implied as much, but I wanted to be sure I understood him perfectly.

He nodded. "Because I can't."

A knock sounded on the door, and we both shut up as they came in carrying our first course. I'd never wanted a waitstaff away from the table faster, and although I was sure they were going at a regular speed, it felt enormously slow.

When they were gone, I stared at my food and started again. "I don't want them sleeping with me because you told them to do it. It was one thing when I thought it was just this odd way we were living. Like, when I thought you had a woman or a man that you were in love with and your brothers wanted to fuck me, so that was fine. It's another thing now. I feel a little bit like a chore they were assigned. Do the dishes, sleep with your brother's wife—I think I'd rather that stop. No more sleeping together. There are plenty of ways I can handle myself if I need that kind of release."

His smirk took me by surprise. "I don't think either one of them would equate sleeping with you as some kind of task given to them. They're both deeply attracted to you. I don't spend a lot of time thinking about these things. It pains my soul to do so, but that I can tell."

"Thank you, but I think before you even knew what I would look like, you told them to handle this part of life for you. They had no idea if they'd want to, but they agreed to it because they love and are loyal to you. Let's let them find their own bed partners and take me out of the equation."

Alejandro scooped some pasta onto his plate. "I'm not going to rescind the permission. If you don't want to sleep with them, say no or tell them you'd rather not. But if I try to pull you back now, they'll both rebel. They want you, Lily. What's more, is I think they really like you."

I liked them too, but was I always going to wonder what was real and what was ordered? I had to think about this. I followed his suit and put some of the pasta onto my plate. To be polite, I took a bite. It was delicious. Flavorful. My absolute favorite kind of food. Still, I had no stomach for it.

"What about you and me? How do we work? I'm your wife in the eyes of everyone. How do we behave? What are the rules?"

He looked up, his dark eyes boring into me. "We share a bed every night. As far as the staff and the outside world is concerned, we're sleeping together all the time. So whatever goes on with my brothers, if it continues, it has to be discreet and not when others are around to see it, not even the staff that will be with us every day. And you sleep each night with me. In my bed."

As we had done the night before. Okay. I understood that. "How do we behave otherwise?"

"How do you think husbands and wives behave?"

At first, I thought he was being dismissive, but then I realized it was a real question he was actually asking me. I set down my fork. "Well, I guess they do this kind of thing. They go to dinner. They spend time together. I suppose, if we can keep this up, and if I can be there for you in whatever way you think would be useful to have a wife, then we can, ultimately, be good friends."

He pointed at his plate. "You should eat more of this. It's really good." It was, but I had no stomach for it. "Yes, let's be good friends if we can. Let's get to that point where we can count on one another. I hope we can."

The waiters knocked again. It seemed like a good idea to stop talking. I had a lot to digest, and I didn't just mean the wonderful food that arrived.

I stared at my husband. *Where do we go from here?*

He waited until the waiters had left again to address me. "Lily, perhaps this doesn't need to be said, but to be completely transparent, I must say it— I can't be cheated on. If I'm made a mockery by my wife, I lose power and something will have to be done about it. If you don't sleep with my brothers, you sleep with no one. And, if you break that rule, well, I think you know what will happen."

I laughed, which was the absolutely wrong thing to do, but I couldn't help it. In fact, I laughed so hard, tears actually came out of my eyes. I wiped them away. "How many times do you suppose you can threaten me in one meal, Alejandro? We're currently at two. Do you think we can get to four by the time they bring the main course, or will we stall at three?" I held up my hand. "This is the last time I'm going to say that you can trust me. After that, you'll just have to see. But if you keep threatening my life, I'm going to decide I can't trust *you*. We're in this together. Don't make me scared for my very existence. You do have an entirely other choice."

Alejandro held my gaze. His eyes hardened when I spoke, but there was also something else… Maybe it was grudging respect. I didn't fold and just cry that of course I wouldn't step out on him. I was too worked up to have lost my backbone at the moment.

"What's that?"

"Send me away. Put me somewhere where you'll never have to deal with me again. I won't bother you or make a fuss. I'm good at staying off the internet. Just be done with me. You've fulfilled your end of the bargain. You married me. Nowhere does it say you have to stay married forever."

He drummed his fingers on the table. "Let's leave that for now. I think you could be downright useful to have around, and we might become, as you said, good friends. But yes, we can be rid of each other if it comes to that." He put his hand out like he wanted me to shake it.

I almost reached for it. "Rid of each other does not mean killing me."

He almost smirked. "I didn't make that threat. We're still at two. I didn't mean killing you. I meant sending you to live in a convent somewhere."

"A *convent*?"

He laughed, throwing his head back at what must have been my utterly horrified expression and tone. "Don't you want to be Sister Lily?"

"That might be a little hypocritical on my part, considering I'm not entirely sure I believe in God."

His smile fell. "Really?"

"I didn't say I'm a nonbeliever, just that I'm not sure." I ate more of my pasta, some of my appetite returning. There was chicken on the table now, and it smelled fantastic.

"We just got married in the church." He dug into his food too.

"Well, no one particularly asked me. I'm not sure what I would have said anyway. If it was important to you, I'm glad we did it."

It wasn't like we were going to have children to worry about raising one way or another, anyway. That thought jarred me. I wasn't going to be a mother. Ever. Not that I'd wanted that tomorrow or anything, but I'd always assumed that one day, it would be an option.

As we weren't going to be having sex, that was off the table.

Well…that was what it was.

"So you believe in what, then?"

These were my favorite first dates. The ones where we did more than comment on the décor or the weather. Real issues that said whether we wanted to see each other again. Only this time, I was having it with my husband. We were going to see each other again, whether we wanted to or not.

"I believe in being good to others. Being as nice as I possibly can be. A little bit of vengeance when necessary. I don't get hung up in what will happen next or won't. There's too much to worry about in the present to spend too much time thinking about that kind of thing."

He nodded. "Our mother was devout. I'm not overly religious, but I am a believer."

I sipped the wine. It tasted better now.

* * *

Dinner had flown by easier after we'd gotten through the hard parts. Alejandro was smart, funny, and pleasant to be around when he wasn't trying to make me afraid. He need not have bothered. I knew just how badly it would go for me if I betrayed his family.

Now that my stomach was very full, I was sleepy. It was dark in the car and after ten o'clock, which was when I'd have started to go out at home, not fallen asleep, assuming it was a weekend. I studied later than this during the week.

I yawned, and Alejandro side-eyed me. "It's been a long day."

"An okay one or a bad one?" I hated that he never had good ones. Even I had those on occasion.

He leaned back. "An okay one. I'm scary, but you don't act that way. You argue with me, you don't take threats the way others do. I think it turned out okay because of you. Thanks for that."

My eyes threatened to close. It was the wine. I'd eaten a lot, for me, and drank two glasses of that wine. It was going to be a struggle to stay awake. Eventually, I lost that battle, and when we finally arrived back at the apartment, I jolted to consciousness, aware that my head was on Alejandro's shoulder and that his head was leaning on my own as he breathed deeply.

We'd both conked out.

It was comfortable like this, even if remaining thus would eventually make my neck hurt. It hadn't yet. Still, we couldn't stay in the car all night. I touched his arm. "Hey, we're here."

He said something in Spanish but didn't rouse immediately. I squeezed him again. If I moved my head, he'd fall over, and that was just not a nice way to get up. "We're back."

Alejandro lifted his head. "Sorry, I didn't mean to…" He rubbed his eyes, and I scooted over so that he could have some space.

"I think that I'm the one who started it. Just knocked right out."

He smiled at me. "Yes, and then you were comfortable so I joined you, despite my best efforts to stay up. I don't fall asleep in cars usually. Too risky."

"Well, you've been carrying a burden since you learned of me that today you got to rid yourself of. It's probably a real hit to your adrenaline."

He smiled slowly. On anyone else, I'd call it a come-hither, sex promising look, but I knew now that wasn't going to be why he did it. "My adrenaline keeps me upright. Can't lose too much of that."

With a tap on the window, he indicated to Eduardo that we wanted to get out. He stepped out first. "Don't open that door. Let one of us get you."

I nodded. This part was going to take a little getting used to, but maybe that was the key. Once I'd been around more than a day, they'd see that I was fine, not a risk to them, and let me have a little more freedom on my own.

A girl could only hope.

We walked together back inside, and if I'd been left to it in the elevator, I might have put my head right on his shoulder and gone back to sleep standing up. This was a man who had twice said he would kill me, but all I wanted to do was curl up against him, even upright, and go to bed. It made no sense, but when the elevator opened to the apartment, I hadn't talked myself out of wanting it.

The television blared loudly in the living room. Both Javier and Francisco rose when we entered, the latter raising his arms over his head to stretch, like he'd been still for too long.

"Hey." Javier spoke first. "All well?"

I nodded. "Yes, it was a lovely dinner."

"And the other things? You get through them?" Francisco lifted a dark eyebrow as he spoke seemingly directly to his brother.

"We did." Alejandro stepped away from me. "I'm going to bed. My wife has some things she wants to discuss with you two. I'm not sure if she wants to do it tonight or tomorrow, but make yourselves available, will you?"

With that said, he strode into the bedroom, leaving the three of us behind to stand there awkwardly. I was tired, but sometimes it was better to just get things over with.

"Guys, I realize you've been put in an impossible situation. You want to protect him, and you love him, you're loyal to him. That doesn't mean you have to…fuck me just because he told you to. All right? You can go back to your lives. Now that I understand things, I'm not going to make you." I sighed. This might have been the strangest day for conversations ever. It ranked higher than the one where Salvatore had told me to get dressed because I was getting married. All right, maybe it had been a week of weird. "No need to give up your bodies to the cause, so to speak."

Javier tilted his head. "Are you under the impression that either of us had sex with you because Alejandro told us to? Like he was some kind of…pimp?"

Francisco laughed. "He says lots of things, *cariño*. Some of them we must listen to. But I don't think even my brother, who will someday be the head of this family, could tell me who to sleep with if I really didn't want to." He took my hand. "There was no hardship. In fact, I can't wait until we can do it again."

I held up my hand. "We really need to think on this. Obviously, I'm very attracted to both of you. There will, however, come a time when you either no longer wish to be with me that way or I feel that way. Then we have to live together. Or you meet a woman you want to marry. Or your father signs a contract this time for one of you. And then there we are…"

Javier's abrupt shake of his head is what stopped me from talking. "You worry about many things. We're all alive today. Today we want each other. Let it be enough for now. If something changes, you are still Alejandro's wife. We'll figure it out."

Wasn't that what I'd been saying to Alejandro at dinner? That I couldn't worry about tomorrow, when all I had was now. Javier had pretty much just parroted that back to me, and he didn't even know what I'd said earlier.

It was a good reminder about how I truly felt about things. "Okay. One day at a time then. See you in the morning."

Francisco motioned toward the couch. "You could watch a movie with us. Sit. Have a drink."

"On another night, I would love to. I'm a little bit exhausted. I need to close my eyes and process things."

Javier tugged me to him. He was warm when he whispered into my ear. "I said things to you today, and I meant them. Don't forget them when you are working this out in your head. I wouldn't touch a woman I didn't crave. You aren't a job or a burden to me. Remember that when this is all too heavy tonight. We'll be up late. You can come out and forget for a while."

I nodded against his chest. "Thank you."

With that, I left them there in the living room. Two men who were becoming my friends that I slept with. My brothers-in-law who both wanted me. I left their gorgeousness out in the living room and went to the room I would share platonically with Alejandro until tomorrow, when we'd go to bed the same way elsewhere.

He looked out into the night, a glass of whisky in his hand, staring at the dark skyline. Where had he gotten the booze? Did he have a secret stash? Better I not know, actually. I didn't want to start drinking at three in the morning when I couldn't sleep.

Besides, this was his room. He could keep his secrets. Right now, I felt more like a guest, and even though this was new and time had a way of changing things, I really felt that wouldn't change. It was why I didn't want to watch the movie, either. Guests should go to bed and leave their hosts to enjoy their lives without infringing on them too much.

This was going to be really, really complicated.

He turned. "Get any answers?"

"Yes, but I'm in no condition to consider them tonight." I walked until I stood right beside him. "It's pretty out there tonight. Is there anything I need to do tomorrow, before I have dinner with the family?"

He shook his head, slowly. "The day is yours. What were you thinking of? Javier will have a phone for you tomorrow, and your laptop should be home when we get there."

"I'd like to see Mexico City. I've never been here before, and I don't know if I'll be back. Just some of the sites like a tourist, is that possible?"

He nodded. "Yes, it's possible, but you will be back often. We come here for business all the time, hence the second home. Or third home. I forget in what order these places were purchased at this point."

"You come back here. Perhaps I will, if you need me. But I don't think you'll bring me on all your trips, will you?"

I left him to open the drawer and take out the loungewear I'd bought for sleep. Long pants and a tank top to wear that were soft, cotton, and white. Excusing myself, I left Alejandro and my unanswered question in the room to change quickly and brush my teeth. I braided my hair for the night and washed off my makeup. My discarded dress needed to be hung up, and I did that first thing upon entering the bedroom again.

"I don't know," was how he acknowledged me, finally turning from the window. "Today, I met with one of your senators. In secret, of course. He had his wife with him. It would have been convenient to have my own. Perhaps sometimes, you will come."

*Fair enough.* That woman was probably there for show as much as I would be, if I'd accompanied him. They might even have their own business arrangement. Perhaps more people did than I ever thought about, and if I were supposed to be shocked that he'd met with a senator, I wasn't. My brother regularly had dinner with the governors of several states.

Everyone was in everyone else's pockets.

He left me there to watch the view while he took care of himself in the bathroom. I shut the shades as he'd had them the night before and dimmed the lights low. Enough that he could see but that it was obvious we'd be going to bed.

With that, I climbed into my side. Having slept in the car, I knew I was exhausted, but this was still a totally new experience for me. Last night, I'd been drugged, but today, I had my senses intact. Was I going to be able to sleep?

The answer was yes, because I was out as soon as my head hit the pillow.

I dreamed of little boys running up a mountain. They were laughing. Three of them, all dark brown hair, one of them had curly locks. They were shouting and laughing but stopped all of a sudden. I chased after them. Why had they stopped? Darkness surrounded us, and even though I didn't know the children, I wanted to protect them. Keep them safe. I reached for them, but they were gone. There was nothing for me to grab.

Then I was in the darkness.

It wasn't safe, but it was familiar.

It was the light that woke me, streaming through the cracks in the shades. I lifted my head but couldn't move very far, as I was the little spoon to Alejandro's big one. His arm was flung over me, keeping me down while we shared a pillow in the center of the bed. I'd done it again, somehow managed to cuddle with him in sleep. This was going to be awkward.

His alarm beeped, and in seconds, he'd let go of me and turned it off. I closed my eyes. Maybe if I pretended to sleep, we could avoid the conversation altogether. It wasn't like I was doing it on purpose. Embarrassment made my heart race. Why was I cuddle seeking? I'd never done it before.

Alejandro sat up, putting his hand on my hip, and since I could hardly pretend I hadn't felt that, I rolled over to look at him. His knees were up to his chest, and he was beautiful in the morning light. We even sort of matched, as he wore white boxers. His leg muscles were thick, like he was a runner, and even that thought made me long to run myself. Maybe tomorrow, when we got to the place they called home, I could do that.

“Did you sleep okay?” He smiled at me. Alejandro didn’t have all his guards up yet. Looked like first thing in the morning, he was somewhat relaxed.

I leaned up on my elbow. “I did. How about you?”

He nodded. “I did. I don’t remember waking at all.”

“Well, I hope you have an okay, fine day.”

He grinned at me, a real smile that was filled with plotting and subterfuge. Maybe that waited until he put on his clothes. “Have fun today. See you tonight.”

Alejandro jumped out of bed, and I snuggled down to my pillow. Looked like we weren’t going to address our situation, and that was fine. He went into the bathroom, and I heard the shower start. This was the first day that I finally understood what my new life would look like, and it was kind of a pleasant start to a new day.

I rolled over. He had to be up, but I didn’t yet. I closed my eyes. It was nice to doze in the morning with nowhere to go and no one waiting for me. Time had a way of moving slow when I was awake and fast when I wanted to rest. I was going to grasp onto these moments.

# 9

I sat in my bathrobe and watched Guadalupe make breakfast. She knew what each of them wanted to eat. We were lined up again at the counter, but this time, Alejandro joined us. All of them looked at their phones, and although Javier had handed me one that was now considered safe for me to use, I wasn't feeling compelled to look at it right then.

Someone—probably Javier—had put the guys' cell phone numbers into the phone before they gave it to me. Also, most of my friends were in there. When I'd asked why some were missing, he'd shrugged and said they were dangerous. It was hard for me to believe that the always stuttering Ryan, who I sat next to in Psych 101 in undergrad, was a hazard, but this wasn't a point I was prepared to argue about right then.

*How does she eat?* I texted the question to Javier.

He looked at it and then answered me fast. *A port. I help her when there are problems.*

Well, one mystery solved. What was Guadalupe's life like to make her feel she needed to go to such extremes? What was it she couldn't say? I had my phone, so I quickly googled what I wanted to say. Opening my mouth, I gave it a try. "*Gracias por el desayuno.*"

While Guadalupe smiled and nodded at me, my accent was apparently so bad that it caused all three of the guys to laugh at me. Guadalupe swatted Javier with her dish towel and exited the room to go do something else, although I didn't know what. I'd only ever seen her in the kitchen.

"That bad?" I held up my hand. "No, don't tell me. I know it was. I'll start working on an app tomorrow for languages. I was trying to be nice."

Javier leaned over and spooned some eggs onto toast. He picked it up and held it to my mouth. "Chew and swallow."

"She ate last night." Alejandro added, "Don't try to speak Spanish around our father and uncle. You'll never hear the end of it. Just wait until you're more accustomed to it."

"He's being polite," Francisco helped. "Trust me, you don't want to be a joke to them. You never stop being one if they find a chink in your armor."

That was good to know. I took a bite of the toast. I hadn't been actively not eating, just distracted.

"She wants to go see the sights today. Francisco, you are taking her." Alejandro was still looking down at his phone.

Francisco grinned, but Javier slammed down his toast. "I could take her."

"No, you're coming with me. We're going to check on some people today as a courtesy, and having you with me will speak well to them. Francisco is going to tour her around, and then we'll all have dinner with Dad and Uncle Geraldo."

Francisco fake coughed in his hand. "I'm sick. I think by tonight I won't be able to make dinner."

Alejandro shook his head. "Nope."

"Fuck. But I get Lily today. So I win." He smiled. "Which tourist places do you want to go to?"

"Hold on." Alejandro rose. "Looks like Dad is moving things. No touring today, I'm sorry. We're going over there now."

I blinked. "Now?"

"Now. He wants us back home tonight, so we are doing the

roundup with him now. Then, off we go." He actually clapped his hands together, which made me want to laugh. Alejandro Hernandez, heir to a drug kingdom, looked like a camp counselor.

I rose. "I'm going to need a minute to get dressed, obviously." My nighttime clothes were not going to work. I'd picked up a few more casual things, and they were going to have to do.

We were going to his house, not a restaurant. I'd make my pants look dressier.

"How long do you need?" He rocked back on his feet.

"I can be ready in ten." I turned my back. I would be, and that was impressive. It was a huge bummer I wasn't going to have the day I'd hoped for, but it was a small thing. I was Alejandro's wife. He needed me to do certain things with them, and this would be one of them. His father and uncle. The ones who hadn't gotten him out of trouble fast enough, so their enemies had tried to break him.

I stood in the bedroom and realized I couldn't remember getting into the room. My mind was so preoccupied with…things, that I'd totally zoned out. I took a deep breath. Was this when it got heavy? I rubbed my eyes. *Okay.* I didn't live through Alejandro's pain. I wasn't going to pretend I had a clue what that was like. I just knew that, if I'd been kidnapped, my family would have paid quickly to get me home and sent me to whatever help I needed. I was pretty sure they'd have done that for any of my brothers too.

I shook my head. This wasn't going to help me get dressed any faster. I rushed into the closet, pulled out the black pants and the dressy tank top I'd bought. The sweater I'd not worn the night before would do too. I shoved makeup on my face and brushed my hair until it was smooth. I was presentable. They knew what I looked like, they'd all been there when Alejandro and I had said I do.

I shoved strappy sandals on and made it back outside in eight minutes. The three of them stood there waiting, and just like the night before, Alejandro was a statue as he looked at me. His brothers made a fuss, Javier putting his arm around me and Francisco kissing my hand.

"So lovely in no amount of time." He smiled. "When next we

return to Mexico City, I will take you to see all the sights. We will spend the whole day, just you and me."

I bumped into Javier when I went to move, feeling his piece beneath his jacket. It was a good reminder of where I was going. These were dangerous men going to see their dangerous patriarch and uncle. I didn't really understand everything about this life yet, but their dad was enough to make Alejandro jumpy. That was important to know.

We walked in silence downstairs to the car that had been cleaned the night before. It wasn't the same driver. "What happened to Eduardo?"

Alejandro side-eyed me. "He was a little too familiar with the lady of the house?"

"What?" I almost tripped getting into the car as his words hit me. "He wasn't familiar with me."

"You addressed him by name. He smiled at you. That's not how this works." The door to the car closed, and he finished. "You're ours. Others don't get to speak to you, not if they work for us."

I leaned forward. I was next to Francisco. Javier and Alejandro faced us from the other side. "I am not going to only speak to the three of you for the next however long I live. That is not a reasonable ask."

Alejandro matched my glare, sitting forward. "That wasn't what I was going to ask of you, but if I wanted you to only speak to the three of us for the rest of your natural life, that is what you would do."

He sat back, and so did I. My heart raced, and all the good feelings I'd built up about him over the last day fled. Wow, he was an incredible asshole. The tears that I didn't want to shed threatened again, and once again, I concentrated on not shedding them. It was all I could think about, and that was okay, because the guys were speaking to each other rapidly in Spanish.

Francisco was tense next to me.

I didn't look at any of them.

Alejandro had told me he was terrible to fight with.

Francisco put his hand on my knee. "No one will expect you to not speak to anyone. He doesn't mean that. We all get a little touchy when we have to go see Dad."

I swallowed. "Just let me know what you want from me."

I grabbed my phone. Back in Chicago, my friends were living their lives. If I couldn't even say hello to a driver without causing some kind of problems, I'd just speak over text to them. I picked my friend Janice first. She was getting engaged any day.

*Hey, it's Lily. How are you?* I sent the text.

Francisco squeezed my knee. "Lily."

They wanted me to look up, so I did. Otherwise, this car ride was going to get long. "I get what you want. I do. Obedience. Yes, sirs. There are very few things I'm going to push back at you about. Most things don't matter to me one way or another. But a man has lost his position because I dared to say hello to him? That's not okay. Your judgement on what I did or didn't do was wrong, and I'm pissed off. But I'll still play my role tonight and every night, even if I'm mad. Trust me, we all have daddy issues."

Francisco snorted and then full-on laughed. "Daddy issues."

"It's not funny." Javier rolled his eyes. "I told you not to talk to him. There is protocol for all of this."

I forced myself to take a deep breath. So it wasn't just Alejandro who was going to be obnoxious about this. It was Javier too. "Do you feel the same way?"

"I don't care one way or another." Francisco shrugged. "I don't like that you're unhappy right now."

Javier shook his head. "You *do* care. That's bullshit." He turned to me. "Did you really walk around Chicago knowing the name of everyone in your family's business empire?"

I sighed. "Most of them, yes. When my father was alive, he'd have these huge get-togethers in the backyard. They were all aunt and uncle so and so. That's even how they were introduced. Sometimes they'd die, we'd all be like *oh that's really sad*, and then someone would say something religious, and then we'd all move on. After my father was gone, the barbecues stopped, and I didn't call my brothers' associates aunt and uncle, because we're too close in age. But they were still part of our lives, like they're family. I didn't have someone driving me around, so that wasn't an issue."

Javier sighed. "I'm glad for you. We used to have that too. But when someone takes a member of your family, and you know you were betrayed by someone trusted enough to have access to you, then you have to start limiting who is allowed to be close. You have to make it clear there aren't people on the inside who can hurt you. Because of this, you don't give them the chance to know you, to take those that you love away from you. Eduardo is probably fine. His family has been with us forever. No, I don't actually think he was going to hurt you because you said hello to him, but I don't want him paying too much attention to you, and neither should you."

Well, Javier had certainly just spit out quite a mouthful. For his part, Alejandro was a statue. If he thought or felt anything, I couldn't read it on his face. I'd obviously made Javier worked up because his accent had thickened when he spoke, increasing as he went on. I attributed their almost total lack of an accent to their boarding school education, but there it was, showing up when he got really angry.

"I said hello to him, he didn't say hello to me. He barely acknowledged me speaking to him at all. And now, because his wife," I pointed at Alejandro, "didn't know the rules or didn't listen to them after you told me, there is a man who has just been essentially demoted. Lost his rank, maybe bonuses, or whatever that means here. What kind of hit is that man going to take to his life because he isn't driving for all of you now?" I held up my finger. "I was thoughtless because I didn't understand the rules. I'm upset about it. I can't fix it because I am powerless here. Not that I ever had any power anywhere, but now I've fucked somebody over. Not to mention, I am apparently now being told that my husband can dictate who I speak to for the rest of my life."

"And we're here." Francisco shook his head. "Just another day at the Hernandez household gatherings. I do love these visits to dear old Dad."

The door opened, and he got out. Apparently, that was all we were going to say on the matter for now. My husband extended his hand, and I took it while his brothers got out the other side of the vehicle. To be careful, I didn't even make eye contact with the driver and his helper. There were two of them with us. I looked at neither.

"Is this a place your father uses sparingly too? Like you guys with where we're staying?" I asked Francisco. I wasn't happy with any of them, but he was the least irritating to me at the moment.

"Yes, he has a compound near ours at home too. When they were being built, he put himself in one with his brother and then ours was for us as adults. We could change it, but somehow, it's worked."

We approached the house, and Alejandro took my arm. "Let's do a history of the construction practices of my family another time."

I took his point. We were in this deception about our relationship for the sake of keeping his private business just that—private. I was mad, but I wasn't vindictive. I'd never be that way. He wasn't sure he could trust me as of yet. This might be an example that he could. Not that I was particularly in the mood to play games, but when I pulled his arm from me, it wasn't to be a bitch but rather so I could take his arm instead. It was a more submissive pose.

They had to ring the bell at their family's home, and Javier did just that. He shot me a look I couldn't decipher, and then we were inside. I made sure to not hold eye contact with anyone very long. Another mistake would be bad. Better to keep my eyes downcast and just get through this evening.

Or that was my plan until Miguel turned to me. I couldn't very well ignore my father-in-law. He put out his hand, and I shook it before he tugged me into a too-tight hug. There were greetings that were made to make me feel included and greetings that were clearly meant to dominate me. I was given the second. It was like he was asserting his right to hold me too close if he wanted to.

I gave him a moment to not make a scene, and then I pulled back, nearly stumbling into their uncle, who I hadn't met before.

Alejandro gripped my elbow. He had to have seen what just happened. A muscle ticked in his jaw. I'd just somehow pissed him off again. So I lowered my gaze and smiled demurely at his uncle.

After this evening, Alejandro might just stick me on a plane to New Zealand and be done with me.

"Tio," he said, addressing the other man. "This is my wife, Lily. Lily, this is my Tio Ricardo."

I knew that word. I'd heard it before. It meant uncle. I smiled at the man, and he smiled back.

"You have the loveliest green eyes. I noticed them in the church. My nephew lucked out with his wife. Looks like we won out in this arrangement."

He smiled at me and said all the right things. Still, I shivered. His eyes were dead. Javier caught my gaze, narrowing his, but I otherwise wasn't sure even Alejandro, who had my elbow still, noticed my discomfort.

"You're too kind." I let my gaze travel down. The perfect wife who wouldn't make a fuss, who would fit in with no issues whatsoever.

"Yes, we lucked out." Their dad spoke again. "We were fairly certain you were going to be ugly."

There really was nothing to say to that. I'd addressed it with Francisco already. They'd all have to be stupid to not know I'd been fixed up.

But he wasn't done. "We wouldn't want Alejandro to have ugly children."

That panged my soul, as I was sure it was meant to do. Yes, any children I had would have the possibility of suffering through similarly unfortunate years as my teen years. Although, no one ever criticized how my brothers looked. On their faces, the nose was striking. Women liked them just fine.

Of course, I wouldn't be having babies, so this was for naught anyway. It was easy to put on my smile and answer him, even as I seethed. This was their fault. They hadn't protected him. This whole fucked-up situation was because of these men here. But I was a good liar. You couldn't come out of my family and not be. "Any children Alejandro has will be gorgeous, I think we can say that for sure." I wished I could make myself blush, but that was beyond my abilities.

Still, it seemed to be the right answer, because his father nodded like that was a given. People were inexplicably proud of their genes, even though they had absolutely no control over the ones they did and didn't get.

"I need a drink," Francisco announced, and his words propelled us from the front hall into the dining room. There were two other lieutenants joining us for brunch. I didn't catch their names as they were brushed past me like either they or I didn't matter. Maybe it was both.

I sat with Alejandro on one side and Francisco on the other. Everyone started speaking at once, and none of it in a language I could understand. I focused on my meal, one I really wasn't in the mood to eat. I'd just had eggs on toast not so long ago, but there was a ton of food in front of me, and I wouldn't be accused of making a scene by not eating it. So I chewed and swallowed while I moved food around on my plate to look like I'd eaten more than I had.

This wasn't an I-have-an-eating-disorder problem. I was just full. Still, the guys ate like they had an endless pit of a stomach, and I envied them for it. There were Bloody Marys on the table, mimosas, and something with tequila. The eggs here were good, but not as tasty as Guadalupe's. I could see why the guys held onto her.

Francisco sat back in his seat, and the movement drew my attention to what was happening across from me. Javier was pissed off. I didn't know why, but his target was the man next to him, one of the unnamed lieutenants. They had Alejandro's attention and he joined the fray, and soon, both his father and uncle were all focused on the screaming match over brunch.

One second, everyone was in their seats, the next, those two were up and on each other. Alejandro darted up, not to stop it but to stand in front of me so I couldn't see it clearly. Or maybe he was trying to block me, to protect me, but it felt like the first option, like he just didn't want me to see. Francisco joined him, forming a wall between me and the other side of the table. Still, I could see between them, and I wasn't the least bit surprised by how it was going. His opponent was big and strong, but Javier was tougher.

He had the other man by the shirt as he pounded on him. That was before he pulled out his gun.

This got Alejandro to move. He shouted some things, and Javier still didn't retreat, not until Alejandro physically moved him.

The other man slumped to the floor. He was breathing, but he was also beaten, badly. Javier stormed from the room.

I wanted to go to him, to see if he was okay, but I had to be careful. No one could know I had any relationship with Alejandro's brother other than sisterly. I turned toward my husband. "Alejandro, would it be okay if I checked on your brother? See if he needs anything?"

He waved at me, still talking to the man on the ground. Whatever had transpired between the men, people remained pissed. I took the wave as a yes and hustled in the direction where Javier had stalked away, leaving the scene behind me. I found him in the back of the house, staring at the porch but not going out on it.

Breathing heavily, he ran his left hand over the knuckles on his right. They had to be hurting. "Are you okay?"

He turned when I spoke. "Fuck him."

I stepped closer. He hadn't told me to back off, which I would have done, if that were what he wanted. "I don't even know what happened."

"We've been losing some money. Someone is fucking with our business. There was an incident in Boston. That's been worked out. Rosa's new husbands figured out some things." He'd put an S on the word husband, which had to be a mistake, but it didn't matter at the moment. "The suggestion was made that it was Alejandro's negligence which caused the incident, and that my father should eliminate him to fix the problem. I won't ever let anyone hurt him, nor even suggest it."

That was so interesting because, next to me, Alejandro had seemed completely unfazed by the whole incident until Javier had pulled out his gun. It was back in place now.

I stepped closer. Was Alejandro not worried about being gotten rid of, or did he know Javier would handle it?

"Let me look at your hand."

He shook his head. "It's fine."

I put out my own. "Please."

This time, he relented, and I stared at his once again shorn knuckles. "He's lucky you would protect him from all things. Not everyone has that in this world. It's a gift. Still, if you keep beating up your hand, you won't be able to do your other job, which is taking care of people. So it dawns on me we should get you some kind of stick, like gangsters used to carry in movies."

Javier blinked. "Like a thick beating stick?"

"Right. A nightstick. You can carry it with your gun. Just whack people with it whenever they piss you off."

He laughed, a good roar, and some of the vibration I could feel coming from his skin cooled a bit. That was good. The adrenaline crash he was sure to have coming was going to be rough. "Alejandro didn't let you kill him."

"Not here, but he'll be dead tonight. Everyone here knows it. He's just sparing my father the bloody mess."

Maybe that was Alejandro's way of taking care of Javier right back. "I'm glad you're okay."

"You two." It was Francisco who appeared down the hall. "Come on. It's calming down in there. He's being removed from the house, and he'll be dealt with shortly. Come back before someone notices you're gone."

I dropped Javier's hand. "Do you beat up everyone you get mad at? Just wondering if I should start carrying ice bags for you."

He shook his head. "You'd never believe it, but most of the time, I'm very calm." Javier walked next to me toward Francisco. "I'm the sensible one."

Francisco had a drink in his hand. It was whisky, clearly his preferred choice when it came down to it, and he was on his second glass. Maybe it was his third. I wasn't keeping track. He drank. Javier beat people up. And Alejandro was silent. I guessed they all had their way of dealing with things. Who knew what mine would be once I'd been here for any length of time?

# 10

Their father wanted us out of Mexico City and home in Culiacán to solve the mystery of whatever was going wrong with their supply routes. We were leaving straight from the house. Francisco thought to tell me our stuff would be packed and brought to us. Truly, I wasn't sure how anyone would ever hide anything at all, considering how many hands other than my own were constantly touching my stuff.

It was a two-hour flight from Mexico City to Culiacán, and we didn't have to fly commercial, so we went straight from their father's home to the airplane. Three people met us there, ready to load luggage we didn't have, and then we were on the plane. I'd been on private planes before, in fact, I'd taken one to get to Mexico days ago. But theirs was bigger. In the US, organized crime spent a lot of time hiding from the FBI and the IRS. No one wanted to be the next Al Capone, going down for tax fraud. That would get them laughed out of the bad men's club.

So we hid wealth a lot. Literally, sometimes in dirt in the ground. They didn't seem too concerned with the law. Sure, there were organizations watching them—or at least I thought there had to be—but they didn't live looking over their shoulders like my brothers did.

Maybe that was why Alejandro was so preoccupied with security up front. Do it right away, and then he didn't have to think about it.

My phone dinged, and I smiled. It was my friend finally texting me back. *OMG, girl, where have you been? Guess what???*

I smiled. Janice didn't just text like that, she talked like that. She actually said 'OMG' instead of 'Oh my God.' It was fun.

*I'm in Mexico. I fell in love and got married.* That was the story, so I'd stick to it.

That was bound to get a fast response, but we were boarding and I didn't want to slow us down, so I turned off the volume and stuck it in my pocket. I'd text her from the air if we had Wi-Fi, otherwise I'd wait the two hours until we landed.

There were eight seats in the center of the plane and two rooms in the back I couldn't see from where I stood. "Is it okay if I have a window?"

I didn't know if we had assigned seats, but I loved to fly, loved to see everything from up high.

Alejandro indicated one of the chairs by the window. "Take this one."

I scooted past him to sit down. With only my phone, I didn't have much to do on this flight, but I'd managed to download my reading app onto it in the car and I'd read. Hopefully, my earbuds would be with my laptop when I got to where I'd be living. Then I could easily tune people out with my music or try to learn Spanish, so I wasn't always waiting for someone to translate.

My husband took the seat next to me, which left his brothers to each have their own rows of seats. Javier moved the divider between the seats and lay down, like it was a bed in which he intended to nap. Francisco didn't do that, but he closed his eyes after he placed earphones in his ears.

Jealousy was unattractive, so I refused to give in to it, but I'd do anything for those music listeners right then. I couldn't remember the last time I'd flown without music.

Alejandro took my hand in his, and he squeezed. I looked over at him. Had I missed something? Why was he doing that?

"I'm sorry."

I stared at him. "Sorry?"

"That I told you that I would dictate who you spoke to. I won't do that. I fully expect you to have friends. They'll be screened, but that is all. I would only tell you that you couldn't see them if they were some kind of spy. Otherwise, your friends are your own."

He spoke in a low voice. His brothers weren't currently paying attention to us, but that was neither here nor there. The low tone did make it seem like we were alone, just speaking between the two of us. Javier let out a snore, and we looked at each other, Alejandro smirking in amusement. The plane took off into the air, leaving the ground and my two days there behind.

What a long few days it had been, and yet also too fast in its own way. I still really hadn't seen Mexico City.

"Do I snore like that?" He looked at his brother and then back at me. "I haven't shared a room since I was a small child, and only then when Javier would crawl into bed to get away from my parents' fights. They did not like each other. No one to tell me if I'm doing that."

I shook my head. "No, you're quiet. Do I?"

"So quiet." He smiled at me. "Do you forgive me, Lily with the green-green eyes?"

I rolled those eyes at him. "Yes, and I will make an effort to not screw up the way things are done for safety reasons. No more talking to the staff. Is Guadalupe okay?"

"It's different with her. She's sort of like an odd aunt to us. Yes, talk to her. It's not like she talks back."

That was a terrible way to put it. "That's not nice."

"I think that is exactly what she wants, though. She could write things down if she really wanted to communicate. She still has both hands. She's literate and capable. Clearly, she sewed up her mouth, more than once, for the purpose of saying nonverbally that her mouth was shut."

That didn't make it nicer. "Point taken, but you know you were being mean."

I stared out the window at the view of the city I hadn't seen disappearing from beneath us. It was cloudy, and that meant we were going to be bumping in the air. Turbulence was the only thing I didn't like about flying. Never knowing when the next jolt in the air was going to come.

Alejandro stared straight ahead. He always seemed to be lost in thought.

"Is it okay for me to ask you what you're thinking about?"

He blinked rapidly and then stared at me. "Yes, of course. I'm worried my temper has made you more cautious around me. I can see how easily you joke with my brothers, but Javier is the only one you've seen really lose it. Why are you so much more nervous around me?"

I lifted an eyebrow. "Is that what you were thinking about?"

"No." He sighed. "I was contemplating who is trying to fuck up my life. I mean…there are the *always want my life* people. They're always on the list, but this feels more…personal. My life was just threatened in my father's house, that's how desperate this has gotten."

*Wow*. In that case, I could see why his mind was forever occupied. "Do you want to talk about it, or would that be an intrusion?"

He frowned at me. "I thought you asked my permission to see Javier at my dad's as part of the show—well done with that, by the way—but I didn't think you were really like this. Ask me whatever you want. If I don't want to answer, I just won't. Or maybe I'll be mean about it. Obviously, I sometimes am, but you don't have to walk on eggshells with me. We did very well together last night, didn't we?"

We had. I sat up a little. "You are in control of my life, Alejandro. It's a scary situation that making you upset with me could mean that I have little to no happiness." As it was, I wasn't expecting to be downright giddy very often, but maybe most people lived lives of quiet desperation. Fuck, I was quoting Thoreau in my own head. "So I'm trepidatious. We had a fight today. I forgave you. That doesn't mean I'm not going to be on shaky ground for a while. Or no ground, shaky air." As if it wanted to agree, the plane shook.

"I know there are couples in this arrangement who are going to be very unhappy based on family history and lots of other things. Your brothers and me? We don't hate each other. There's no love or trust lost, but it's okay with our families. I want you to be happy. I don't want to make you not that way."

He seemed so sincere in that moment that I decided to believe him. Or at least to believe that he believed what he was saying.

I swallowed. "Most of the time, you would suspect other families in the business. Others here in Mexico who want what you have."

"Yes, they'd be the list. Only, they don't get this close. We have plans in place and contingencies after that. Someone has to know what is happening. They are specifically targeting me too. Not Javier's runs. Not Francisco. Not my father or uncle's. Just mine."

I could eliminate a jilted lover from the list of possibilities. "Who has the most to gain from your losing power? From you being eliminated?"

"Javier, but you've seen him. He is loyal. We would walk through fire for each other. Francisco too."

I stared at him. "It's more than loyalty. They love you. You love them. It matters." I didn't know from personal experience, but I'd seen it. Love was real. It was all powerful.

"True." He smirked at me. "It just isn't particularly macho to talk about loving my little brothers."

Now it was my turn to laugh. "Fair enough."

"I see what you're saying. If I eliminate them, who gains by my death? Lieutenants? This is what I'm thinking about."

It was a lot. "I'm sorry this is happening to you."

His smile was slow and soft. "Thank you."

The plane shook violently, and I closed my eyes. "This is the only part I hate."

"Come here." He opened his arms. "I've got you."

I did as he said, lying down so that I was in his embrace. He even took his seatbelt and buckled me in with him. "I like the turbulence.

You don't know when it's coming, and it's just a reminder that you're alive and you're not on the ground. That you are doing something that our ancestors couldn't."

*Interesting way to look at it.* I wasn't tired, but I closed my eyes to not think about the shakes. There was something comforting about Alejandro when he wasn't threatening my life or yelling at me.

"Tell me something about you that I don't know. You're a graduate student studying anthropology. You grew up in Chicago. You have friends that you miss. Three brothers who you are avoiding speaking to. You are agnostic. Funny. Good at playing the games we must in this life. Javier's temper doesn't frighten you, but you don't like mine. You seem to see that Francisco is really smart when most people dismiss him. Those are some of the things I have cataloged. Tell me something I don't know."

That was a pretty good list for how little we knew of each other. "I like cats."

"Not dogs?" He still spoke in that low soothing voice.

"I like dogs, but in my heart, I'm a cat person. Which do you prefer?"

"Truthfully, I like cats too. We don't have any animals right now. Perhaps we should amend that? And I'd gladly have a dog, they are just needier than cats. I like how it has to be the cat's idea to get attention. The independence of it."

"When I was a little girl, I used to get scared of all kinds of things." I hadn't thought of this story in a long time.

He placed a comforting hand on my arm. "Like what?"

"Like of monsters coming through the roof. Or serial killers. Or demons possessing me while I slept."

Alejandro laughed. "This from the girl who doesn't believe."

"I was little. Anyway, my brother Salvatore told me that cats had a sixth sense about things. That they somehow knew if there was evil in the house. I believed him, because back then, Salvatore knew everything. So I loved having our cat around, because if the cat wasn't scared, then I had no reason to be. Plus, the fact that she loved us meant that we weren't evil, either." I shook my head. "Salvatore was obviously full of shit, but I believed him for years."

Alejandro was so quiet, I wondered if I'd put him to sleep. When I started to turn to check, he spoke. "I don't know if I've ever comforted my sister. She was quiet when she lived here. Last I saw her, she was different. Happier. But not here. I was caught up in my own things, and then away at school for long periods of time. She was alone at home with Francisco until he went off too."

He continued, the soft rhythm of his deep voice soothing me as much as his words. "Thanks for doing this. What other falsehoods did you believe as a child? My father once convinced me that a particular lake we were on would suck me down until I drowned because he didn't want me to jump in and get wet. We had somewhere to go when we got off the boat. It was really a business thing, and I was very likely to jump in just for the fun of it. That was before I was taken. I wouldn't have jumped after that."

I lifted my head. The air was calmer now, and he let me get up. "He let you think you would drown?"

"He did."

I stared at him. "You understand that's fucked up, right? I mean…you don't tell the kid they're going to drown if they're not really going to drown. He could have put you off swimming altogether. Maybe that's how you even create some kind of phobia in a kid."

"Oh, we can't have phobias. We'd be put down for sure. We all have to be strong and sound, hence the secrecy about the way I live."

I always thought my was family fucked up—and they were—but theirs really took the cake.

"What other falsehoods did I believe?" I had to think. "Socks prevent nightmares? I got told that too. If I wore socks to bed, there was a chemical released that prevented me from having nightmares. Then I never had one again. If I had one, I'd get up and put on socks to stop them. I believed that one for way too long."

"I like that one. Seems like the lies they told you were to make you feel better. Good lies."

That was true. In our world, there were good lies and bad ones.

He closed his eyes. "I worried I wouldn't be able to sleep next to you. That it would be too hard to be vulnerable around a stranger. The first night, I didn't because you were walking around, thanks to that pill I suggested you take. I kept worrying that your prediction about taking a sleeping pill and drowning in the bathtub was going to come true. But last night, I slept better than I had in years. Yet, as I sit here, I'm tired again."

"Go to sleep. I'll read and leave you alone." I sat back in my chair and leaned toward the window to give him lots of space.

"I don't want to." He opened his eyes. "Tell me more stories."

Ultimately, he fell asleep halfway through my next one, which had been purposeful on my part. If he was tired, he should sleep. Talking about anthropology tended to put others to sleep, especially if they weren't interested. Javier still snored loudly across the aisle, and Francisco hadn't moved at all, his eyes closed. That might be because of the booze he'd ingested at brunch. I pulled out my phone.

Janice had texted me back.

*What number is this?*

*You got married?*

*WTF. Who is he?*

*WHOA! I got engaged.*

*When can we talk?*

*Ugh you aren't seeing these.*

*Lily!*

I smiled. I hadn't seen her in a week, but it felt like longer. Checking my phone, I noticed there wasn't Wi-Fi on the plane. Maybe they never used it for business? Maybe it couldn't be secured enough? At whatever thousand feet I was at, I couldn't text her back. It would have to wait a few hours.

Alejandro sighed in his sleep and then rolled over until he could put his head in my lap. He settled down, his arms around my waist, and continued sleeping. I stared at him. Maybe I wasn't the one who kept clinging to him in our sleep. Maybe the secret cuddler was my husband.

I liked that thought. We couldn't ever be together, but it didn't mean we wouldn't be close.

* * *

I ended up dozing but not sleeping until we landed. Not one of the guys stirred from their unconscious states, which was crazy to me. I'd never slept through landing. But their deep rest meant I had to wake them, which proved easier thought than done.

"Alejandro." This was very reminiscent of the night in the car. "Time to get up."

His eyes fluttered open, but he wasn't immediately cognizant. It took a second, and then he rubbed his face and sat up.

"Hey." He smiled at me. "Guess I ended up on your lap."

"Did you?" I winked at him. "I hadn't noticed."

"I still want to hear that story." He grabbed his bag that was in front of him. "My falling asleep does not indicate my lack of interest or anything."

It was fun to tease him. "Sure, it doesn't."

I touched Javier, and he roused all at once. "Did we take off?"

"We're there." I stroked his cheek. "And you, Dr. Hernandez, snore. You should get that looked at."

He shook his head. "I don't snore."

"If you say so."

I left him to wake up, even though he looked rumpled and so not put together that all I wanted to do was kiss him. We were in public. But when I touched Francisco to wake him, he wasn't so easy to get up. When he finally opened his eyes, it was to pull me onto his lap and kiss me, hard.

I should have pulled back, but he caught me by surprise, his warm mouth meeting my own, and before I could think, I'd pressed myself against him, meeting his immediate heat with my own.

"*Te voy a coger.*" I didn't know what that meant, but I knew how his body tensed against mine, his mouth on my neck and his hands traveling down until they were about to slip under my pants to find my most sensitive spots.

"Hey, lover boy." Javier leaned against the seat. "Can't do that here. Remember where you are."

Francisco's hands fell away. "Fuck."

"Yes, we got that gist. Let her up. Come on." Javier pulled me off Francisco. "Pick it up later. And no more questioning whether we want you. He's barely awake, and all he can think of is fucking you."

The youngest brother fell backward on the seat, groaning before he stomped his foot. "Damn it."

I scooted around Javier and met Alejandro outside. This was a private airport. We were the only ones there. A dark black car sped up to pick us up, and as we stood there, Francisco came off the plane and straight over to me.

"Sorry. I was still half asleep. Just knew you were there and that I… Well, that I wanted you. Badly."

I smiled at him. "All of this is going to take some getting used to." He smelled great. Or maybe it was just that he'd turned me on and now my body wanted him. "Maybe we can find some time."

Alejandro whirled around and extended his hand. "Time to go home."

I took his fingers in mine, not sure what to make of the blank expression on his face, or the way that Javier watched us like he might at any second take me away, or what to do about Francisco's gaze following me in the car until he couldn't see me anymore.

The ride home was quiet, even as I stared at things like I'd never been out of the house before. This was going to be where I lived from now on.

My phone dinged, and I stared down at it. Janice still wanted my attention. I turned to Alejandro. "My friend is getting married. Is that the kind of thing I can attend, or should I tell her right off the bat I can't go?"

If he said no, I'd argue tomorrow. Not today. Too much had happened today.

"Yes, of course you can attend a friend's wedding. I'll take you." He looked away. "Deal with some business in Chicago while I'm there."

Well, that was better than no. Would he have wanted to go if it weren't in Chicago? If she were getting married in some fictional small town where no one did drugs and therefore there was no business to do at all? Such a place didn't exist. Besides, why was I making myself nuts by asking that sort of question to begin with?

Finally, we arrived at what they had called the compound. It wasn't really that. I'd pictured huge scopes of land behind a gate with no one around for miles. What their compound turned out to be was three houses lined up together that shared a backyard. It was huge for the city but not like the kind of place I'd had in my mind.

Did they all have different houses? There were three, after all. I quickly discovered the answer to that was no. The other two houses were for guests. For the sake of safety, we all lived together. There were six bedrooms in the modern looking house, and unlike the place in Mexico City, this one was clean but lived in. There was stuff here. Books on shelves, paintings on walls, pictures. It was clear that this home was somewhere people spent their time. It also had a pool, a hot tub, a gym, wine cellar, and tennis court.

My stuff had been put away in Alejandro's room. Hung up and gently placed in drawers. My laptop was open, my screen saver of the Alps on display, and my hair products sat waiting in the bathroom. It was like I'd always lived there, even though I'd never set foot in their home before.

There was no staff to be seen.

"No one is here." Francisco informed the room as I came out of the bedroom, needing space from how easily my life had been transported. Why was it so easy to just move me there when I hadn't even known this place existed?

Like I'd never really been in Chicago. As if I had no roots in need of transplanting. I was overthinking this.

"No one is here?"

"Not today. They'll be back tomorrow." With that, Francisco threw me down on the couch.

I gasped. Javier and Alejandro were walking around. Was this okay?

He tugged down my pants. Obviously, he thought it was. "I want to put my mouth on you. It's all I can think about. Let me make you come."

It was hard to think he was being forced to sleep with me when he acted like this. "If that's what you want."

"It's what I want. Badly."

Who was I to argue?

# 11

I swallowed. “Is this okay?”

“Everything is okay with me.” His grin was huge as he tugged down my pants and discarded them onto the floor. Then he did the same with my panties.

*Wow.* He was just going to get right to it then. There was a coffee table in front of the couch, and he kicked it away so that it slid into the wall with a bang. He jumped off the couch and was on his knees in front of me. “Sit up.”

I swallowed as I did what he asked, my mouth suddenly gone dry. “Francisco?” I wasn’t even sure what I was asking for.

But he seemed to know because his mouth was on me. I caught my breath, grabbing onto the couch like it was a lifeline. He pushed my knees apart further and then further again, then pressed his mouth right against my pussy. I cried out. Sometimes, oral sex felt like too much. There was no way to pull my head back from it, and there was an intimacy with his tongue on me there that I just didn’t experience when I had sex in other ways.

I grabbed onto his head, not so that I could dictate what he was doing, but because somehow, it grounded me. I could touch him, feel him as his tongue caressed my slit. I needed the connection.

And he didn't seem to mind because his tongue was then on my clit. I know some women needed more than clit stimulation to come, but that wasn't me. I could come from touching my clit alone, and right then, he had that little bit of nerves right where he wanted it. And where I wanted it too.

Francisco seemed to always understand my body. This was our second time being together, and both times, it was like he inherently knew just what I needed, when I needed it. I quickly lost the ability to think rationally. There was only *oh yes* and *more there*. Not that he needed my direction. I only so much as thought about what I wanted and he did it.

A noise caught my attention, and I opened the eyes I hadn't realized I'd closed. Striding toward us, his pants tented as he watched, was Javier. "Oh those noises you make. Best fucking sounds ever."

He stood over us, getting harder as I watched him. "Can you get her there, or do you want me to take over and show you how it's done?"

Francisco's only answer was to nip the tip of my clit. I cried out. No one had ever done that to me before, and fuck if I didn't like the bite of pain. I was so wet, I had to be dripping into his mouth, yet he didn't seem to mind at all.

Javier sat down next to me and kissed me hard. His tongue took possession of my mouth, and even though my eyes kept threatening to close—seeing anything was too much—I stared at him through the slits in my lids. He pulled himself out of his pants, and with the hand that wasn't holding my head against his, began to stroke himself. *Oh, fuck. That is hot.*

I squirmed, and Francisco held me still, putting more pressure on my thighs. He moaned, and it was almost my undoing. These two men wanted me so much. It was a heady sensation to feel this level of desire. So much that it might have been intimidating if it weren't so fucking hot.

One last nip, and I came hard. I leaned back and practically shouted my pleasure. Francisco drew it out. He didn't let up, even when I felt swollen and done. He wrung me dry until I had nothing left to give him. Javier drank my cries in his mouth until he was coming in his hand, moaning into my mouth as he brought himself pleasure at the same time Francisco gave it to me.

I could hardly breathe, but I yanked Francisco up. He smiled like he'd just won some kind of prize. "Your turn."

He tilted his head. "What did you have in mind?"

It wasn't easy to get him to switch places with me, since my legs were wobbly as though I'd just run a race, but I managed it. I tugged down his pants just as Javier lay back on the other side of the couch.

Francisco shoved his arm. "Did I need help? Fuck, no. I could teach you a few things."

"Doubtful, but I do love how you made her moan. Lily makes the best noises." He closed his eyes. Was he settling in for a nap?

It didn't matter. Francisco had just gotten me off, and if Javier wanted to sit there while I did the same for Francisco, that was fine by me. It had actually been really hot, how he'd stroked himself to the sounds of my pleasure. What a head rush that was.

I pulled Francisco's zipper down with my teeth. He caught his breath. I looked up to see I had officially knocked the smile off his face. His gaze had turned hot again. *Good.* That was just what I wanted. I pulled down his jeans to his ankles. Gently, because I certainly wouldn't want someone yanking hard on my lower leg, I pulled them all the way off. His cock was hard, pressing against his briefs, and the view made me smile.

Just to tease him, I cupped him on the outside of his briefs, and he hissed in a breath. Tugging them down all the way, just as I did with his pants, I carefully set them aside. I was naked from the waist down and should have been embarrassed about that, only I wasn't. In this moment, there was no such thing as being self-conscious. I just had to go for it.

Javier took that moment to get off the couch. He winked at me as he walked away. I didn't look to see where he was going. Why would I, when the view of Francisco's cock was so incredibly all-consuming? He was big. I'd known that from the last time we were intimate, but now I had to face the daunting trial of putting him in my mouth.

Practice made perfect. If I wasn't great this time, I'd be better the next time. Besides, I was pretty certain that even a mediocre blow job was pretty fucking wonderful for the person receiving it. I'd never heard of anyone complaining.

I took his head in my mouth. I'd never given a blow job to an uncircumcised man before. All of the men I'd been with this way happen to have been circumcised. But Janice had once told me that the foreskin was really, really sensitive. I guessed I would find out. I started with the tip. Licking him made him say something that sounded an awful lot like a curse. Still, he didn't ask me to stop. I guessed maybe what I'd heard was true. I hadn't done much yet, and Francisco really seemed to like it.

Having been successful once, I did it again. And again. He really seemed to like the licking, so I kept doing that, but I wanted to feel more of him. What was his penis like throbbing in my hand? I pressed my hand over the top of it where I'd been doing a pretty good job of licking. He was warm, and he pushed against my hand.

I wouldn't forget how this felt, but I kissed the head to get back to what I was doing. I licked and licked him. Finally, I took him in my mouth, and I sucked. He shook his head. "Go back to the licking."

His accent was thick, and he petted the back of my hair. Over and over. I did as he asked, and it didn't take long. The licking seemed to be what Francisco wanted. I licked him until he came, all over my face.

I fucking loved it.

I'd no sooner finished than Javier appeared to hand me a towel. As quickly as I could, I wiped myself up, but I was going to have to shower because I was going to be sticky. That was okay. This was the best kind of mess.

"Welcome home, Lily." Francisco grinned at me.

I highly doubted this would ever feel like home, but it was certainly a nice way to begin my time there.

* * *

I swam, back and forth through the pool. I loved swimming, but we couldn't do it much in Chicago. At least not outside. If I wanted to swim when it was cold, I went to the gym. And that was how I'd ended up becoming a runner. I just hated changing in the locker room. It was easier to run and just go home in my clothes than having to go through the whole process at the gym.

Here, it was warm, and I loved swimming in this pool.

A pair of feet obscured my view as I reached one end again. I looked up. Alejandro stared down at me. He wore a black pair of pants and a white T-shirt. It was actually among the most casual of the outfits I had seen him in.

I stared back. "Hi."

"Hi." He bent down. "You like the pool?"

"I do. Do you need me?"

He nodded. "In a bit. We need to go introduce you to the other wives. They want to celebrate our wedding. All the lieutenants and their significant others… I was hoping to put it off for a while, but I guess we can't do that. So we'll go tonight. I wanted to give you enough notice to get ready."

That was fine. I could get myself together before then. I could pick from my wardrobe. That wasn't a problem. "Sure. Tomorrow, I need to start studying again. I can do that in the bedroom, but the truth is that I study better elsewhere. I don't want to disrupt anything here. I can take my laptop anywhere, but can you give me a place to do that?"

He ran a hand through his hair. "For sure I can. We'll get you your own office. I don't like to work in the bedroom, either. Guadalupe will be here tomorrow. If you want any particular food in the house, leave her a list. I can translate it for you."

"Thank you." I smiled at him. "Do you have a vision for tonight? How you'd like me to be?"

His smirk surprised me. "The men are all going to go home wishing they could fuck you. All the women will want to be you. Just be you, Lily. I trust you to know how to be. Someday, you'll be the queen of this organization."

Well, that was a lot to take in. He was probably not correct. I'd never be that woman, but if he needed me to pretend for a night, I could try to play the role.

I finished my swim.

Later, when I got out of the shower wrapped in a towel, I stopped abruptly. The white dress that I hadn't bought because Javier said it was too sexy hung over the wardrobe. Had Javier gone back and gotten it? I stared at it and grinned. Was this going to do the trick?

My hair was straightened, my makeup was well done. I just had to decide if I was going to wear the white dress or not. I put it on and stared at myself in the mirror. I'd liked it in the store, but I hadn't been sure. Now, however, I felt strong and powerful in it.

Alejandro wasn't shy. If he didn't like it, he'd tell me to go change.

But when I stepped out of the room, I once again got no reaction from him at all. He said he trusted me to know what to do, only when it came down to it, I wasn't sure if he really gave a shit one way or another how I looked. Maybe in the sense that it added to his power if everyone in there wanted me, one way or another, because it would make him looked at as an even stronger leader?

I made eye contact with Javier, who walked over to me with a strong stride. "Perfect."

That was what I wanted to hear. Francisco entered the room, took one look at me, and whistled. "It should be illegal to look like that in a dress."

"Thanks, guys."

I strode forward. I was almost used to how this would go from now on. "Ready?" I asked Alejandro. "Let's go."

He must've been, because he followed me out. It shouldn't

matter that he said nothing to me, especially because of the fuss Javier and Alejandro had made. How needy had I gotten? I knew he wasn't into me sexually, that he'd spent years not letting his mind go to those places because of his inability to do anything about sexual feelings. I really just had to get over myself.

I hadn't even asked where we were going, but it didn't really matter.

Javier put his hand on my back. "Somehow, you look even better in it now than you did in the store."

"When did you do this?" I smiled at him. "It shocked me. I thought you said you'd kill people for looking at me in it?"

Francisco laughed, but Alejandro shot Javier a look saying he wasn't amused. I was finally starting to be able to read their facial expressions.

"Some of these people, I'd be okay with them dying. But I will restrain myself, either way. Besides, I have to play brother-in-law, and that means that I keep my hands to myself and my eyes off your curves. That's going to be hard." He brought my hand to his mouth and kissed me lightly on the hand. With a solemn look, he dropped it just as we exited the house.

I came up short. Standing in front of the car was Eduardo. I dropped my eyes. Not making eye contact with him was probably the best thing to do, considering the past response to a simple thank you. Francisco leaned over to whisper in my ear. "This is how Alejandro says sorry."

I didn't even know Eduardo, but I was incredibly glad to see him. This was better than Alejandro liking my dress.

* * *

The celebratory dinner was taking place at a local restaurant. It was dark inside, with low light, and the room hushed when we entered. Generally, I didn't get nervous at these sorts of things. We always had my father's business associates at home.

But this time, I wasn't being admired for being the daughter or sister of a powerful man. This was downright hostility, and not from the men. No, it was from the women.

I steeled myself. This was going to be a long night.

Alejandro played his role well. His hand on my back, he led me into the room like he was actually proud to be there with me. We were supposed to have fallen in love and had a whirlwind courtship, so I supposed he needed to act the part.

I smiled at him and leaned over to whisper in his ear. "They all hate me, and I haven't said a word."

"Let them," he whispered back. "Every one of them wants to be the lady of the family. They want their husbands to be us. If any of them are overtly rude, they'll be dealt with."

One of the ladies up front approached me. "Oh, you must be Lily. I'm Josephina. I bought your clothes." She smiled at me, and her teeth were very, very white. Her accent wasn't local. I was going to guess she was from some place in eastern Europe. She was beautiful, blonde, and other than the teeth being just a little too bleached, she could have starred in a film about gorgeous people.

I'd no sooner said hello than she was pretty much pushed aside by the next woman. "I'm Verónica." Her smile was forced, but her teeth were normal. "I told Javier where to take you to buy clothes."

"Oh, Javier," Josephina purred. "He is so handsome. Lucky girl you were, to get to go shopping with him."

One by one, the women introduced themselves. I was never going to remember all of their names, because it turned out that I didn't have to. They were happy to talk, all of them, and about each other to me, even though they were at most two feet away from where I stood. My head spun, but I kept smiling. All of them could speak English and all of them wanted to be my new best friend, which would be great, but I could feel the hate coming off them.

For married women, they certainly liked Javier and Francisco.

Alejandro was spared their constant ogling.

It was only later, when Josephina grabbed my arm, that I understood why. "Alejandro was always going to get married fast like he did. So religious. He's never even kissed anyone publicly. Lucky girl you are to show up here and get the boss' son."

I took a deep breath. "Other than the boss' son, I would say that we are in the same situation, right? You're not from here, either. How did you end up becoming a member of the family?"

"Oh, my husband was in my town on business, and what can I say? I fell in love." She didn't say that with much affection. I didn't usually like to jump to conclusions, but I'd say if she were ever in love, she wasn't now.

Sometimes, it could feel like hours were minutes, but this time, it was the opposite problem. The minutes dragged by. But like everything else in life, time did move.

Javier arrived at my side. He said something to the group in Spanish, which made them all laugh, and then he handed me a plate.

"My brother requested that I make sure his bride has food."

I smiled at him. We both knew which one of them had sent me this plate, and it wasn't Alejandro. He'd never have thought of it, and if he did, he'd expect that I would simply handle getting myself fed if I wanted it. "Thank you, Javier."

"You're welcome." He smiled at me, and in that moment, there was so much not said. Javier knew that I knew it was him who was taking care of me, and that we'd never be allowed to let anyone know.

It was so much more complicated than he and Francisco taking care of my so-called sexual needs. I couldn't speak for them, but I was falling hard for both of them. Even if this setup worked for the moment, at some point, it all was going to blow up in my fucking face.

Only I couldn't deal with it right then. I had to focus on the dozen witches who wanted to be my friends in name but not in reality. It hadn't occurred to me that I would be living like this. Not that anyone had given me a choice, but I certainly didn't sign up for this. But it was getting easier to see how lonely I was going to be.

Javier stepped away. He crossed the room to Francisco and

picked up a conversation. Alejandro was nowhere to be seen. I turned my attention back to the hell in front of me.

An arm came around my shoulder. It was Alejandro. "Ladies." He spoke to them in English. "I hope you're being kind to my new bride and not scaring her off when she just joined us."

They all pretty much sighed in unison. I smiled at him like he was the best thing I'd ever seen. In that moment, I could almost see it as it might have been. Sure, we'd been forced into the marriage sight unseen, but marriages like that weren't unheard of in our world. He was the son of a very powerful man. I was the daughter of one. In a better world, maybe the thing between us could have been real.

As it was, Francisco caught my gaze over his brother's shoulder. He was serious, an unusually distant expression across his face. It was like he'd slightly checked out of the moment as he looked at us. By contrast, a muscle ticked in Javier's jaw. He was pissed about something.

What was this world we lived in going to look like?

Alejandro squeezed my arm, bringing me back to the present. I continued to grin, and everyone else laughed and laughed.

"What can I say? I saw him across the room and knew he had been made for me. Sometimes you just know these things."

That wasn't actually a lie. I'd seen him across the church and known just that.

As Eduardo drove us home later, the car was quiet until Francisco spoke. He actually seemed remarkably sober for a change. The last few nights, he'd been pretty drunk, but as far as I could tell, he was stone cold sober at the moment.

"I have to leave tomorrow night. I know you've got class, but maybe in the evening, I could show you some things?"

I met his gaze. "Sure. I'd like that."

He nodded. "Good."

Javier yawned. "I'm working tomorrow too. We're all working. Honeymoon is over."

I giggled. If this were a honeymoon, it was one of the strangest in history. I leaned back in my seat. "Sorry, that just struck me as funny."

Alejandro turned toward me in the seat. "You did well tonight. You continue to do so. Thank you for that. What were your impressions of the people you met?"

I stared at him. It was dark in the car and hard to see each other's expressions, but he seemed mostly at ease. I didn't think I was going to get my head bit off for being honest.

"I think that the women are all phony. Maybe not *all* of them, I think it will take some time to know which ones are for sure. Most of them seem like they are pretty preoccupied with Javier and Francisco. I think you could probably have any one of them that you wanted. And, Alejandro, your cover has worked. I heard several times about how you were very religious."

He leaned closer to me. "I'm not *not* very religious, but yes, I've let them believe I'm more dedicated to my faith than I am, for obvious reasons."

Francisco stared out the window as he said, "Any one of them that I wanted, I had a long time ago. I'm not interested in other pussy, Lily. Just yours."

I opened and closed my mouth. I didn't know exactly what I was supposed to say to that. Javier groaned. "I might not put it like that, but that's what I want too. Just you."

"Then I am so happy this arrangement is working." Alejandro sounded bored. "Looks like you might be living the dream of those ladies, since they all seem to want to fuck you both so badly." He shook his head. "You'll watch the women for me. If you get the sense that someone is betraying us, I need to know who. This bullshit of my shipments disappearing stops now. I'm not playing around. Francisco, I'm going to need your help, in particular."

He nodded. "Yes."

Javier leaned over and squeezed my knee. "This will get easier."

"It's not hard. Just a little bit…I don't know…full of bullshit? My friend Janice in Chicago is getting married. I'm not there celebrating with her, looking at dresses and spoiling her, because I'm here with Josephina blowing smoke up my ass while she looks for any edge to make a fool out of me. Don't worry about me. I know how to survive."

It looked like it was going to be a very useful skill to have.

# 12

"Want to watch something with us?" Javier knocked into me gently when we got inside.

I shook my head. "Thank you, but I'm just going to go to bed."

"Do you not like television?" Francisco laughed. "We can find something you'll like."

I smiled back at him. "I do. Soon. I'm just tired. Thanks for asking me."

If I stayed long enough, they'd be able to convince me, and I'd spend the whole time feeling like I shouldn't be there. My head wasn't on straight. Maybe I'd feel like being domestic once I understood the rules of this new reality. I just wasn't there yet.

Alejandro clearly wasn't either. He hadn't even hung out long enough to be asked. I found him in a similar position to the one I'd walked into last night. Different apartment, same position. He stared out the window. What did he see that I didn't see?

He looked handsome and strong. No one would ever know the secrets he carried. After I grabbed my night attire, I walked into the bathroom and took off my clothes, hanging my dress back up and changing fast into a pair of shorts and a tank top. There was a plus to this arrangement—well, other than the fact that I had two men who wanted me badly, making me come every time they could—and it was that I never had to worry about being sexy in bed. With no rush on my time, I took the time to moisturize.

It was so nice to have my own stuff around me, and I put my hair into a braid to go to sleep. It would be easier to deal with in the morning that way.

When I came back out, Alejandro gave me a small smile and traded places with me. Like before, I closed all the curtains and got into bed. Houses had noises that were normal and noises that weren't. I'd never been able to stand a flashing light in the bedroom while I slept. I could take light as long as it was steady, and fortunately, I didn't see anything flashing in this room.

The ceiling fan made a nice *whoosh* sound that would help as white noise if I couldn't sleep. Alejandro came out, and like the night before, he wore boxers. He turned off the light and climbed in next to me.

"I hope it's okay I took this side of the bed. We never really decided it."

He leaned over on his arm. "Yes, this works for me."

"Great." I rolled over to face away from him. For some reason, the awkwardness that hadn't been riding me during our marriage had hit me tonight. Sleeping next to him like a roommate was going to take some getting used to.

"I keep thinking about what you said to me."

I rolled back over to regard him. It was rude not to look at someone while they spoke to me. "Which thing?"

"Who has the most to gain?" He sighed. "Anyone in that room could take over if we were gone. I have to say *we*, because if I did, it'll be Javier, and he'll rage vengeance on the world. Francisco too. They'd have to end all of us."

I stared at him in the dark. "Have you had threats against your lives?"

"Not that I know of, but going after my earnings is enough to put a price on my life."

That was an interesting way to view it. I was sure he was right. This was his existence. "Who would kill you for lack of money?"

He abruptly lay on his back. "My father, I guess. I don't like to think about that."

I bet he didn't. "So explain to me what happens exactly? You send someone out to deliver product, and then what happens to it?"

"The trucks are vanishing. Just *poof.* Nothing. The guys who bring the product—and good job calling it that—are either found dead or they're so beaten up, they can't work anymore. Honestly, taking care of them is going to start to become too expensive, and I won't be able to get people to do it. I don't know. It seems to be entirely directed to me, like I have become a bad bet to move it."

Something like that, it would take planning. "Let me dwell on this. If the guys themselves aren't betraying you, because they're the ones ending up dead or destroyed, then maybe it's a question of cutting someone out who is talking and shouldn't be? How many people know what you're going to do before you do it?"

He was quiet for a moment. "Four. But…only family."

The only people he trusted. "Like I said, let me dwell on it. I…I might have some thoughts."

"Great."

The room went quiet. I guessed we were done talking. "Goodnight."

"*Buenas noches y hermosos sueños.*" I didn't know what that meant but it was pretty.

I closed my eyes but didn't fall asleep as the minutes passed. My mind was consumed with his problem. There was a solution, and I loved coming up with them. It was just how my brain worked. His breathing evened out, and he slept deeply, the way I'd heard him do a few times so far. The deep even breath said Alejandro Hernandez, my husband who no one really knew, was asleep.

A few more minutes passed before he tugged me against him. In his sleep, he arranged me until I was pressed against his body, my stomach to his. He muttered in Spanish and then settled again. I'd been right—I wasn't the cuddler. He was. Since I was awake, this was going to be hell. He was a beautiful man I couldn't have physically. I closed my eyes. It was going to be torture, but I liked his warmth.

I'd take care to fall asleep before he did going forward, so I could be less aware of the fact that his chest was hard, his arms were huge and comforting, and I'd never know him more than this.

* * *

After spending the morning watching class virtually in the office Alejandro had set up for me next to his, I spent an hour swimming. Guadalupe silently puttered around the house with four other staff members. Eduardo was outside with five other guards. I didn't talk to any of them.

When I finally showered, I put on some jeans and T-shirt because I didn't have anything I was expected to do that night that needed me dressed up and pretty. It was then that Francisco took me to see what he wanted to show me.

His cars.

It seemed Francisco had a hobby. I didn't know the first thing about cars, but I could admit these were beautiful, in the way that artwork was. I ran my hand gently over the Lamborghini in front of me. "You have all of these beauties, and you let people drive you around all the time."

"I don't, actually. Only when I've been with you. I drive myself as much as possible. I'll be headed across the border tonight, driving myself. I wanted to show you. I don't just buy them." He smiled and motioned to the side. "Sometime, I'll take you for a drive in one of the ones I fixed."

He motioned to a row of cars in the process of being restored and some that were done. *Wow.* This was impressive. "Amazing."

"It's not, but I like doing it." He rocked back on his feet. "And I wanted to show you."

Was he feeling insecure? I walked over to him and took his hand. "Take me for a ride now?"

He widened his eyes. "I'd love to. Which car do you want to take for a spin?"

I couldn't help my smile. This was the most fun I'd had since I'd arrived in Mexico. "Surprise me."

We ended up in his red Dodge Viper. It had two black stripes down the front, and being in it made me smile. Francisco had worked on it a little bit, but he didn't restore the whole thing. I wasn't sure where we were going or where he intended for us to end up, but we drove for hours. Sometimes we talked, sometimes we didn't. Eventually, we stopped outside of town on the side of the road to eat what he called the best tamales he'd ever had, and we sat side by side on the front of his car.

By the time we finished eating, I'd learned he absolutely hated broccoli and loved brussels sprouts, didn't remember much of his mother, and was loyal to a fault to his brothers. His favorite American movie was *Casablanca*, and he'd visited every continent in the world—including Antarctica.

"I want to read the books you're reading for your masters so we can talk about them, but that means I have to read the undergraduate ones too."

I leaned my head on his shoulder. "That is a lot of reading."

"I like to read." He entwined our hands. "This is wonderful. I have to leave soon, but I'll take this with me and be better on this trip because of it."

I lifted my head. "Are you okay?" This wasn't the spin a circle, laugh all the time Francisco, and that was fine. But we'd had fun in the car driving around. Had I done something wrong since we'd parked?

He shook his head. "I hated last night—all those vultures around you—and there wasn't a thing I could do about it. Alejandro has a higher tolerance for this bullshit than I do. He holds to traditions and the ways things have to be done. I hate some of it. In public, there is nothing I can do to show those people what I feel for you, how I would like to protect you. I'm going to be honest—when he told me I could sleep with his wife, I didn't expect to feel like this. I didn't know that I'd feel this for you. I've been with lots of women and felt nothing. But you…you do something to me."

I didn't have a right to feel a pang because he'd been with other women. I'd been with other men. I was sleeping with one of his brothers. But my emotions weren't always reasonable, so there was the pang whether I wanted it or not. I ignored it.

"Is this too much for you?" The sad truth was Francisco could get out if he wanted to leave. I couldn't. And even though it had just been days that we'd known each other, I would miss him if he left. It would be like an ache to my soul to lose him.

I wouldn't say anything to make the situation harder on anyone. I'd give him that, because I liked his sweet smile, the way he kept things moving, and the fact that he had a million small qualities that I just kept discovering that easily made him one of the most interesting people I'd ever known.

He shook his head. "It should be, but I won't give you up."

I put my face in my hands. "You should. If this is causing you pain, you should. I can't do anything to fix it. Not one thing. I don't want to cause you pain."

He ran a hand down my back and then back up again, rubbing my neck. "Let me worry about my pain. I'm used to pain. It's an old friend. This isn't that."

I lifted my head. "Francisco…"

"I know." He nodded. "You have those feelings for Javier, too. And you might even have a quiet infatuation with Alejandro, even though things are going to be complicated there. It's okay. We're all going to be better for having you in our lives."

I leaned over close to him. "You can't know that."

"I can see your soul."

He was so beautiful with the sun setting behind him. "I don't know if we really have souls."

Francisco ran a gentle finger down the slope of my nose and stopped to cup my chin. "We do, and yours is beautiful."

He kissed me gently. Not the hard claiming kiss that I'd gotten used to from him. No, it was a sweet, easy adoring joining of our lips. "I am going to kiss you now, *mi cielo*. Just kiss you here because I can. For as long as I can."

I loved that idea. And when he kissed me, I kissed him right back. On the hood of his car with the sun setting like we were in some kind of fantasy I hadn't known I had.

A car pulled up to the tamale stand, which was manned but obviously didn't concern Francisco for prying eyes. He stopped kissing me and looked over his shoulder. The men ordering were talking, not looking at us where we parked a slight distance away.

Francisco's whole body tensed up. I gripped his arm. "What's wrong?"

"Somebody is here who shouldn't be here." His jaw was hard as stone, the sweet lover of just seconds earlier gone.

"Who?"

He jumped off the hood. "Get in the car, Lily. Now."

With an order like that, I wasn't going to fight him. I jumped off the hood and got right in the car. Francisco did the same, but he pulled out his gun before he got in. Were we about to have a big problem?

"Francisco?"

He pulled the car onto the road before he answered me. "If I were alone, I'd try. Those men are two of the biggest assassins in Mexico. They have no business being here. They are banned from our territory, and if they are here, that means bad things. However, they were clearly not looking for me or I'd be dead. They were eating dinner. I mean, what are the fucking chances of that? Low. Alejandro needs to know they're here. If I shot one and missed the other, there is a chance they'd hit you. I won't risk that."

Keeping one hand on the wheel, he set down his gun and picked up his cell phone, which he held up to his mouth. In seconds, he'd dictated something in Spanish that was sent over text.

"Motherfucker." He pounded on the steering wheel. "Alejo was right—his life is in danger. You only bring the Pérez brothers here for him. They're too much money to waste otherwise."

That was the first time I'd heard that nickname, and I was betting

I was only hearing it now because he was so worked up. I chewed on my lip. "Do you think it likely they didn't recognize you?"

"Actually, you might have saved my life. We looked like two nobodies making out on the hood of the car. This isn't a vehicle I take out very much. They'd know me more in my Porsche. We weren't worth paying attention to, not in this."

I leaned back in my seat, my head starting to pound. "What will you do now?"

"Let's see what Alejandro wants me to do." He took my hand. "Don't be afraid. This is not the first time we've had to deal with this kind of mess. Plus, we got lucky today. We are ahead of them. You are our good luck charm."

I hoped he was right. I'd never been good luck for anyone, not even myself.

* * *

"Checco," Alejandro met us by the door and embraced his brother. "If they had seen you…"

That had been my concern as well. Also, I was getting small doses of their nicknames. Alejo. Checco. They'd probably been using those names since they were children. It was adorable, but it wasn't the time to focus on them.

Alejandro turned to me next, dropping his brother. "You're okay too. When I got his message and realized it was the two of you, I was not a happy man."

"To say the least." Javier stepped toward us from where he had been in the back of the house. "I was also not a happy man."

We walked farther into the living room. Alejandro wasn't done talking, since he ignored Javier's remark. "They would've left you alone unless they accidentally hit you. They are actually assassins with honor, which is something of a problem because that means they won't leave the job undone. They can't be paid off. If they are here when they know they are forbidden, they mean to leave with a dead body."

Javier sat down, stretching out his legs. "Or bodies. Are they just here to kill Alejo or all of us?"

"I don't intend to find out. They will be dealt with tonight or tomorrow. I am not playing. In the meantime, Lily, you'll stay in the house where it is safe. We have our own assassins we can hire or I'll kill them myself."

Francisco raised his hand. "I'm better than you. I'm a better shot."

"I'm not staying home," Javier stated. "They need me at the clinic. I'll stay inside and you can send extra security with me, although if we're not trusting people, then what is the point? You're the one who needs to stay home, Alejo."

He crossed his arms over his chest. "I'm not frightened of them."

"You should be frightened." Francisco's yell startled me. "This isn't run of the mill bullshit. Someone hired them to kill you."

My husband shook his head, getting in Francisco's face. Seconds ago, they'd been hugging, but now, they might come to blows. It was serious enough that Javier got to his feet.

"Maybe it's not me. Maybe it's Dad or Tio."

Francisco laughed, but there was no joy to the sound. "Maybe they're the ones who did the hiring."

Alejandro went very still. "They wouldn't do that."

"No? Do you think you were left in that place being abused all those years ago because it just took that long for them to receive the money? Or was Dad actually negotiating for the price of your life? We all have numbers attached to us, and you and I both know that you're only as good to them as the money you bring in. How many grams are you currently worth to them?"

Their yelling quickly changed to Spanish, and that was my cue to exit. The situation involved me, but only to a point. I was Alejandro's wife, Francisco and Javier's lover, but I was also still just a visitor, or at least that was how it felt.

Javier nodded to me, which told me that I was probably right in my desire to exit, so I did just that. I made it into Alejandro's room and lay down on the bed we shared. It was absolutely not time to sleep, but this seemed like the best place to stay out of everyone's way. I chewed on my lip. Maybe I should have gone to my study space?

My friends texting was all as to be expected. No one had run into assassin brothers while they were on a date with their husband's brother. I answered all of them, pretending to be in love, and read about the goings on at school—actually on campus—from the ones who were in grad school with me.

With really nothing else to do, and with the yelling continuing in the living room, I downloaded a Spanish app and decided to finally take advantage of the huge bathtub in the adjoining bathroom. I stepped inside. Was this okay for me to do?

I filled the tub. Much as I was terrified of drowning in bathtubs—which was why I avoided them if I'd had alcohol or drugs in my system, thanks to what happened to my friends—I also loved a good hot bath. That was what I made the water now, and when it was ready, I sank into it. With my earbuds in place, I started to learn some Spanish.

Of course, learning 'the dog is under the table' wasn't going to help me understand what was happening most of the time, but baby steps with languages. I had to start somewhere.

*El perro está debajo de la mesa.*

I listened and repeated. Over and over. The app was great. It had pictures to go with it. I could see the dog under the table. I hadn't taught my first class yet, because it was supposed to be my next step in grad school. I'd be a teacher's assistant at some point, but I hadn't the slightest idea how other people learned things yet. Maybe the pictures with the audio helped? It didn't matter, so I set it aside. I was in a hot bathtub trying to learn Spanish while two guys wandered around unbothered in the world, prepared to kill one of the people out there in the living room. Or maybe they weren't. We really didn't know.

I closed my eyes. I wasn't tired and I certainly wasn't going to sleep, but sometimes things aren't easy to see.

The world was hard to look at right then.

My stomach clenched, feeling too full, and it had been a long time since I'd eaten those tamales, which told me it wasn't actually food I was feeling. It was the stress. It was so easy for me to give in to the instinct to not eat. Everyone had their personal battles, and this one would always be mine.

A knock sounded on the door, and Javier stuck his head inside. "You okay in here? Don't be scared. The house has bulletproof windows. You're very secure."

"I'm not scared for me." I rolled over to look at him. "What will you guys do?"

"Well, now that those two are done fighting—see, it's *not* just me—they'll work out a plan. I haven't seen an assassin yet who has stood up against the power of them when they're on the same side. We fight loudly and love that way too." He came and sat on the edge of the bath. "This will be over soon."

I needed to think about other things, since I couldn't fix this. I wished I could be that person. Wield a gun, head outside, gun down the bad guys like I was some kind of fierce avenger. The stuff of fiction. No one was really like that. Maybe we were even the bad guys? Or at least as bad as the ones wanting to shoot at us. Most of the time, problems were solved with the exchange of money and occasionally with the exchange of daughters or sisters.

Pointing at the door on the other side of the room, I asked an obvious question. "That door is locked. Who's in there?"

"An empty guest room. We never use it. Guests don't stay here. It's just kept cleaned and locked up."

*Interesting*. "And someone thought the guest room should share a bathroom with the master?"

"No." He took my hand. "I think it's probably intended to become a nursery. For babies. Easy access for mommy, and on the other side of that, also locked up, is another guest room, the last room in the house. My guess is that was probably for a nanny, in case mommy didn't want to get up with baby. That room has its own bathroom too."

I might never get used to this house. "Did your mom have a nanny?"

"Like ten of them. She wasn't much into childcare." He squeezed my fingers. "Are you thinking about running away?"

I hadn't, actually. "Where would I go? I don't have a person in the world who would take me in. My friends don't know who I am, and if they did, I wouldn't risk them. I'm afraid you're stuck with me."

"If you ran, I would follow. Either to bring you back or stay with you. Francisco too. Probably Alejandro, in truth."

I shook my head. "So if he's Alejo, and Francisco is Checco, what childhood nickname is going to show up for you?"

My question had thrown him. He blinked. "They used to call me Javi."

I could see that. "Cute."

"What about you?"

I reached for the towel and pulled myself out of the tub. When I was ready, I stepped out. "Lily is too short to nickname."

"Well, then we'll have to come up with one for you."

I kissed his cheek. "Maybe when you're not plotting how to end assassins."

"Fair enough."

# 13

I woke up the next morning once again with Alejandro's arms around me. I was getting downright used to his nightly embrace and might miss it if he stopped. Gently, I released myself from his snuggly hold and went into the bathroom. Dark circles marred my eyes. I'd been getting plenty of sleep, just clearly not rejuvenating when I rested. Stress tended to do that to me.

Today, I would run on the treadmill when I got done with class. When I came back out after brushing my teeth, Alejandro sat with his knees pulled to his chest in that way he seemed to do when he first woke up. It wasn't time for his alarm to go off yet.

"The bed was cold without you."

I stopped on my way to the closet. "We're getting used to sleeping together."

He lay back. "Maybe." Alejandro rubbed his face. "You were out cold when I came in last night."

"Should I apologize?" I sat on the edge of the bed.

His smile was fast. "Sure. Go ahead and apologize for falling asleep without me. You didn't look relaxed. Are you afraid?"

The way I answered his question would be important, but I wasn't going to lie to make myself look better. "I'm not *not* afraid. I know that doesn't explain anything, but that is the best way I can explain it."

"I actually understand you."

I was glad that he did, because I wasn't sure that I could say the same and I was the one feeling it.

He stretched out his hand, and I took it. "I was worried for you. I knew Francisco was okay, because he'd sent the message, but you didn't send one. I wasn't sure if that meant you were not okay or how you felt about the situation. I should have said that when you came in, but it was easier to free my temper on my brother. I'm not great at expressing myself."

This was the Alejandro I only saw in brief moments alone in our room. Late at night and now early in the morning. He'd be distant and uncommunicative for the rest of the day if he kept up as he had been. "That's okay. I don't expect you to baby me."

"You're my wife." He said it like he'd been talking to a person who just couldn't understand a simple concept.

I nodded. "I know, but—"

He interrupted me. "We're going to be good friends. I care about my friends." Alejandro looked down. "I didn't expect for my brothers to fall for you the way they have. I thought it would just be sex. They seemed to be able to do that. But I can tell they're crazy about you. Do you feel that way too?"

"This is such a strange conversation."

He squeezed my hand again. "No avoidance. Just truth between us."

"I do."

His nod was fast. "Good. Marry one of them if they take me out. They'll take care of you. Both of them can easily leave this life. Listen to me, this is important. There are three accounts they know nothing about. I'm only telling you because no one will ask you, but it might be important for you to know. Three—one for each of you. It's bailout money. Javier doesn't have the temperament to run this business. He's much happier helping than hurting. Checco actually could, but that's what scares me for him. Don't let him. Take them away. Go."

Since this was a time for truth, I asked my question. "Do you think they'll get you?"

"No, but I need someone to know just in case."

That was fair enough. "What about you? Should you be running this organization? When your father is gone?"

"Yes. There's no one better for it anywhere."

He was telling me something about himself, but not what he thought he was telling me. Probably his fears were for the same reason it scared him to think of Francisco running it—the fact that it would change him, make him darker, destroy him in some ways—was what he thought of himself. What I saw was the burden of responsibility and a person who would never shirk something he saw as his responsibility, ever.

"I have a thought about your situation with the shipments." I almost asked him if he'd like to talk about it. Hesitancy had happened with how I dealt with Alejandro. I'd seen that one slip up had temporarily cost Eduardo his job. I didn't want to do that to anyone else. Mistakes had consequences here. Big ones.

"Tell me." He scooted closer to me. "I can't talk to them about this. They'll worry endlessly. We take care of each other. Javi will do something stupid trying to make this better. They can't know my level of concern. I'm grateful you've thought on it at all."

"If I wanted to figure something out, I'd determine what I could eliminate to understand the person behind the disruption. I think you can eliminate the mystery quite easily. It's not the people driving, because they're the ones dying. So it's someone on this end, before you release the shipment of product. The drugs." We might as well call them what they were, just once. "First time out the door, tell no one your plans. Give them to the driver and set them loose. If the drugs make it there with no problem, you can confirm it is someone here causing the problem. Next, tell Javier. We know it's not him, but we have to eliminate everyone, right? Start with him. Tell just him. Then on from there,

Francisco. Your father. Uncle Ricardo. One at a time. Eventually, someone will show their cards. Don't tell them that's what you're doing. Act surprised. *I thought I told you*, or *Didn't you get my message?* By the time you've crossed them off as the betrayer, they then can know about all future movement. So they're only aware minimally and for a short period of time that they're out of your loop. Go from there. Don't even tell them afterward that it was a test. Just tell me."

He nodded. "That's very methodical. We deal so often from our guts in these situations. I almost always know who the traitor is, but I can't figure it out on my own this time. It's very unlike me."

Now it was my turn to squeeze. "Because it's so close to you."

"Yes, that's why." He nodded. "I'm not stupid. I know what you heard Francisco say has some truth to it, but I don't accept that they sold me out. Decisions were made, but they wouldn't have hung me out to dry at twelve. I was a good kid. I did as I was told. Bright." He smirked. "That's not bragging, just truth between us. They knew I'd grow up to be good at leading our company. I think mistakes were made, but not purposeful ones, and I have let that go…as I've let many things go."

I thought I understood what he was saying. "And since your brothers don't have the burden of leadership, it's different for them and why they can't understand."

"You understand."

I leaned my head on his arm. "I worshiped my big brothers. Until recently, I believed the world started and stopped with them. If they liked my boyfriends, I felt like I'd won a prize. If they were proud of me, I could live on that for a week. When I disappointed them, I felt it inside." I put my hand over his heart. "Different with boys, I'm sure, but I think you might be underestimating how much they take it personally that their big brother was left there. Francisco was young, but Javier not so much, right?"

He frowned. "I'll think on it."

I dropped my hand. "Nice talking to you this morning, Alejandro. *El perro está debajo de la mesa.*" I tried out the one sentence I'd learned yesterday.

His grin was huge, like he'd actually understood what I was doing instead of thinking I was nuts. "My dentist makes a lot of money."

"What?" I gasped. "Was that the first thing you learned in English?"

"Yes. It was in a book." Alejandro laughed outright.

His alarm went off, and his face fell. "Back to it."

I nodded. *Indeed.*

* * *

It was amazing how easily we could fall into a routine, even with the threat of death looming over us. A week went by. I studied, I swam or ran, I ate food with everyone, had sex with Francisco and Javier, and slept with Alejandro. It actually wasn't a bad life.

One morning, as I browsed the internet while eating oatmeal Guadalupe made for me, I stopped and stared at my phone. One of the pretty men I used to date was on the cover of a magazine. What was his name? I couldn't even remember it now. But I must have gasped because that brought Javier to my side to peek over my shoulder.

"What?" He'd be leaving soon to go to his clinic, a place I hadn't seen yet.

"I know him." When I would have swiped the screen, he took it from me.

With a lifted eyebrow, he stared at the man. "How do you know him?"

I leaned back. "We used to date. I can't even remember his name."

He put my phone back on the counter and blocked me in with his body so that I couldn't move. "I'd kill him if he looked at you right now. You are mine. I have to share you, but I will not allow strangers to even think about you that way."

Javier smelled great, and if we'd been alone, I might have considered what I wanted. But there was staff around. Guadalupe for one, and several of the maids on top of the usual staff who guarded us. I couldn't make out with Javier right then and there. In fact, it was shocking he was breaking protocol like this to be all over me.

"You were the one to give me the white dress. You sent me out that night for *everyone* to look at me."

My phone had been dinging with messages ever since that night from the wives of lieutenants, all wanting to do various things with me. For now, I was able to get away with not having to go with any of them because I was so wrapped up in Alejandro. Or that was what they thought, anyway.

Someday, I'd have to come up with a different excuse. Certainly, I couldn't always say it was because I was wrapped up in Javier.

"Yes, but that was my choice. I wanted you to be seen that night. If other men do it without my permission—spoken or otherwise—I will have to kill them."

He leaned over and kissed my neck. "Go through your life knowing that. You're mine. You are part of my family."

With that statement, he left me there, breathing hard. I swallowed, a lot hungrier than I'd been when I woke up.

Francisco was out doing something, which was amazing since Alejandro had all but bound him to the house, and my husband was locked away in his office. As if I'd conjured him, Alejandro appeared. In two strides, he was by my side. "Morning."

"Good morning." *Everyone is being so friendly today.*

"It worked. The shipment got there." He hugged me fast and then let me go. "The plan is underway. Thank you."

I shook my head. "I didn't really do anything."

"You got me out of my own head, and for that, I thank you."

That was a lot of thank yous for Alejandro. "You're welcome."

"I need to go out now." He'd also been home since the threats. "I'm taking two of the security with me, but I have to go see my father and drop off this news. I don't trust anything right now, not even my texts. I'll see you shortly. Want to have lunch?"

Funny how quickly you could fall into routine and how fast you could fall out of it. Lunch with Alejandro was a new thing. "Sure."

"Great. See you later." He seemed so genuinely happy.

In the meantime, I was bored in school. Maybe it was the virtual nature of it? I didn't like doing school online. I missed the camaraderie of my fellow students, and I knew that I wasn't going to be able to continue remotely learning next semester. So really, was there a point to doing all the work if I'd never meet the goal and get my degree?

Guadalupe came out right then. Seeing her every day over the past few weeks, I'd gotten to the point I almost didn't notice her stitches. *Almost.* "Thank you for breakfast."

I was allowed to talk to her. Where the line was over what I could and couldn't discuss, I wasn't sure, but this much I could do. I got off my chair and cleared my place. She never let me do the dishes, but I always tried. Was I becoming a shut-in? Was I really going to be fine staying inside this house forever?

At the moment, the answer seemed to be yes.

I used to have quite a life, but it had been weeks since I really thought about doing anything at all.

That was when the gunfire started. Funny how I could hear the sound and not immediately recognize what it was. *Pop. Pop. Pop.* Loud. Insistent. Not stopping. I lifted my head, and I wished I could say that I recognized right then what it was.

But I absolutely did not.

It was the look on Guadalupe's face that finally woke me up. Then the battering ram hit the door. I gasped. This was bad. Someone was trying to get in. *Shooting. Oh, fuck.* I didn't have a gun. That was a thread I'd dropped. Everyone here was armed except me.

Guadalupe was frozen, her hands over her ears. With them beating down the door, it couldn't have been about just catching Alejandro, who I had to hope had gotten away. Worry flooded me. Had he? Or had they just killed my husband outside?

I didn't have time to consider it. Instead, I grabbed Guadalupe and moved her body like I would a statue. She was bigger than me, heavier, but in that moment, I was stronger. Maybe it was adrenaline. I couldn't think, I just reacted.

There was only one place I could think to go. I hustled her into Alejandro's bathroom. It was a big tub. And I had to get her into it. Under the bed was going to be obvious. Would they check the bathtub?

"Stay here. Okay? Just stay here. No one wants to hurt you." She didn't speak English, but I kept talking. "Don't be an accident."

Alejandro's office was open. What info had he left out that he wouldn't want these people to find? There was nothing I could do. If they could get into the house, they'd get in there with no trouble. The battering ram was still happening, so no one was coming to rescue us in the immediate future. I couldn't get out the front door, and all that would happen if we went out the back was that we'd get stuck out there.

We were stuck in the house.

What was I supposed to do? Armani had given me no training for outright home invasions. None. Where was I supposed to hide?

I crawled into the closet. I spent so much time thinking about my stupid clothes, it would serve me right to die with them.

Gunfire sounded in the house. The fuckers were shooting up the walls. I put my head down and made myself small. There was nothing to do but wait in hiding and hope that help arrived before we got killed. Or figure out how to fight back from the man with the gun? There was more gunfire, this time from outside. How many people did they have of ours already? Were all of the guards dead? Or had they been in on the betrayal? I didn't know.

Didn't know.

Couldn't breathe too loud.

Had to be small.

*Please don't come in here.*

*Please. Please. Please.*

Who was I asking *please* to? Did I suddenly think there was someone listening? It didn't matter right then. I just needed this to end. *Lily Hernandez, wife to drug lord Alejandro Hernandez, was found dead in her home.* Gunned down. Live by the sword, die by the sword. Friends were shocked. Brothers didn't care. Husband and family…did they care?

My thoughts were just nonsense. I had to stop. Had to. More gunfire. This time louder. Lots of gunfire.

And then it stopped.

*Why did it stop?*

Where was my phone? I could call for help. Would the police come? No, I couldn't speak to them anyway. Not enough Spanish. I'd gotten to some basics. *El clima es agradable hoy*. Not going to help me.

"Lily!" Javier's voice thundered through the house. "Fuck. Lily! Are you here?"

I had to force myself to move, force myself to speak. "Here." Could he hear me? "Here!" I tried again.

There were loud footsteps, and Javier was there, pushing the clothes away from me. "Fuck. Fuck. You're okay. Did you get hit? Are you hurt?"

I shook my head and pointed to the bathroom. "Guadalupe. I put her in there. Is she okay?"

He called over his shoulder, and there were more footsteps. Javier never took his eyes off me, but after a lot of calling back and forth, he looked at me. "She's fine."

That was when he hugged me so tightly that I could hardly breathe, but right then, I didn't need to breathe. I closed my eyes as he said things to me I simply couldn't understand. He shouldn't be holding me like this. It would start conversations Alejandro didn't want anyone to have, but I just didn't care.

He rocked me like I was a baby in his arms. I had to pull it together. Tears threatened, and I sucked them back. "Can't cry."

I didn't realize I'd said that aloud until he asked, "Why not? Yes, you can. Cry if you want to."

"No." I pulled back. "I can't."

Because the day that dam broke, it would never close again.

My body shook in his arms. "Trust me. Neither of us want that right now."

He whispered in my ear again. "I thought you were dead."

"Did you get them?"

A door slammed open, and Francisco was there, on his knees in front of me. His eyes were huge. "You're okay." He pulled me out of Javier's arms and into his own. "I just heard. I heard, and I came. Too late. I thought I was too late."

"I got one of them," Javier said, answering my question. "The other is still out there."

Francisco let me go, and I almost fell over before I righted myself.

"What?" He jumped to his feet and was out of the room so fast, it was like he hadn't been there at all.

After that, things became sort of a blur. At some point, I made my way back into the living room and sat down, staring at the holes in the wall from the bullets, when Alejandro stormed through the door. He spoke in Spanish to Javier, who was next to me, and then he held my face in his hands.

"Lily, are you okay?" His hug was tight, and his body vibrated against mine. "I'm sorry. I'm so sorry."

I wasn't sure for what.

* * *

No one had suggested I take a pill, but as I lay in the dark, I almost considered asking for one. Alejandro lay next to me. I could tell from his breathing that he was also not sleeping. The house was surrounded with guards, that much I'd been told. Javier was in his room, and I had no idea about Francisco. No one talked, and I didn't ask. Someone had taken Guadalupe home.

Assassins came into the house. One of them had gotten away. The other was dead and burned in our backyard. I could still smell the scent in my nostrils, even though I suspected it was a phantom scent, since the actual aroma of burning flesh had likely long since dissipated. The assassins hadn't been alone. They'd hired a crew. As far as I knew, those men were now all dead too.

Alejandro rolled onto his side. "It'll never happen again. No one will ever come into our home and hurt my wife again. Hurt you."

"I kept thinking that your office was vulnerable. Was it?" That was a stupid thing to ask, but it had occurred to me in the middle of gunfire that his papers might be taken. "Did they get any information they shouldn't have?"

He scrunched up his face. "You were worried about my office?"

"Never mind." I'd known it was nonsensical when I'd been thinking about it.

Alejandro cupped my cheeks. "My things are fine. Everything is backed up and backed up and backed up. I've hidden it from every hacker and major government organization in the world. Those assholes weren't getting anywhere near it."

That was fair enough. "Stupid. Of me."

"No, it wasn't. It was sweet. Smart, actually. The truck makes it across the border and on its way to Chicago—yes, there, because I picked your brothers to go first, so they'd get their product if the plan worked—and then someone comes in here and guns down the house."

I didn't understand. "Are you saying it is related to my brothers?"

"No, what I'm saying is it isn't a coincidence that once I successfully delivered product, they then came to my house thinking I'd be here." He ran a hand through my hair. "I'm sorry. I should have been here with you."

I could picture the scenario just fine. "You'd have gone in, guns blazing, and everyone would be dead now. I hid. So did Guadalupe. It's why we're still here. They weren't looking for women cowering in bathtubs and closets."

"You make it sound like you did something wrong when you did everything right." He pressed our foreheads together. "Just as you should have. And you saved Guadalupe. You thought through a situation where others would have folded."

I closed my eyes. "What happens now?"

"Well…"

A door slammed outside, and I jumped like something had

exploded. Alejandro darted to his feet, grabbing the gun off his side table where he'd put it earlier. We didn't usually sleep with his gun obviously present. He swung open the door before he spoke to me. "It's Francisco. Where the fuck did you go? What happened to you?"

He stormed into the room, his clothes torn and covered in blood. "I killed the other fucker."

I sat up straight. "What?"

"I found him, and I killed him. Dead. I got a few others who were with him too." He was breathing hard. "They won't be bothering you anymore."

Alejandro pulled his brother into a hug. "You are okay?"

"I'm okay." They embraced for a moment before they broke apart.

"Good." Alejandro ran a hand through his hair. "Did you get any information? Did you ask him who hired him? Did you get any information at all?"

"I…" Francisco's shoulders slumped. "Honestly, it didn't occur to me. I'm sorry."

Alejandro held up his hand. "It's okay. You did the important thing. You ended this threat. I don't expect you to interrogate. No one has ever asked you to do that. That's not your job…but neither was it your job to go kill him. You're my brother. You are more important than a hired gun."

He pointed at me. "They came into our home and shot at my woman. I would burn the entire world for less."

Alejandro nodded. "I know. You are so much stronger, so much braver than I wish you had to be. But, brother, once again, you have come through for the family. Thank you."

Francisco's eyes met mine. "No one takes what is mine."

"*Gracias*, Francisco," I whispered.

He bent over and kissed me. His lips were cool, and I could smell the night on him. The cool air, the way it hung to his clothes, even with the other scents on him. "Don't ever thank me."

# 14

The assassins were dead, but from what I could tell, that didn't alter Alejandro's feeling about how things had to go from there. The next morning, he woke up with his face pressed into the back of my neck, breathing deeply, and I didn't know it, but he'd already made a safety decision. I wasn't going to be separated from him unless I was with one of his brothers, and that included within the house.

Negotiation gave me alone time in the pool and the bathroom. I couldn't have one of them on top of me at all times. Not if they didn't want me to freak out. My brother Armani texted me that morning too, but I ignored him. I wasn't unhappy in my life, but I wasn't ready to let him off the hook yet, either. I was still being shot at and living a life I couldn't tell anyone about, as though what the four of us did was shameful. I'd get over it eventually, but I wasn't ready to forgive him for not warning me yet.

That made me petty. I knew it.

But the biggest change was that my office where I studied was now inside Alejandro's office. Like *we* shared a bedroom, *we* now shared an office. The trouble with this new setup was that once again, I felt like I was visiting his space instead of having anything of my own. In reality, I was in less danger than I'd been before, but he seemed to need me close and they were all more relaxed if I wasn't alone. I guessed the fact that I'd been by myself had really thrown them off.

Guadalupe had taken to making me very special meals. I hadn't realized that before she'd been making the guys their favorite meals regularly. Now, it seemed like she was trying to figure me out as well.

"I don't eat very much," I told her one day when Javier was sitting with me. "I have an illness. Or at least an issue? However you want to put it. I fight it, but making food for me is wasted. I just might not be able to eat that day, or not be able to eat very much."

She leaned over and swatted my hand before she wagged a finger at me. I lifted my eyebrows. "Because you don't know what it's like at all to battle back issues?"

That earned me a nod, and she walked over and hugged me, sort of bumping Javier out of the way to do so. They were being less and less careful around her, like they no longer cared if she knew that I was intimate with Javier and Francisco. I understood why—it wasn't like she was going to tell anyone anything.

But our new security measures meant spending my days watching my professor talk from the comfort of a desk in Alejandro's office. For his part, he wore earbuds, talked very little, and when he did, it seemed to make the people on the other side of the phone very nervous. He definitely had a tone that said he was annoyed. I'd heard it a little bit when he'd argued with me, but never to the extent he used with his business contacts. So far, in no surprise to him or me, Javier and Francisco didn't betray him. When it was only them who knew the details of the shipments, they got there with no problems. The process of elimination left his father and uncle. I didn't bring it up, but I knew he realized it too.

I disconnected my connection when class was over and glanced at my husband. "I think I'm going to quit."

He pulled out his earphones. "Why?"

"This is a huge amount of work, and I won't be able to go any further once I finish it. I love it." I did love to learn, I always had.

"But I'm finding it pointless. I'm just going to go intensive on my own to learn Spanish."

He crossed his hands in front of him. "And then what?"

I spun in my chair. "I guess that I'll bleach my teeth too white and spend too much time thinking about the lives of people that have nothing to do with me." I grabbed my breasts. "Maybe I'll get more work done. I could go up two sizes to better fit in with the wives."

Alejandro groaned. "That is not you, Lily. Get whatever work you want done, but I think you will be very bored very quickly."

"If I can get enough of the language under my belt, I can find something to volunteer to do locally. Be some sort of constant volunteer."

He tilted his head. "Don't quit yet. Think on it."

I rose. "I'm going to go swim."

He shook his head. "Later. I want to give you something."

Well, that was surprising. I had everything I wanted and then some. What more could he give me? "Really?"

"That look on your face tells me I need to give you more gifts. Think of it as our two-month anniversary present."

That was even more surprising than the present. "Has it been two months?"

I loved when he got the sardonic smile on his face. It always meant he was about to say something amusing. "Does it feel longer or like less time?"

"Less time, I guess. I feel like…like it just happened. But I guess it didn't. We've been married for two whole months."

He walked over to me, a bag in his hand. "In a normal marriage, we'd still be on our honeymoon."

"That's a long honeymoon. Most couples are back to work long before two months. They get a week, maybe two, stateside."

Alejandro shook his head. "My wife should have had a year. You got no time at all."

I shrugged. "It's not like we're in a traditional marriage. What would we have done with all that time, anyway?"

"Gotten to know one another even better, although I do love our morning and evening talks. I look forward to them every day."

I did too. "What is it?" I stared at the bag.

He held it up. "Open it."

I did as he suggested, pulling out an M&P Shield, a handgun I was familiar with. It had a thumb safety, and I was sure other features I hadn't discovered yet.

Alejandro smiled at me. "Now, I want you to promise, in the unlikely event that someone comes here and bangs down doors again, that you will hide in the closet. Then, if they come to the closet, you will shoot them. This is until I have a panic room installed here, and then you will go there and no one will be able to get you at all. Deal?"

I stared at the lightweight gun in my hand, and the threat of tears came again. I was getting good at pulling them back. Tears wouldn't be welcome in this life. They'd just make me seem weak. Even when Javier had told me I could cry on the day that the bullets flew, I'd known better than to believe him. I certainly wouldn't give in to them now, not even if I wanted to cry for a different reason.

"This is so thoughtful and exactly what I needed." I smiled at him. "Thank you." Without thinking, but like I'd do with any friend, I leaned over and kissed his cheek. "So sweet of you. I will feel better having this, but I promise not to act like a hero if it's going to get me killed."

His face had gone blank, like he'd disappeared behind a shield I couldn't read. I stepped back, realizing my mistake. "Sorry, Alejandro. I shouldn't have kissed you. I…I'm stupidly affectionate sometimes. I just used to hug and kiss everyone. It won't happen again."

He put out his hand and grabbed my wrist when I would have fled the room. "I liked it. The easy affection, like you have with my brothers. It startled me, but I liked it. Don't resist doing that if the mood strikes you, okay?"

We never talked about how we slept at night. It was like that was a sacred space we'd carved out for just us. Daytime was daytime, night was night, and never the two shall mix.

"Okay." I smiled at him. "Really, really thoughtful."

"You're so surprised by it that I clearly need to be regularly giving you things."

He let go of my wrist, and I tried not to notice the warm imprint where his hand had held my skin. "You do."

"Like what? What have I given you?"

Did he really not understand? "Alejandro, the only thing that you had to do was marry me. You could have decided to lock me in a closet or starve me or send me away to any number of awful places. Instead, you've been kind to me. If everything isn't perfect, then that's just the way life goes. You've made this arrangement very pleasant for me. Thank you for that. I don't have anywhere to go, or anywhere I want to go, I don't need more stuff. Just…it's enough."

"Considering the way things are…I'm the lucky one, Lily. You could have been totally different than you were about it."

I held up my gun. "Now I officially have everything I'll ever need."

He pointed at my hand. "Do you like your ring?"

I glanced at the simple gold one that I wore since we'd gotten married. "Oh, sure. It's fine. Yes, thanks."

He had a matching one. I had no idea where they'd come from or who had picked them out for us. "You don't have an engagement ring."

"We didn't get engaged." Why had this conversation taken such a left turn?

"We did, but it was ten years ago, and neither of us was present." He took my hand to run his finger over it. "Was this what you would have chosen for your wedding ring?"

I hadn't thought about it at all. Not once, even. "I mean…probably not? But it's really not worth thinking about. Who cares about my wedding ring?"

"What would you have chosen?" It was like he was completely ignoring the things I was saying to him.

"I'm not a pure gold person. I like platinum, silver is even better.

But it's nonsense. This is lovely." I pulled my hand back. "It's fine. Don't give it another thought. Going to go swim now. See you later."

I nearly collided with Javier, who rushed into the room. "Hello, Lily sweet." He'd been doing that lately, adding things to my name. "Sorry." He leaned over and brushed a kiss over my mouth. "Alejo, Dad just fired Arturo."

My husband gawked at his brother. "What?"

"Yes, gave him the boot. Told him to get out of Mexico or he'll kill him. No one can believe it."

Alejandro shook his head. "Why would he do that?"

I didn't know Arturo, and if I left, they could speak Spanish to each other, which they had to prefer. I was getting stronger in Spanish, like I now had the ability to talk about as well as a one-year-old, but it was something. They never complained, and that was, again, more than I could have asked for. They were speaking something other than their primary language at home, just for my sake.

It was time to swim. I didn't have to think when I swam.

* * *

Guadalupe had once again outdone herself. The chicken she'd made was amazing. Plus, she'd actually passed me a note. It was in English, and it just said 'Happy.' Was she happy, or did she want me to be? I didn't know, but it was the first time she'd tried to communicate with me.

"Do you want to watch television with us?" Francisco asked me.

I shook my head. "No, but thank you."

Javier pointed at me. "We have English language television here too."

"It's not that." I took a sip of my wine.

"Then what is it?" Javier tugged on my hair. Usually, this was the point that Alejandro disappeared, but this evening, he wasn't leaving. By contrast, he'd been extremely engaged at dinner. I'd never seen him so chatty.

There was a commotion outside, and I tensed. The last time I'd heard anything outside our doors, we'd lost five guards. Not Eduardo, who'd taken my husband to his father's. I was slightly preoccupied with his well-being. It was like I'd already screwed up his life once, so I wanted to be sure it wouldn't happen again on my watch.

Francisco jumped up and ran to the door. Throwing it open, his gun was in his hand and drawn, but he quickly lowered it. "Javier."

Javier rushed the door, while Alejandro stood to see what was happening. He pointed at me. "Stay here."

I nodded. I had no desire whatsoever to get myself tangled into another mess. He wanted me to stay right there, that was what I would do. Absolutely.

But I didn't expect to see the hollering man, shaking violently, being brought into the room. Two guards carried him, and in seconds, he was placed on the ground in the living room. Blood was everywhere. What was happening? That was when I saw the bullet wound. Right in that man's gut. I'd never seen anyone with a bullet wound before, but I'd seen lots and lots of blood in my life. It didn't make me sick.

Javier barked orders that I couldn't understand and spoke to the man in a gentle voice. I jumped up. Yes, despite the fact I'd been told to stay put.

"Alejandro, I'm grabbing towels," I called over my shoulder while I grabbed a bunch of towels I'd seen Guadalupe put away earlier. I hoped they weren't her good towels. That was a funny thought. Technically, they were my towels, yet they didn't feel that way. They were hers. She was much more in charge around here than me.

I handed Javier one, put one under the head of the man who was shot, and tried to figure out where else I could help. Javier jumped to his feet, and then I heard screeching tires outside.

The men who'd carried him in carried him out, this time with Javier running after them. All of it had been really fast and so surreal, I almost couldn't believe it had happened.

"What happened?" I still held three towels.

Alejandro tapped Francisco on the arm. "Go."

"Alejo?" I used his nickname without thinking and winced when I'd done it, but he seemed not to notice. "What's happening?"

He visibly swallowed. "We have a thief. Someone just took from our warehouse who didn't belong there." He shook his head. "Francisco is going to go get the son of a bitch and take care of it, but I know who hired them. Javier will fix our man who was shot. I'll make sure his family is well taken care of, and I'll handle the asshat who did this. Now, how quickly can you get changed? We're going out. I need information that I'm only going to get in a social atmosphere."

There were so many abrupt changes happening that I could hardly keep up with it all. Despite my confusion, I nodded. I was always capable of getting changed and going out. It might be the thing I was best at in the world, and that was a special kind of sad I couldn't afford to think about right then.

"I'm confused." I still didn't really understand what happened. "I mean, I get it. Okay. He was shot. Why was he brought here, and not to the clinic Javier runs for all the people who work for you?"

"He was panicked. He only wanted Javier, so they brought him here. It was a mistake, but it was not the first time it's happened, actually. You might be surprised how many people have ended up bleeding on my floor since Javier became a surgeon. He's really a jack of all trades in medicine these days. That's an expression, right?"

So this was going to be a thing? "Yes, it is. Just give me a minute. What kind of place are we going to?"

"A club." He sighed. "I fucking hate clubs, but like Javier and the injured on our floors, you might be surprised how many times I have to do this."

I wasn't, actually. "My brothers practically had to live at the clubs sometimes. I know what to do."

Still, I stopped short. There was blood on the floor. I had the towels. With no one there to clean it, I'd get it taken care of. It meant a few less minutes to get pretty, but I couldn't leave the blood there.

That man had been shot, he'd come for help, and I couldn't leave evidence of what might be the worst day of his life just sitting on their floor as if it didn't matter.

I scrubbed hard until Alejandro grabbed my hand. "Go get dressed. I'll do it."

The heir to the drug lord empire was going to do it? I stared at him. "You sure?"

"I'm capable, yes." He took the towel from me. "Some things we can scrub away, some we can't. None of us will ever be normal."

I rose, leaving the mess and Alejandro there. "At this point, would you want to be?"

He didn't answer me, and I left him there to go get club ready. I had a collection of things that were nightlife appropriate, and if the wives had been any indication of what to expect, the women tonight would be equally stunning. I ended up throwing on a pair of black pants that were so tight, I couldn't wear underpants with them, and a gold shirt that tied around my neck, making my boobs look bigger than they were. The opening in the back and cropped top displaying my stomach meant lots of skin.

I stared at myself while I hooked on my strappy black shoes that I wore everywhere because they worked with almost everything. Yes, I looked okay. My hair wasn't particularly frizzy today, and I was good at getting striking makeup on fast. When Alejandro was ready, so was I.

I didn't expect him to say anything about my outfit or about how I looked. I knew better by this point. His brothers weren't there, so I was just going to have to trust my own eyes that I'd pulled this off. The blood was gone. I grabbed a bag out of the closet and shoved my wallet and gun into it. I wasn't going anywhere unarmed from here on out. If Alejandro could carry, so could I.

We got in the car, and Alejandro put his arm around me. "This place will be loud, and no one will speak English, but I need you with me. My image of the super religious guy who didn't date has to now look like I can't be away from the woman I married as fast as I could."

I understood. My job was going to be to be quiet and sit still or stare adoringly at him. "If we have a long marriage, there will be a time I might not be able to pull off a club outfit. What would your mother be doing if she were still living? Did she go to clubs with your father?"

"My mother was practically a saint. She was not in clubs." He smiled. "They didn't do things together, and my father's reputation is quite different than mine. He would have been there without her and with many other women instead. That was something that he would've done. Now, he rules from his house expecting me to handle these kinds of situations. One day, I will delegate these tasks to someone else. And I'll make them do it so we don't have to."

I almost asked him who he might trust enough for that position, but I really didn't want to bring up not having kids right then. Besides, even if he had kids, would he have wanted them to do this kind of job? We were in the zone, did that mean our families had to be forever? Or would they never be okay being so-called normal because once you knew this life, you couldn't really know anything else?

Deep thoughts in the car from me. It was going to be like this all night. I wouldn't be talking, which meant I was going to spend too much time thinking.

But I did need to know one thing. "Who hired the thieves?"

"My father fired a man named Arturo. He's been around since before me, and that might be the only reason my father didn't kill him. He kicked him out of Mexico. He's trying to take some product to start over somewhere else. I could have predicted this the second I heard, because I knew Arturo wasn't going to leave quietly."

Okay, now I was following. "He'll be at the club?"

"No, but the people who know where he is will be there." He shook his head. "Baby steps to find him, but I will."

I believed him.

After ten minutes in the club, we were seated in a booth. I stared at the lights and practiced staring at Alejandro like he made the world turn. I didn't anticipate him sticking a knife right into another man's hand. The younger lieutenant bellowed so loudly, I could hear him over the music. I gasped and darted backward, wanting to run, except that with his free hand on my knee, my husband kept me by his side.

He yelled at the other man, whose face paled minute by minute while he remained basically pinned to the table unable.

"This is my wife, Lily." Alejandro spoke in English to the man. "I know you understand me. I am going to go get my coat, so I can take my wife home. In the meantime, you are going to stay here and be polite to Lily. By the time I get back, you'll have a location for me. Don't fucking move, or the next knife I'm jamming in you will be in your fucking dick." He looked over at me, his eyes softening dramatically. "I'll be right back, sweetheart."

The man with the knife in his hand shook violently, his body vibrating so hard, he knocked over a glass that then spilled all over his legs. I wasn't sure what exactly I was supposed to do. I'd really thought I understood what it took to fill the role of his wife, but I hadn't. Really, I didn't have a clue. This man had a knife in his hand.

He stared at me, and I stared at him. Was I supposed to say something? He was silent, and so was I. Quiet seemed to be preferred, but I had to give him credit. I didn't know if I could have stayed that quiet. Minutes passed. *Is Alejandro fucking kidding me with this?*

Enough was enough. How long did it take to get a coat? If he was biding time to make this man sweat, it was too long. I grabbed my purse and turned to the knifed man. "Don't move. It's not a good idea."

I stormed toward the coat check and stepped inside the small room, and then I came up short. Alejandro was there, and an older man stood in front of him, his back to me, with a gun pointed at my husband's head.

Alejandro didn't look concerned—the far away, bored look on his face could mean a million different thoughts. My brother Salvatore had taught me many lessons in life, but one of them really poured out of my head in that second. *Don't raise a gun you have no intention of shooting*. I was sure whoever this gentleman was had the same lessons at some point.

And Alejandro's gun was obviously not accessible, or he would have pulled it out by now. Where was his? I didn't know, didn't see it. Had this ass managed to disarm my husband?

It didn't matter. Those thoughts floated through my head so fast that they were gone as soon as they showed up. I should have felt a million things, but in that moment, it was like I'd become a robot. Alejandro's life was in danger. He was my husband. There was just one thing to do. I opened my purse, raised my gun, and even before he could turn around, I shot him in the head.

It was that fast. *One. Two. Three. I killed a man*. My mind went blank.

# 15

I didn't remember getting back into the car.

But that was where I was.

It wasn't moving, and I was alone. I looked left and right before I grabbed at my head, covering my ears as if I could block out the sound of my own thoughts. I'd just killed someone. I could actually feel the gun imprint in my hand as if I still held it. My purse was next to me. I stared down at it like it was a foreign object, but with shaking hands, I opened it, seeing the gun inside.

Had I lost my mind? Did I not fire it? Was I hallucinating? Snapped?

The door opened, and Alejandro got inside. Just seconds later, we skidded out of the parking lot.

Alejandro tugged me against him. "Do you understand what I'm saying now? Are you back?" He smoothed my hair off my face.

I nodded. "I'm here. I don't remember getting here, but I'm here." I pulled back. "Are you okay? You had a gun to your head."

He cupped my cheeks. "I am okay because you saved my life, which you should not have had to do. I went to get the coat, and I found the coat check woman dead. It distracted me, and he took my gun. Had my own fucking gun to my own stupid head. Guards all over that place, and there wasn't a thing I could do. I deserved to be shot in the head for being such an asshole."

I gasped. "Don't say that. I didn't know we had guards."

"They were all over the place, but I waved them off before I entered the coat check. I was pretty convinced my number was called, but then there you were. And I was terrified he'd turn on you. Then you saved my life. Do you realize what you've done?" He kissed both my cheeks where his hands had been. Somewhere in the back of my mind, I realized that was a first. I'd kissed him on the cheek once, but he'd never reciprocated before.

I swallowed. "Who did I k-kill?" Okay, I was stuttering.

"That was Arturo. He came in to see the man who I stabbed in the hand. He heard I was there and lay in wait, the fucker." He hugged me tighter. "Thank you, Lily. Thank you for saving my life."

It was hard for me to think, like my mind was clouded up, and I couldn't see through the fog. "Of course."

He shook his head. "There is nothing *of course* about it. Most people would have let me die. If you had let him kill me, you'd be free. You know that, right? You wouldn't have to stay here if you didn't want to. You'd break my brothers' hearts, but you could get out. You would have nothing obligating you to stay here."

"Alejandro." I had to make this clear. "I really, really like you. I care about you." It was probably more than that, but Alejandro would balk at a declaration of love and I didn't want to turn the conversation in that direction. There was a dead body at a club, and I needed answers. "I would kill anyone who tried to harm you."

An expression I couldn't interpret crossed his face, and I was afraid I'd just stepped in a minefield I hadn't realized existed. Hurriedly, I explained, "Wouldn't you kill someone who tried to kill me?"

His nod was fast. "In a heartbeat, but I'm the kind of person who does that sort of thing. Rather regularly, if you want me to be honest. You aren't."

I laughed. It wasn't funny, but I wasn't right in the head right then. "Maybe it's a new start for me. Maybe you can send me out on jobs like you do Francisco."

He pulled me tight against him. "Never. I can promise you that. Never."

"The body. The police?" Maybe I wasn't making sense, but he seemed to understand me.

"There will be no body, and the police won't know a thing about it."

That was good.

* * *

I stared at myself in the mirror as the water ran hot into the sink of the bathroom. Leaning against the counter, a fully dressed and serious Alejandro observed me silently. Unlike my husband, I was already dressed for bed. My pajamas were simple—a pair of old shorts and a white T-shirt that had seen better days. If others had comfort food, I had the equivalent in clothes. These were them.

Dark circles beneath my eyes made me look a thousand years old, and even I could see my glassy, non-focused eyes in my reflection. No wonder Alejandro didn't want to leave me alone. He must be worried I was going to fall over.

I shut off the water and looked over at him. "We've never been in the bathroom together before. I think that for some normal couples, it breaks some kind of rule. Stay out of the bathroom, keep some mystery alive."

He shook his head. "I didn't follow you in to watch you pee, just to make sure you're okay in general. I'll leave if it bothers you."

I'd already peed when we first got in the powder room, back when I'd thought I wanted to eat something. I had to be crazy thinking that. It was the last thing my stomach wanted.

"Thanks." I stepped away from the sink. "I'll go to bed. You can do whatever you need to. By tomorrow, it'll be like nothing happened to me. You'll see."

He stalked over to me and took my hand. With a tug, he drew me to him. "You don't have to be fine by tomorrow. You don't have to be so strong about this. I'm not judging you. My brothers, when they know, which they don't yet, won't judge you."

I lifted my chin. "You would, even if you don't know that you would. We both know you eat the weak. You were annoyed that you were about to be shot in the head because you did something stupid. You weren't even scared. I won't be something you come to despise for my weakness. I'll pull it together in the morning."

He didn't let me go. "Lily, someday, you will trust me with your tears. I wish that could be tonight, but if it's not, it will be someday."

I sincerely doubted that. I didn't trust anyone with my tears.

I crawled into bed, forgetting about the curtains and the light. I was just done.

I'd shot someone in the head, and even though I'd had this idea I could be some fictional version of myself, Gunmetal Lily or whoever I'd thought that was, I wasn't badass. I was just tired.

A few minutes later, Alejandro came out of the bathroom and did the things I hadn't done. He closed the curtains and turned off the light. In the quiet of the room, with the swoosh of the fan above us, he crawled in next to me, immediately making the bed warmer.

He tugged me against him. Usually, he didn't reach for me until he'd fallen asleep, but I guessed tonight warranted different circumstances.

"I'd be more worried if you felt nothing at all. You're wrung out. It will pass, yes, but you don't have to pretend to be fine if you're not. There is enough lying around here. I'll trust you to know if you need help and to tell me."

I lifted my eyebrows. "You *trust* me?"

"I do. You are added to the list." He maneuvered me until my head was on his arm and his arm was around my waist. "You said we'd be very good friends."

I closed my eyes. What I really needed right then was more than friendship. The thought struck me—yes, sex would have been a huge stress relief that would certainly have taken away the thoughts of that man's brains blowing out of his head. I pushed the image away. Yes, this was going to take a little practice to stop obsessing about.

I'd work on it. Tomorrow.

* * *

I didn't dream, which was nice, and when I woke up, gentle light streamed through the windows. Less than when I closed the curtains. Maybe Alejandro had a knack for it that I didn't have yet. I'd have to ask him to show me if there was a trick to it.

But then I realized I felt something else. I caught my breath. Alejandro and I hadn't moved all night. We were right where we'd been when we fell asleep. His eyes were closed, his breathing even, and he was hard against me.

I wasn't crazy—shifting slightly, I could still feel him. His cock pressed against my body.

*Well…that's new.* Alejandro told me he just didn't get hard, didn't wake up that way, and had managed to train himself never to think about it. He'd never once been aroused when we woke up, and we were always tangled up in each other in the morning.

I'd have to tell him the news. He *did* get hard, he just didn't know it.

His eyes blinked open, unseeing for a moment, but then he focused on me with a small smile. Then he blinked again, his brow furrowing. Maybe I wouldn't have to tell him, because I was fairly certain that he'd just become aware of his altered state right that second.

I wasn't sure what to do, so I stayed absolutely silent.

"Lily." His voice was low, practically a whisper. "Something that never happens is happening."

I nodded. "Yes, I noticed. I can feel it." I moved my hand just a little to run it gently through his hair. "Maybe this happens more often than you think, and you just don't know about it."

He shook his head slowly. "No, trust me. It doesn't. I had tests done. Never mind. I don't want to think about that right now."

That made sense. He was hard. It never happened normally. "Were you dreaming about something in particular?"

"You." His voice was low. "I was dreaming about you in ways I don't usually dream."

I cleared my throat, my mouth gone dry. "Sex dreams?"

"Yes. Wow. This is just… Wow."

I bet it was. I scooted closer. "Alejandro, would you like to do something about it?"

We really had to find a better way to describe what was going on between us. He was hard. Normally, I could use really dirty words, but I had no idea what Alejandro liked and I didn't want to scare off the hardness, in case this was a one-time thing.

He lifted his thick eyebrows. "Like what?"

"Like I could touch you, stroke you. Or, if you wanted to do yourself, that would be fine too." I really hoped he picked the first one, but this was his show.

Alejandro nodded, slowly. "Lily, would you? I mean…I'm not sure how this is going to go."

I had a pretty good idea of how it was going to go, but easing him into this seemed to be the right choice. "Let's just see."

I reached between us. He always slept naked on top, wearing boxers below. That was convenient, because there was a slit to reach for his cock without having to pull the whole thing off. Still, I didn't just want this to be me pulling him and going for it. Maybe he'd like to be seduced a little bit.

His skin was warm, and I ran my hand down his chest, feeling his muscles jump beneath my touch. I squirmed. He wasn't the only one rapidly getting turned on. He'd been dreaming about me, and then he'd gotten hard for the first time in who knew how long. My nipples hardened. Yes, this was working for me, but it wasn't about what I needed. Not right then, anyway.

I touched each of his thighs before finally pulling his cock out of the hole in his boxers. He was hard and thick in my hands. With the covers down, I let myself take a long look at him. Yes, he really was as big as he felt. His gaze held mine, and I saw in them something I wasn't used to from Alejandro—uncertainty.

"So big, Alejo," I whispered back to him. "So thick in my hand."

He wasn't circumcised, that meant that his tip was the most sensitive part of him. I wanted him to have the whole experience. That meant that I started at his balls and traveled upward to the tip. He sucked in his breath. Yes, he liked that. I did it again. Over and over, until I found a rhythm that made him squirm.

"Lily." He said my name as he closed his eyes. Now it was my turn to squirm. He yanked my head toward his to kiss me. It started out soft but quickly hardened until our tongues danced with each other. I continued to stroke him, playing with his tip as much as I could until he was moaning in my mouth while his hips ground his cock further into my hand.

I was wet, practically dripping from touching him. Had there ever been a moment quite like this one? And then he was coming in my hand. I didn't stop what I was doing, keeping it up until he stopped. My hand was covered in his cum, but it didn't matter. I'd clean up later.

Alejandro pulled me into the tightest hug. His body shook almost violently, and he clung to me like I was a lifeline and he couldn't do without me.

I hugged him back.

We stayed just like that, neither of us admitting where the day was headed. Eventually, his alarm went off, shattering the cocoon I'd been imagining for us.

He lifted his head a second before he turned it off. "In case you ever wondered if I trusted you, I think my body just told you more than I could express in words. Like no one else in the world, I would say."

I kissed his cheek, my mouth still tingling from where he had kissed me. I needed to clean up and rolled away to do so. When I came out of the bathroom, he lay on his back staring at me. Alejandro put out his hand, and I took it, letting him draw me back down on the bed.

"Lily." He kissed me right on the lips. "This morning should have been all about you. I didn't even think to try to make you feel like you were making me feel. After what you went through, it should have been all I was thinking about."

I smiled at him. "Tell you what? I hadn't thought about it. I actually feel sort of great. You dreamed of me and had that happen? What a compliment for my fragile ego."

"Your fragile ego?" He rolled me over so that I was beneath him. "How can you have a fragile ego when you know you are the most beautiful woman in any room?"

That wasn't even a little bit true. I decided, since honesty was our policy, to tell him as much. "That is sweet, but we both know that's not the case."

"Lily…"

A bang sounded outside, and Alejandro nodded his head. "That will be Javier. It's quite likely he's heard what happened to you last night, which means that he will be…"

The door flung open, and Alejandro rolled off me. "Good morning, brother."

"Are you okay?" Javier rushed over. He only had eyes for me. His older brother adjusted himself and got out of bed.

As he walked to the bathroom, he stared over his shoulder. "You could knock."

Javier full-on ignored him now. "Lily?"

I sat up. "Yes, I mean I'm fine. Which is more than we can say for Arturo, who is dead. I didn't get hurt, and Alejandro didn't die, so yes, I'm okay."

He furrowed his brow. "Lily…?"

"She's stubborn," Alejandro shouted from the bathroom.

Javier sighed and lay next to me on the opposite side of the bed from where Alejandro had been. "You don't have to be okay."

"I know." I ran my hand gently over his head. "Did you save that man? The one with the shot in his gut?"

"It was touch and go, but yes, I did." He closed his eyes. "It took a long time, most of the night, and then I had to visit with his wife to make sure she was all set up."

I didn't know if visit was the right word, but I wasn't going to correct him. He was exhausted. I could see the dark circles under his eyes.

"Well done. The good news is no one will be stealing again. Even before the encounter with Arturo, Alejandro jammed a knife right into someone's hand."

Javier winced. "Ouch."

Alejandro came out of the bathroom and headed toward the closet. "It made my point. I left him like that. What are the odds he's still at that table?"

He had been pretty terrified, and with Arturo dead, maybe he *was* still attached to that table. I shuddered at the thought.

Next to me, Javier snored. His eyes were closed, and he was out cold on my pillow. I sat all the way up. That had happened fast.

"He's always been like that." Alejandro was half dressed as he spoke in a low voice. "One second, up, the next, out."

I smiled. "Do we just leave him in here?"

"I would. No need to bother him." He leaned over and kissed me. "See you in the office in a little bit. If that never happens again, I am always going to remember that it did. You're like a miracle."

Another bang. Francisco was home. I smiled at Alejandro. "I'm never going to forget it, either. And maybe it won't be the last time."

"Can't get my hopes up."

As his youngest brother charged through the door, Alejandro shushed him, pointing toward their sleeping brother. I put out my hand and let Francisco help me off the bed. "You okay?" I asked him in greeting.

"I can't believe how he snores when he's exhausted. Yes, I'm fine. I heard you took care of our problem. Thank you, Lily."

That was so Francisco. He didn't ask if I was okay. He just assumed I had this under control. I preferred that. I was shaky, but the morning with Alejandro, who winked at me on his way out the door, had reset some of my thoughts. Maybe I could trade one memory for another.

I didn't know if it worked that way.

But *maybe* was the key word.

"Did you get him? The guy who did the actual thieving and shot Javier's patient?"

He nodded. "Oh yes, he's dead. And some of his friends too."

I was going to try to be like Francisco about the situation. He would be my role model.

* * *

I tried to watch my class but ultimately ended up shutting off the computer. Alejandro was busy, so I left the office quietly and headed outside to the pool. I wasn't going to swim, but it was about all I could handle right then. The guys had dragged umbrellas around one chair for me so that my redheaded self was basically ensconced in shade. The sun wouldn't get me there.

Still, as I lay down, restlessness threatened to make this not a place I wanted to sit, either. I wasn't sure what I was going to do with myself. I couldn't just be a person who walked up and down the halls of a house with nothing productive to do.

Maybe I should wake Javier or Francisco. Only that wouldn't be nice. Neither one of them would complain about a quick romp in the sheets to handle my energy, but they needed to sleep more than they needed to be inside of me right then. Plus, sex could be a distraction, but it couldn't be all that I was doing with myself. Did I need to come up with an answer right that second?

Alejandro appeared next to me. I blinked. "Where did you come from?"

He pointed. "That door. You're distracted. What are you thinking about?" He plopped down in the chair next to me. "Class end early?"

I closed my eyes. "Class is ending now permanently. Why am I putting so much time into something that will go nowhere?"

He lifted an eyebrow. "Because you love it."

I groaned. "That is what you had to say? The one thing that would make me want to go beat myself up studying for tests that I'll never use to obtain an MA, which is the whole point?"

"Lily." He waited for me to look at him before he continued. "Stop whining."

With those words, he threw me into the pool. I shrieked, realizing what the fuck had just happened a second before I got wet. I swam almost every day, but not in my clothes. I surfaced, spitting out water and glaring at him. I hadn't been prepared to get wet, but I couldn't stay mad at him because a second later, he was in the water with me.

I shrieked before I put my arms around him. He'd thrown me in and jumped in after me. That was stupidly adorable and not something I'd have expected from Alejandro. We floated together, my arms around his neck.

"You threw me in."

He nodded. "You needed it. So did I." His smile was slow. "Stay in your class. Next semester will work itself out. And if it doesn't, then you'll figure out your next move, but you're going to be miserable if you drop out now. You're not the kind of person who leaves things half done."

He was right. "Can I kiss you?"

He grabbed my hand as an answer and brought it to his lips. "Yes."

So I did. I kissed and kissed Alejandro until I was lightheaded from it. He pushed back. "You know how I was worried that I wouldn't be able to get hard again?"

I could hardly think. "Yes."

"Not a problem, evidently." He smiled before he kissed me again. "It's all you, Lily. And that shirt of yours showing your nipples doesn't hurt, either."

I caught my breath. "Do you…do you want to have sex with me right here?"

"In the pool? No. I don't want anyone seeing you when we're together. Call me a prude, but that's how I feel. Our time together belongs to just us. My brothers like to pleasure you together. I can't imagine wanting to do that. I want us to be us when it's just you and me. Is that going to be a problem?"

I dipped under the water and came back up. "No. It can be just you and me when we're together, but I'm not giving them up without a fight."

He tugged me to him. "You won't get a fight. They'd probably murder me if I suggested such a thing. We made this arrangement, and it stays as it is. You want to love all the Hernandez men? Well, God help you, Lily. Yes, I just said God." He smirked at me. "We are a lot to take."

"You are nothing I can't handle." I splashed him and swam away. "And who says I love you?"

He laughed, throwing his head back. "You do. You killed a man for me last night."

I pointed at him from the other side of the pool. "You'll say it first. Mark my words."

I loved his grin. "We'll see."

# 16

I stared at myself in the mirror, putting cream under my eyes, when Alejandro stormed into the room. His expression was stern, and I didn't have to be a mind reader to know he wasn't happy. A huge change from how he'd been the rest of the day, which had been downright joyful, but something had set him off now.

"Problem?"

He picked up a container from his bureau and tossed it across the room. "The shipment was taken."

With everything that had been going on, I'd all but forgotten that Alejandro was still dealing with trying to figure out who was betraying him. I rose and picked up the container. "Who was it?"

He visibly swallowed. "My uncle."

I wasn't the least bit surprised. He had dead eyes. I wasn't a huge fan of their father, but the uncle was off. I couldn't always go by my first impression of people, but sometimes I was right. Still, he'd been on the list of people that my husband thought he trusted, and it had to be a blow.

"Any idea why he'd be doing this?" I passed him the container. "In case you want to throw it again."

He quirked his mouth. "No. He's a very rich man. Powerful. My father always treated him more like a partner than an underling. He always gets the first of everything. I was desperate for a brother when I was young because I was envious of their relationship. I don't remember much from that time, but I remember that. Then, of course, I got Javier and Francisco. I always wondered if he was envious of me because I had two and he only had my dad." He blinked. "Stupid childish thinking."

I took his hand. "It's not. Maybe you were actually more right than you thought. Maybe he's envious. You're the heir. If your father were to die, what would happen to him?"

He scrunched up his face. "He'd keep his business. I don't want to take it from him. That would be ridiculous. I mean… Fuck."

We might never know the answers. "What are you going to do?"

"I'm going to kill him. Tonight. I'm going to get Francisco and go do it now."

This was part of our lives. We just went around killing people when necessary, until such a time as someone would decide they should kill us. Hell, people had already decided that. They just hadn't pulled it off yet. It wasn't for lack of effort.

I tugged on his shirt, just feeling like I needed something to do with my hands. "Is this something you should discuss with your father?"

"I think, in this case, he won't blame me. We have a long history of eliminating those who harm us. He'd kill me if I'd done the same. And yes, I can say that. I understand my father, mostly. The power he holds. The way that he runs things. But he would kill any of us that got in his way."

I went up on my tiptoes and kissed him. "Then just be careful."

He kissed me back, hard, on the mouth. "And finally, the easy affection that I've so craved from you. I will be careful. As much as a person can be in an execution." He kissed me again, this time slower. "See you later. Javier is here. He'll stay to make sure you are okay."

I nodded. At some point, we were going to have to figure this out. How was it possible that they had so much money, so much power, and I couldn't be left at home without one of them here to watch me? But it wasn't the day for that conversation. There was a time and a place for these things.

The discussion could take place *after* Tio Ricardo was dead.

I followed him from the room back out to the living room, where Javier patted next to him on the couch. I snuggled up next to him as Francisco came over to kiss me.

"Got to go do this thing. Then we'll be back, and tomorrow, you're coming with us to look at the horses."

I didn't know what that meant. "What horses?"

"There is a horse track not far from here. It's not a big one or anything. But years ago, Alejandro negotiated with them to bring in a lot of older racehorses that aren't able to race anymore, past their prime. Time for them to be out for stud, so to speak. They get brought here before they are sent off to wherever they're going in the world to deed. People come to see them here and make deals on them. Some of it is decided beforehand, but some of it is decided here."

That sounded really cool. "And you guys take a cut?"

"Actually, no. It's the one thing where we don't. We just like the horses. We have a dream of buying a racehorse someday, but not till Dad is gone. We don't want to give him a cut of it." He smiled. "So it'll be our horse. Your horse."

He put on the television, and his brothers left. Was it appropriate to wish them good luck killing their uncle? I just didn't know the protocol, so I stayed quiet. Javier put on a movie I hadn't seen. It was in English, so I settled down to watch the men in the film kill zombies. There wasn't much dialogue. Just a lot of shoot 'em up, bang bang.

"This is nice," he said, and his voice was low while his thumb traced circles on my arm. "Why don't you watch movies with us at night?"

They'd asked me that a lot over the last few months, and I'd been able to pivot and dodge the question. But I was tired of avoiding the conversation. I had to answer. "Because I happen to think that guests should go to bed so their hosts can breathe."

He jolted. "What?"

"I said—"

Javier held up his hand. "I heard you, I'm just shocked. You're not a guest. You're family."

I sighed. "I *feel* like a guest. I've never been able to think of myself as permanent here. I feel like everything is temporary. Maybe it'll change? Maybe a year from now, this will feel like where I live, but right now, it doesn't and I'm not sure why."

He got on his knees. "You are permanent to me. This is not how I live. Before you, I alternated between getting shit faced and working. I was pissed that Alejandro asked me to be with you sexually, because I thought it might get in the way of my getting laid by other people." His accent thickened, revealing what he said to be emotional for him. "Then you were like sunshine to my soul. All I wanted. I've told you this. I'd have fought him for you if I couldn't have you too. Now all I want to do is make love to you and watch movies with you, since Alejandro won't let us sleep with you. He says that's his domain, whatever that means. So…yeah. You are permanent to me. Are you planning on leaving?"

I shook my head. "No, but I wasn't planning on being here, either. I have come to believe that people are loyal to each other, love each other, until they just don't anymore. My brothers raised me after my parents were killed on that boat. One of them in particular took care of me all the time. Then I came home one day to find my things packed, and I came here. My brothers would probably tell me they love me if I asked. We don't really have those conversations anymore, haven't since my parents died, but I'm sure they would say they loved me, if they were pressed. *Yes, I love my sister*, they'd say. I'm sure you love Rosa, but you gave her over the second you had to. You love me, Javier, and I have those feelings for you. That doesn't necessarily lend itself to permanence, not in our world. It doesn't mean that something won't happen that will make us not an *us* anymore."

His face fell. "Lily sweetheart. There isn't anything besides death that would take me from you, and even then, I would wait for you on the other side."

These men and their faith. I'd never been where they were in their belief. Actually, I admired it. What was it like to be sure of something? "Javier—"

He kissed me rather than let me finish my thought. "All will be well. You'll see. And my sister? She is so in love. Did I know that when Alejandro took her off? No, I didn't, but I am hugely relieved. I'm also not sorry about any of this because it brought you here to be with us. It's not like we would ever have met otherwise. Even if I had come to Chicago, you wouldn't have been allowed to see me. If we'd bumped into each other, you would've been hustled away. This is the only way this," he motioned between us, "happens. You aren't a guest. You aren't impermanent. You are it."

I sighed. "I'd like to believe you. I hope that I can, eventually. That a year from now, we'll laugh at this while I talk about whatever I've figured out to do with my life."

He shook his head. "You have to finish school."

"I'm quitting. Why bother? I can't actually finish school. This is a lot of work for no payoff. I've got to figure something else out, because I can't just sit around here all day."

Javier kissed my face, all over it. "Finish your class. You don't know what could happen next semester."

"I thought I did know. I'm going to be here with you, right?"

He smoothed the skin out under my eyes with his thumb. "Yes, that we do know. The rest of it we don't." He kissed me, and I let myself get lost in Javier. It was easy to pretend all was fine everywhere and with everyone when I got to be with Javier like this. He could almost make me believe that everything would be just as he imagined it would be.

Javier pressed a finger over my breast, pinching it from the outside of my shirt. I closed my eyes and let him love on me. It was so fucking hot.

* * *

I woke later to the feel of the bed dipping beside me. Alejandro pulled me against his chest.

"You're okay." I hadn't really woken up yet. My head was fuzzy, but he was there and that was everything. "Did you get him?"

They'd been gone a long time for what should have been a point and shoot. He kissed my neck. "No, he was warned somehow that we were coming." Alejandro flipped me over. "We tried for some time to track him, but so far, no luck. Coming home to this is so fantastic."

I wrapped my arms around his neck. "Does that mean you're still…interested?"

"Very." He kissed my neck. "And I want to learn your body. I didn't earlier. That was a big error on my part. I was so overwhelmed by the feelings and you took such beautiful care of me, but I've had all day to get used to this happening. I'm still floored by it. But I want to take my time now and make sure you feel as good as I do."

I cupped his cheeks. "I was so wet from what happened. Believe me, it meant a lot to be part of that moment with you."

"Part of the moment? You were the whole moment. The reason it happened. Then you were there with your small hand wrapped around me like you knew just what I needed. You brought me so much pleasure."

I kissed his chin. "It was you who made that happen, not me."

He moved until he could kiss my neck more directly, and then moved down. He pushed aside my shirt and then must have wanted it totally removed, because he threw it aside. Alejandro squeezed my breast. He wasn't gentle, and I grinned. Alejandro took what he wanted in all things. He wanted my breast, he wasn't going to play around it, he was going for gold.

I closed my eyes, pleasure moving through me. My breasts weren't always sensitive, but they were tonight. His touch really worked for me.

"So pretty," he whispered, and I lifted my lids to gaze at him. "Every part of you is so gorgeous."

My heart rate kicked up. I tugged on the back of his neck, bringing his mouth to my nipple. He was smart, and he'd catch on fast to what I wanted. His mouth, my nipple. Right. Then. Alejandro sucked hard, and I sighed. Yes, that was just what I'd needed. He palmed my stomach while he did as I'd wanted.

Eventually, he lifted his head to pay attention to the other nipple. I ran my hand through his hair, and he must have liked that because he leaned slightly into the touch. For years, he'd denied himself any of this. Alejandro had to be touch starved. I hadn't considered that before.

I moved, which stopped his attentions to my breasts so that I could spend some time touching him too. I tugged on his shirt, and when he finally took it off, I wrapped my arms around him tightly so that we were chest to chest.

He ran his hands up my back, and I did the same for him. "About your tattoo?" I couldn't see it from my angle, but I knew it was there.

"Yes, it is the family crest, so to speak, as I told you before. Part dragon, part snake."

I'd been thinking about that. "Should I get it put on me?"

"I'd love it, if you did." He pinched my hip. "Right there." When I yelped, his smile grew broader. "If you want to be technical, it is the feathered serpent wrapped up in a snake."

He laid me down, and I let him. His words were intoxicating, the sound of his voice as much of a turn-on as anything else. "Dragon is a powerful but good ruler. That is in direct contrast to the snake, who is found in all kinds of mythology and is often the bad guy. It speaks to the family. Little bit of good, little bit of bad, but always both parts at war with each other."

I shimmied out of my pants. "Right now, you are being very, very good."

He took off his own pants. Normally, I'd want a condom, but I knew that Alejandro was clean, and I was protected from pregnancy with my IUD. He was hard, and I'd barely touched him yet.

"All day?" I asked, and he didn't misunderstand me as he nodded. "Poor guy."

"It was fantastic." He lowered his hand, stopping on the outside of my thigh. "Tell me how to do this for you, and I will make you come. It's very important to me."

I took his pointer finger in my hand and pressed it inside of me. It was so much better when men asked for direction rather than fumbling around if they didn't know what they were doing. I'd much rather it be this way.

He closed his eyes for a second when I placed his finger on my clit. "This is heaven."

I smiled. "Glad to know."

With a little help, I showed him the speed and direction I wanted him to move. He followed where I led and had it down in seconds. Leaning my forehead against his shoulder, I just let myself feel. It didn't take long for me to be swollen and ready. He kissed the top of my head as I started to grind against him.

"Yes, just like that." I'd always been a person who could come from clitoral stimulation, but right then, it hit very intense. Almost too much. Still, I wanted it not just for myself, but for him as well. I wanted Alejandro to get me off, and I was sure that he wished for it just as much.

He spoke to me in Spanish, whispering in my ear, and I had no idea what he was saying, but it sounded so hot. I ground against his hand, and it was just the pressure I needed before I exploded. "Yes," I cried out, clinging to his body. I shook and writhed. He held me, his own shaking with mine.

Finally, when it stopped, I stared into his eyes. "Thank you."

"Thank you? No. That was…that was everything I needed. You like that. Those sounds. Yes." He kissed me, and I reached between us to feel his cock. Yes, he was hard. Plenty ready to be inside of me. I kissed him gently.

"Come here."

He didn't scoot over, and I tilted my head. What was going on? "Do you want to do this? It's okay if you don't."

Alejandro nodded slowly. "I do. But…seeing as I never have before, maybe you could be on top this time."

Oh, I loved that idea. I so rarely got to be on top. It was going to be like a special treat. I smiled at him. "Absolutely. Love to. Switch with me."

We changed places, and soon, I was on top of him, gripping his cock in my hand before I pushed myself down on him. Since I was in charge of the movement, I didn't have to stop to fit him inside or worry about what would or wouldn't hurt. I knew this would go well, and I was so jazzed to have this moment that I knew, despite the fact that he was really big, he was going to fit without trouble. I sighed as I took him in, and he let out a moan like I'd never heard from him.

Alejandro widened his eyes. "Lily… Wow."

Yes, those were my feelings as well. "You feel amazing."

I started out moving slowly, wanting him to adjust to what was happening, but it became clear very fast that he needed no such consideration. He gripped my hips, and in seconds, he moved me the way that he wanted it. I grinned. Why should I be surprised? This was Alejandro Hernandez. He may have been temporarily waylaid, but he always knew what he wanted and he got it one way or the other. I shouldn't have expected sex with him to be any different.

I shifted slightly so that his thrusts would hit my clit on their way in and out. He flipped me over as I cried out, and I giggled at the suddenness of it.

"This way," he said, and I nodded. Yes, I'd sort of expected this was how he'd want to do it. I would bet he would want to take me from behind when we got even more experienced together. I wrapped my legs around him tightly and held on for the ride, my body becoming molten lava with each pass and coming together. I might actually be on fire and that would be fine with me.

We moved together, like our bodies had muscle memory and knew how the other one liked things, even though that was impossible. An unspoken language we somehow already understood.

Eventually, I cried out. An explosion of pleasure overtook me, and I practically begged for my release when it happened. He gave me everything I could have hoped for and then some. Finally, he followed me over the abyss, my name a prayer on his lips.

Sometime later, he whispered in my ear. "I didn't know it would be so amazing."

I smiled. I had known it would be, and the experience hadn't let me down at all.

We fell asleep wrapped up in each other, and I woke up in the middle of the night once when he pressed a finger inside of me. I smiled. Yes, that was the absolute best way to wake up. I'd rolled over and let him take me just as he wanted to, fast and hard.

I wasn't sure what woke me, but I wrenched my eyes open to find that Francisco and Javier stared over at our sleeping forms. I lifted my head. "What's wrong?"

"Nothing. Came in to tell our brother that we might have a lead on our uncle, and, ah, I guess we were surprised." Javier rocked back on his feet. "I take it things have changed."

Alejandro said something that sounded like a curse. "In the hall. Both of you. Now. Knock next time."

Javier listened, but Francisco just grinned. "You know this means the sleeping arrangements are changing?"

I shook my head. "What did that mean?"

"He gets you every night because that's the only way he can be with you and he doesn't want the staff to know, but we can figure out the staff part. If he's having sex with you now, I want the nighttime cuddles too."

With that remark delivered, Francisco left the room. Alejandro grinned at me and then groaned. "Last night was incredible."

I kissed his chin. "It was."

He got out of bed. "We'll sort this out, all of us. Maybe I'll make some kind of schedule. If we use the bedrooms we never use, the ones connected to our bathroom, we might be able to pull this off. I'll think on it. But I don't know if I can sleep without you anymore."

That was so sweet. "Alejandro—"

He kissed me to cut me off. "Francisco will be here with you today. I have to go check out product. He'll bring you to meet us at the horses later, then maybe we'll eat out. Like our version of a normal couple. You, me, and my brothers. The Hernandez men wanting you more than we know what to do with."

"I might just lie here for a few minutes."

I needed to find my equilibrium. Things had shifted and that was fine, fantastic really. But the way things had been just two days ago were gone. I was married to Alejandro, and if I were honest, I'd fallen head over heels for him, but I'd done the same with his brothers. I was sleeping with all of them. How would that work out in the long run? In the world with restaurants and visits with strangers?

We couldn't spend every day locked in the house, but I didn't know if I could actually pretend to just be Alejandro's wife when we were out if his brothers were there. Was I supposed to sit across the table and not touch Francisco's hair or lean over to kiss Javier on the cheek?

Alejandro got out of bed, and I rolled over onto my stomach, grabbing my phone from where it was next to the bed. It was fully charged. Quickly, I sent my friends texts in response to the ones they'd sent and then paused over the name I needed to consider contacting.

My brother Armani. He'd been texting, and I'd been ignoring him. It was probably time for me to reengage. Most of my anger had cooled, and it was just getting petty on my part. I wasn't built for long lasting resentments.

I sent him a quick message. *So do you think the Bears have a chance at winning this year or will they eat us alive?*

For the moment, that would have to do. Hopefully, he took it as the peace offering it was. I stared at the sun coming through the window. I was going to take a shower before I faced this day. Things tended to make sense after a hot shower, or at least I hoped they would.

I knew one thing for certain—I wouldn't change a thing about how it was between me and these guys, even if it was complicated.

# 17

With my hair wet, I headed toward the kitchen. Javier and Alejandro must already be gone, but Francisco greeted me with a big grin when I finally made it to the kitchen.

I pulled my hair back and started to braid it. I was just going to leave it like this today. Tomorrow, I'd blow it out, and maybe I'd be able to leave it untouched for a few days so that I didn't have to think about it again. "Morning."

He leaned over and kissed me. "Morning."

Guadalupe entered the room, and we stepped apart. This was just what I'd been worrying about. The longer our entanglement continued, the more I would tend to forget the rules. Besides, why should we have to live with any rules? Weren't they powerful men? I knew the answer to that—they were only as powerful as their people continued to earn for them and keep them that way.

Francisco patted the seat next to him. "I'll braid your hair for you."

When I shot him a look, he shook his head. "I used to do it for my sister. Perfectly appropriate thing to do."

Yes, I imagined it would be, although my brothers didn't do that kind of thing. Still, I was pretty sure there was nothing about it that would feel at all the same with Francisco's hands in my hair. I passed him the hair elastic I was going to use and sat down for him to get started.

That was when I heard the noise.

The click.

I turned my head. Francisco heard it too. Someone had cocked a gun.

I just couldn't have predicted it would have been Guadalupe. It almost seemed surreal. She had a gun pointed right at Francisco's chest. I had to turn to see it fully, and then, for a long second, I couldn't move at all.

Finally, when I could think, I stared at Francisco. He was very quietly speaking to Guadalupe in Spanish. I had no idea what he was saying, but I didn't hear fear in his tone. It sounded almost like he was confused. So was I, but that gun had me plenty nervous. My hands shook, so I shoved them in my pockets.

I had no idea what could have caused her to pull a gun. "Guadalupe." I had no idea if she could understand me. In this case, she didn't even look at me when I spoke. "Francisco, tell her that we're not doing anything wrong. That we're not cheating on Alejandro or anything. We didn't do anything wrong."

It had to be what she'd seen when she came in, that must have been what set her off. Where was my gun? I didn't know. I hadn't seen it since I used it at the club—when that man's head had exploded. I shook my head. No, couldn't think about that right then. No. It wasn't helpful.

I had to stay present. In our current mess.

Francisco frowned. "I don't think that is what this is about. I'm not sure what it is, but…"

"It's about me." Sauntering out of Alejandro's office like he had every right to be in there was a person who absolutely did not belong—their uncle Ricardo. "She follows my orders. Always has, always will."

Francisco whirled around, reaching for his gun where it always was, attached to his buckle in his back. But Guadalupe was fast.

She'd had the gun pointed already, and his movement stopped him from being shot in the chest, hitting his shoulder instead.

I didn't think, just reacted. I knocked that gun right out of her hand and tackled her to the floor. The impact had taken Francisco down, and once I secured the gun from Guadalupe, I turned to point it at Ricardo. But I stopped immediately, dread filling my pores. Francisco's face flared in agony. His uncle held his gun at his nephew's head, his dead eyes acting like nothing was happening at all.

No one said a word.

The threat was understood. If I fired, he'd fire, and no way would I be fast enough to prevent it. With a glance at Guadalupe, who didn't seem to have reacted at all, I pulled myself to my feet.

"Why are you doing this?" I supposed it didn't really matter, the why of it. Still, I wanted to know.

"Lily," Francisco implored me. "Go. Run."

Yeah, I wouldn't be obeying that order. "Why?"

"I'm here for you." Ricardo answered me, but he didn't look at me. Instead, he kept his gaze on Francisco. "It is time for me to break you."

I knew that language. I'd heard it when Alejo described what they'd done to him. Breaking him. His uncle had been right in the middle of that. I cocked my head to gesture at Guadalupe. "Like you broke her?"

She lifted her lips in that vacant smile thing she did with her stitched lips. I thought the expression endearing. I didn't now. It was evil, mean. She'd shot my love. A man she'd known since he was a boy. He was bleeding on the floor right that very second.

Sure, she'd been broken. Maybe I should have sympathy. I didn't. If that made me a bad person, then so fucking be it.

I looked back at the man who'd threatened me, and he nodded. "Just like I broke her. Guadalupe has been my broken doll for decades. You'll be my next plaything."

*Like hell, motherfucker*. "You didn't break Alejandro."

"No. I shouldn't be surprised. The boy is our blood. He would survive it. You, my dear, will not."

Francisco snarled at him. "She's not going anywhere with you."

I could see what would happen next as if it already happened. This fucker was going to shoot Francisco in the head and take me. There had to be a way to stop him. Even with my gun, he'd somehow manage it. Guadalupe would tackle me or something else terrible would happen. But the worst part of it all would be living to know that Francisco died because I'd failed to act. I couldn't handle that. He had to be fine, whatever else happened.

And that was love. That was how I'd define it from now on, if someone ever asked me what love meant—it was knowing what happened to you didn't matter, not if you'd protected someone important.

I held up my hand. "I'll come with you. I won't even put up a fight, but you have to let me get him help."

"No!" Francisco's eyes were wild with rage. He loved me too. The thing between us was real. Funny, I had spent so much time questioning the nature of our entanglement, when I should have reveled in the fact that it existed. I was a fucking idiot.

"I don't know how Guadalupe got you in here undetected." Unless every guard here was one of his broken dolls. That was too horrifying to think about, so I had to assume he'd been snuck inside by her. "But I will go with you without kicking up a fuss. If I do, you have to let me get Francisco help." I repeated myself twice, lest the man was an utter idiot. A psychopath for sure, but maybe he was also dumb. One could only hope.

"Fine."

He kicked Francisco in the head hard, knocking him out. I gasped. That hadn't been at all what I'd said to the man.

"Get him help."

*Okay*. He'd told me to do that. Just what I wanted. I grabbed my phone out of my pocket. A bunch of unread messages filled the screen, but I couldn't stop to see from whom or what they wanted. There was no time.

I shot out a text to his brothers. *Francisco has been shot and knocked out. Your uncle is kidnapping me. Get home to F fast. Guadalupe in on it. She works for him.*

It was hard to text with my shaking hands, a telltale giveaway that I wasn't calm. Not at all.

"Now put the phone on the counter. The gun too."

I'd agreed to this. With just a glance at Francisco's still form on the floor, I did as his uncle told me. Nothing good would come from obeying, but I didn't see any other options.

I steeled my back. "Now what?"

With a pull on the trigger, the asshole shot Guadalupe right in the head.

This time, I screamed. I might not have anticipated his action, but it made sense. She'd been made. He didn't need her anymore. After all her years spying on them for him, she'd stopped being useful, so he ended her.

"Why are you doing this? They would've let you keep your business. No one was taking anything from you."

He tilted his head. "They already took from me, from my brother and me. This should always have just been us, but then the boys came. Then you. There are too many people. It is always just my brother and me."

I don't know why I wanted rational thinking, but I wasn't getting it.

Ricardo continued, "It was clear to me things would have to happen. There are too many people involved in our lives. The second that they signed that contract, it all became too much. I was happy when he asked me to get rid of this deal. Your brothers will never forgive them for losing you, and they will eliminate them for their weakness. It will all fall apart now. And then it will just be me and my brother, just as it always should have been."

Who the fuck was he? Who had approached him? I was so confused. "What?"

He didn't answer me. "Walk."

With no choice, I did. Although I left my heart bleeding on the floor and knew that the other parts of it would be rushing home too.

I didn't know if I'd ever see any of them again.

I was going off with a sick, evil man who was obsessed with his brother. *Talk about family issues*. Nothing should be funny right now. But that was.

Ridiculously so.

* * *

I didn't know how long I had been wherever I was. The thought woke me. I'd long since stopped rousing from every sound I heard coming toward me. They had to shake me awake to torture me. It was like my body had gone into survival mode, declaring that I would have as much rest as possible to live through this, even if that were contrary to what I should be doing.

But I didn't know how long I'd been like this.

I smoothed my hands over the blanket that I'd laid on top of on the floor. It wasn't soft, but it had become home to me. I'd been there at least long enough for my small, windowless room and this blanket to become home. My body hurt. They beat me yesterday. They tended to give me a break between beatings, so that I would just start healing when they'd go at it again.

Ricardo and his friends. All of them sociopaths. All of them brutal and uncaring. They hadn't broken Alejandro, but they had raped him. As a child. I shuddered at the thought. No one had raped me. At least not yet. I got the impression their sick preferences ran more in line with my husband when he was twelve than toward a woman's body, anyway.

Was Francisco dead?

I didn't know.

No one would tell me.

If they knew.

I hummed to myself. It was a song my mother used to sing that I hadn't thought about since she died. She loved the Beatles. "Here

Comes the Sun." It was funny, really, how I lay there singing. I was pretty sure they were surprised by how long I was lasting. Most people went fast, apparently.

They wanted me to be unable to say the names of my guys. I didn't stop. I said their names aloud as frequently as I could.

See, the thing was that I wasn't just some girl that they'd decided to torture. My family was just as dark as the Hernandez family. Maybe darker, depending on the day. That darkness lived in my blood. Even my mother's family was connected—they weren't the superstars that my father's family became, but they were tough too. Survival pulsed in my blood. And revenge.

There would be revenge for this.

When I could pick up my hand without it hurting, I became pretty sure they'd broken something this time.

Ricardo had done it himself. *Stupid fucking asshat.*

It hurt, but it was almost like I'd become so accustomed to pain that it took more and more of it for me to notice it. I closed my eyes as the door flung open.

"I told you not to hum," Ricardo yelled at me, in a loud, annoyed voice.

I couldn't roll over, so I didn't. I just hummed louder. He roared, grabbing onto my body.

"Rico." A voice I didn't expect to hear spoke his name. "Put her down."

He did, dropping me on my back. Ricardo answered his brother in Spanish. I could make out a few words in between others I couldn't. *Hermano. Aqui. Problema.*

Was I the problem? I had no idea how I could be. I was just there, on the floor, being broken or whatever they were doing to me.

My father-in-law didn't answer him, instead looking at me. "Young lady, you have no idea the difficulties you have caused me."

I stared back at him. "Fuck you." I didn't have it in me to be polite or pretend to be. Anything short of *I am here to rescue you* meant he could just go fuck himself.

He rolled his eyes. "There is no business happening. Everything has dried up since you were taken. All three of my sons are refusing to work. They are outright losing money by the day. Alejandro burned down several of our houses. Who burns down *houses*?"

I couldn't comment on that. I had absolutely no idea why Alejandro would be burning anything. None what-so-fucking-ever. All I could hear was that Francisco was alive. All *three sons* refused to work. That meant Francisco had made it.

My head hurt, and if I was feeling it, that meant it was really bad.

"Burning things." He shook his head. "He burned a warehouse full of product. Product!" He shouted the word the second time he said it. "And so something must be done."

I laughed. "What do you propose?"

"Things will get better when there is finally a body. My brother will disappear, and your body will appear. Everyone will mourn you. My sons—all three of them, and I can't figure out what that is about—and your brothers. I will make amends to your brothers. There will be a financial reconciliation with them. But people come out of mourning. Everyone will start earning again."

I really hated this man. His brother was a sicko who had hurt me for however long I'd been gone, and I was sure this fucker had enabled it. Now he was talking about earning while they had hurt me—truly, deeply hurt me to the point that I wasn't sure if I would ever really recover from the things they'd done.

Holding on as tightly as I could to sanity, I answered him. "How much do you plan to pay the boys in Chicago for my life? What is the going rate for killing your daughter-in-law?"

He scowled at me and lifted his gun. I closed my eyes. I wasn't going to watch myself be killed. Maybe he'd get me right in the head and I could drift away fast, not thinking of the regrets I had that would never go away.

"Get that gun away from my wife." Alejandro's voice hit me like a bomb going off, and my eyes flew open before I'd even registered that he was there. Actually, he wasn't alone. I drank in the sight of Alejandro, Javier, and Francisco, who all seemed perfectly fit. All three of them had weapons raised and pointed at their father.

For his part, my father-in-law scowled but lowered his weapon. "Okay, boys, it's time to negotiate."

"Javier," Alejandro said, ignoring his father. "Go."

Javi lowered his weapon and made his way over, kneeling down next to me. "Love." He spoke in a low voice. "You're going to be okay. I'm going to make all of this better."

I tried to smile, but it hurt, so I gave up the attempt. "I don't think that's possible."

He kissed me gently on my temple. "Yes, I can. I swear it." He picked up my wrist and placed his thumb over it. *Oh, he must be taking my pulse.* He smelled clean, fresh, and like a dream.

"There will be no negotiation. None of any kind. Francisco, take our uncle. Put him in the car. He will have no mercy. He will know only pain until we kill him, and that will not be soon. It will be ugly." He spoke directly to his uncle. "All of your people are dead. No one will help you."

Francisco looked at me. "Lily, all will be okay now."

I didn't believe him, but it was a lovely thought. "I'm so glad you're alive."

Heat flared over his gaze, and he grabbed his uncle hard, speaking low and in words I didn't understand. My head was starting to feel heavy like I might just lose consciousness. That was a funny feeling. Why was that happening?

"You left me to his people all those years ago, and now you allowed him to take my wife."

His father flared his nostrils. "I thought he'd bring you back, and when he didn't, I would eventually negotiate for your release. My brother doesn't care about money. I misjudged that. Besides, your wife was not someone you wanted. I didn't think you'd care this much."

A muscle ticked in Alejandro's jaw. "You have no idea how much I care."

"Lily, look at me." Javier caught my attention, and I smiled at him. "How many fingers am I holding up?"

I'd been communicating just fine before, but now it was a little bit harder. "Two."

"Good girl." He nodded as he gently touched parts of my body, making note of where I hurt and where I didn't. His hands were gentle, but most of me hurt.

"You have no idea how much each of us cared. I almost collapsed from the need of her, from the lack of a vital presence in my life, but I knew something. I knew if I made things hard enough for you, that you would eventually lead me straight to her. You were so fucking predictable. You see, Lily taught me something, and that was that in the end, you would all do just as I knew you would, and all I had to do was trust myself."

I'd taught him that? Wow. That was nice.

Alejandro smiled at him. "In the end, I will do as I would have been predicted to do too." With barely another glance, he shot his father in the head.

And my world fuzzed out for a long second before it officially went black.

* * *

*Alejandro*

Waiting was impossibly hard, and I hadn't gotten better at it in the eight weeks she'd been gone. Now, as I could do nothing but sit and watch her in the clinic that Javier ran, it was somehow even more interminable than the endless minutes I had to obsess over what might be happening to her while my uncle kept her.

The man I'd trusted because I'd been too blind to know that I shouldn't.

I'd heard it my whole life, family came first, and I bought into the idea completely. It had never occurred to me that they'd betray me—which proved to be a fatal error. I'd always believed it would be the

Hernandez family until the end. In some ways, that worked completely. My brothers were everything they should be. Loyal. Good. And now in a relationship with the woman I loved. A relationship I'd put them in and wouldn't dare extract them from. I'd known they were all in, but these last weeks proved it beyond a shadow of a doubt.

They loved this woman, and it was obviously going to take all three of us to keep her safe.

Maybe less hard, now that I was fully in charge of the family and had demonstrated I was willing to burn the world for her.

Literally.

Francisco stared out the window. He'd been so silent since she was taken. Not that any of us wanted to chat much, but he was utterly silent most of the time.

I wasn't the kind for platitudes, and I'd use none to describe the current situation. I didn't know if everything would be okay. It often wasn't.

My phone dinged. Her brothers were threatening to invade if I didn't produce her, and my texting that I rescued her hadn't stopped them. Only the threat of all-out war kept them home. That might not last much longer.

I would send them my uncle in pieces. That would probably help. A little.

Javier came in and placed a hand on her forehead. She slept so quietly, it was almost like she wasn't there. Only the beeping machines assured me of every breath she took and that her heart still beat.

"They didn't rape her. No evidence of that. Otherwise, it is as it seems. She's beat up so badly that I want to throw something or beat someone. And she is concussed. I'm worried about her broken nose, and I've called in a plastic surgeon to consult. I know her nose was important to her. I don't really care from my end."

I lifted an eyebrow. Did he think that I did?

"I'm the one who made her uncomfortable about that." Francisco closed his eyes like they pained him.

I patted his arm as I rose. "She'll be okay, then?"

"Physically, yes, eventually." Javier held my gaze. "But you know better than most what can happen mentally."

I took her hand in mine. She'd gone into shock at the warehouse, but since then, the drugs kept her knocked out. Hopefully, they also kept her pain far away from whatever she dreamed. "She is the reason I started to heal. We will be that for her. No one will ever again touch what is mine. If the world thought my father brutal, then they just don't know how awful I will be if someone comes near her again. She can walk down the street in any country in the world from now on, and every human being will give her respect and a wide berth. If they don't, they will die."

Francisco stepped to her other side. "I will kill anyone who looks at her funny."

Javier spoke softly. "She's going to sleep for a while, and I am going to the basement." We kept my uncle there. "There are medical tools I'm just dying to try on him."

I smiled. That sounded delightful. "When you're done, I'll take a turn."

There would no longer be any mercy. No one would get a second chance. I'd been raised to be brutal, and my uncle had seen to it that I was also heartless. She had thawed that part of me, so only she would reap the rewards of my finding my soul.

To everyone else, they would learn to obey.

Or they would die.

Badly.

I kissed her hand. *My love. My one. My only.* She was more than I could have imagined any human ever being.

The beeping told me she lived. It was the most precious sound, so I would hold onto it until her lids lifted and I could see her soul staring back at my own again. I would wait right by her side until that happened.

# 18

*Javier*

"Did you kill him?"

I turned at the sound of her voice. I'd finished with my uncle and was back in Lily's room. She awakened sooner than I would've expected, and I certainly didn't intend for her to see me covered in blood. I finished washing my hands and disinfected before I turned to regard her, half expecting her to have fallen back asleep.

Since I was done, my brothers had gone down to take their turns. In a place like ours, no one paid attention if someone was screaming. Besides, it was unlikely anyone could hear Tio yelling, anyway. There were very thick walls.

But Lily was awake still, and I approached her fast. "How are you feeling?"

"Terrible." She didn't lie, which I appreciated. "But better, I'd imagine, than whoever's blood you're wearing."

She still had her sense of humor. "I didn't kill him."

But I'd wanted to. More than anything. He might wish he were dead, but he was still breathing and I intended to keep him that way a long, long time. Yes, this was the worst kind of revenge, but I'd never acted like I was anything other than who I am. A part of me would always be brutal.

Lily told me not to fear my dark side. I never feared it, but I liked that she didn't.

She made a sound that told me she was in pain, a fact I already knew from how high her pulse spiked. "On a scale of one to ten, how bad do you feel right now?"

Glossy eyes met mine, but she understood me. "A ten, but I don't want to end this addicted. I've told you, I don't want to drown in the bathtub hyped up on too many pills."

"And I told you that I would take care of you. I will. That includes accidental drownings in the bathtub. But for now" —I put her hand on the machine that would dole out medication when she needed it— "push that and take as much as you want to ease your pain."

She nodded, hit the button, and closed her eyes. "He didn't know."

"Didn't know what?" She might already be out. I pushed over a chair and sat closer to her. I could sleep anywhere, and since I had taken care of my need to cause Tio pain, I could remain by her side for a while.

She sighed, a sweeter sound. "That I was strong. He thought I'd be weak, but I was strong."

I took her hand in mine, running my finger over her knuckles. I was pretty sure where I touched her wasn't too tender. Her other hand was broken. This one appeared okay.

I kissed the not tender spot. "You *are* strong. Incredibly strong."

"He forgot that I'm not just some girl. My people…they're pretty brutal too."

I shook my head. "Only in our circumstances would that be something that we would consider a plus. But yes, for us, it's a real bonus." She tried to smile and winced. I wished she'd take a little more pain meds. Knock herself out for longer.

We would bring her home tomorrow or the next day. Well, back to Mexico City. We didn't currently have a home there, not since Alejandro had woken us up and told us to get out because he was burning it down. It hadn't seemed like a great idea in that moment to argue with the man who'd clearly crossed into a mental territory that was beyond normal. As it turned out, he'd been incredibly brilliant in pretending his madness. Father had led us right to her.

"Don't kill him." Her voice was low. "I want to kill him."

Now that was a shift. I'd wondered how our life would change her. For all that she'd been raised in the business, she really wasn't part of it before her marriage to my brother. Her brothers had done a good job of keeping her from these things. We'd thrown all of that away, even if we hadn't meant to. She wouldn't be who she was before ever again.

But she was always going to be mine. "I love you. And we'll see."

"Love you too." Her eyes fluttered closed. That was good. I settled in to sit with her until morning. There was absolutely nowhere else I needed to be. Ever.

* * *

*Francisco*

We weren't able to take her home because the plastic surgeon that Javier had called in arrived. They decided to operate on her again. The change of plans extended her stay in the clinic by a week. On one hand, it was a good thing, because she had more time with the nurses, and the doctor thought her face was going to heal with no trouble. I rubbed my eyes. I was the one who'd made that stupid remark about her being prettier than I'd thought she was going to be on the first day we'd met.

As she'd endured the pain of more work being done on her, I couldn't help but think it was my fault. I'd tried to tell her that it didn't matter, about how she didn't have to go through more pain.

She was gorgeous, yes, but I would love her no matter what she looked like. We all would. Still. She didn't listen to me.

But we were alone now. Javier was taking more of his frustration out on our uncle—I was done with that. If I saw him again, I was going to kill him—and Alejandro was moving product where it needed to go. He was the man in charge, and there had to be business or he would lose the role. He could work some from the clinic, but work called for a face-to-face meeting, so he needed to leave for a while.

She stared at me. "At some point, you're going to have to speak to me, Francisco."

I lifted my head. "I've been talking to you."

That got her attention. "Have I been ignoring you?" She winced. I couldn't be sure if my words caused it or if the uncomfortable expression stemmed from physical pain that still rode her. She'd be in pain for a long time to come, and I couldn't change that.

"No." I rose. "You've been pretty out of it."

She held out her hand. "What have you said that I haven't heard?"

"That you didn't have to fix your nose." I pointed at my own. "Or go through any more pain. That it wasn't necessary."

She squeezed my fingers. "I needed it. I wasn't going to be okay leaving it like that. I'm vain, you know that."

I sank down into the chair closer to her bed. "We're all vain, in one way or another. Maybe someone out there isn't. I'd like to meet that someone someday."

"I'm so glad that you're okay." She sighed. "I worried, not knowing."

Well, we were finally getting to the heart of what she and I had to say to one another. I wasn't going to bring it up until we were home and she was feeling better. "We can talk about that later."

I rubbed at my shoulder. It didn't hurt. Sometimes it got stiff, but that was it. I'd been lucky, but I should have been dead.

"Let's talk about it now. You and I don't do sullen and silent. Talk to me. What is it that you want to say?"

It was hard to even speak. I'd carried it for so long while she was gone, and part of me didn't think I had the right to really ever let it go. But she wanted my truth, so I would give it to her. Lily could have whatever she wanted, whenever she wanted it.

Even the words I didn't want to speak.

"You should have let me die and saved yourself." There, I'd said it. "My job is to protect you, not the other way around. They took you because I failed. For that, I ask your forgiveness, and I would have your promise that you will never, ever do that again. That you will watch out for yourself."

She opened and closed her mouth. "Francisco, there is no need for an apology. You certainly aren't responsible for what happened, but no, you can't have that promise."

There were men in the world who would cower rather than speak to me that way. Lily did so with no fear whatsoever. Just *no*. That was all there was to it. "Lily…"

"I love you. That means that I get to decide what risks I take and what is worth it to me. Saving you? That is worth it to me. I will do that every time, all the time, whether you like it or not."

I blinked, her words bringing up tears that I didn't dare allow to the surface. Had anyone ever cared so much about me? I didn't think so. Lily loved me like I mattered. It was beautiful and all-consuming. I could hardly breathe from the power behind her words.

"I love you too."

I kissed her because I had to. Her lips were sweet, and her sigh was all I needed to survive another day.

"We'll just have to take care to never end up in that situation again, then, Checco."

I loved when she used my childhood nickname, like she'd always been with us. "We'll have to take care, yes, but we've done something to make sure you will always be safe."

"Like what?'

I kissed her nose. "You're just going to have to wait and see."

She pretended to pout and then shifted her attention to the door before looking at me again. "Can you do something for me? There is something I want to do before I go home."

"Anything." I meant it.

* * *

*Lily*

I stopped in the doorway of the room where my torturer was being tortured. I don't know what I expected to see, but the man slumped over in the corner wasn't it. For two months, he'd put me through hell, yet he looked pathetic rather than terrifying.

Javier stood in the corner. He said something to Francisco in Spanish, who in turn, shrugged. Javi wasn't happy that I was there, but Checco didn't much care. There had to be a period that I could put on this sentence.

Tio Ricardo lifted his head to stare at me. They'd done damage to this man. Beaten. Cut. Dried blood on his hand, some dripping down his face. Lest I ever forget that my husband and his brothers were dangerous, the proof sat before me. They were as dangerous as to be expected in our world, just more circumspect about who deserved their violence.

It would never be me.

I turned slightly toward Francisco. "Let me use your gun."

He pulled his out from its usual spot and handed it to me. I stepped closer to the man on the floor. They'd chained him up like an abused dog. I'd have more sympathy for an animal. This monster deserved it. Not just because of what he'd done to me, but because of all the others. The ones who weren't alive to make him pay.

"You hurt me," I said, as if the list of his crimes started with myself. As Francisco said, we were all vain, and I'd add to that premise that we were all also narcissists, but that wasn't all that we were. At least the people in our world. We had to choose which sides of our light and darkness would be embraced.

I continued, "I forgive you for that."

He hadn't asked for my forgiveness, and perhaps he didn't deserve it. Still, me saying the words freed me of him.

No one spoke, giving me the time to finish speaking. "There is, however, no forgiveness for the other things you've done. The people you've hurt. What you did to a person that I love." What Alejandro endured trumped anything I'd been through. "Those women that you made into your dollies? There is no forgiveness for that, not any that I can give you, anyway. Maybe you're a believer, so when you meet your Maker, you'll face the Almighty's consequences. Maybe you're not. I don't know, and honestly, I don't care. All I can think when I close my eyes is about that woman who sewed her mouth shut so that she'd never accidentally betray you, after you'd warped her mind."

Guadalupe might have been our enemy, but I had no doubt she'd been the biggest victim of the situation. I'd survived. Alejandro had too. I didn't have the names of others who hadn't. Guadalupe represented all of them to me. She hadn't come back, not really.

"You made them your dollies." I lifted my gun. "So I'm going to make you nothing. A footnote in our life that no one remembers even lived. Your life was nothing."

I fired.

Long after the bullet tore his head apart and the ringing stopped in my ears, I still didn't move. Finally, a gentle hand touched my wrist, catching my attention and taking the gun from me. Alejandro was there. When had he arrived? He handed the weapon back to Francisco and then took me in his arms.

"Lily, that was brave."

It hadn't been. I was at no risk. Nothing was going to happen to me. That defined bravery to me, not what I'd done. It had, however, solved that problem for me. I couldn't move on while that man lived. He was gone. That was enough.

I'd needed to be the one to do it. To end him myself.

Tears leaked from my eyes, and I dug my forehead into Alejandro's shoulder. "I guess you can have my tears now."

He pulled me even closer, his strong arms holding me so tightly, I couldn't move if I'd wanted to—which I absolutely didn't.

"Give them to me," he whispered in my ear. "I love you, Lily. Every single thing about you."

I closed my eyes and smiled. "Told you that you'd say it first."

He laughed, shaking his head. "You did. That is true."

"I love you too."

* * *

*I'm fine. I just don't want to talk about it.* I sent the same message to my brothers that I'd been sending all day. They were like a dog with a bone, not wanting to let this go. I could tell them about what I'd been through, but the truth was that they weren't the ones I wanted to talk to about my experiences. I would need some kind of therapy and I'd see to it that I got the help I needed, but listening to my brothers' feelings on the matter was more than I could handle right then.

I appreciated that they loved me, in their own way. We were all victims to the whims of our fathers.

Alejandro stared at me from across the room from where he worked while I wrote a paper. Well, sort of wrote it. One-handed was a problem, so I dictated it. Strangely, it was as if since I couldn't use my fingers, then I couldn't get it done. The thought process that went from my brain to my fingertips was incredibly different when I needed my mouth involved. Somehow, it short-circuited my brain.

"They still harassing you?"

I laughed. "They don't want to let it go."

"I can tell them to stop." He closed his laptop and pulled out his earbuds that he used to not hear me speaking aloud to work on my paper.

"No, that's extreme. Something or someone will distract them eventually." Wasn't my oldest brother supposed to be getting married too? To the daughter from New York? I was pretty sure that was on the agenda for him very shortly. How was that going to work out?

Alejandro tilted his head. "Have you checked your email today?"

"Not for a little while. Why? Is there something there that I need to see?"

The door opened and closed, and both of his brothers entered the room. The setup felt a little fishy. "What do you guys have going on?"

"Open your email." Javier sat down on the couch, and Francisco winked at me before he did the same.

"You guys can understand why I don't love surprises, right?" Sometimes they landed you in a wedding dress you didn't know was coming.

Alejandro shook his head. "Lily…"

I held up my good hand. "Checking it now."

There wasn't much in it—a lot of junk, some offers on clothing that I might look at later, and then finally, a letter from the university. I clicked on it, not expecting much. They made announcements all the time. The goings on that took place on campus didn't really concern me anymore.

However, this time, it absolutely did.

My mouth fell open. "What the fuck?"

"I love when she curses. It makes my cock get hard every time." Francisco grinned.

Javier held up his hand. "Too much information."

The university was making a huge announcement. They had decided they needed an even bigger international presence and therefore were opening satellite campuses around the world. As it was, my particular degree could now be achieved on the campus in Chicago and also, taught in English, in Mexico City.

I stared at the words almost not believing them and then back at my husbands. Alejandro had joined them on the couch, so they were all lined up together, looking as innocent as if they had no idea what I'd just read.

Which one of them had done this? I pointed at them each individually. "How did you do this?"

"What are you talking about?" Alejandro stretched his feet out to put them on the coffee table. "Javier, do you think she needs to go lie down? Is she sick?"

Javier nodded, slowly. "Maybe."

"Looks pale," Francisco said, agreeing with the other two.

I rose. "Seriously. Who did you threaten? What did you do?"

"It's not always about threatening. Sometimes it is about paying the right people to do what they didn't know they wanted to do ahead of time." Javier yawned. "So, you finish your paper, since you're going to be able to do what you wanted to do. You'll just do it from here."

Faster than I had been moving lately, I threw my arms around all of them. "I should be angry at all of you. You didn't have to interfere. Only I'm so glad that you did. I'm incredibly glad. Thank you." I kissed them on their lips, one after the other.

Their arms all came around me, which was awkward but also fun. I wasn't sure how things could get any better.

* * *

Music and voices blended to become a wall of sound in the club, but I still didn't know why I was there. When they said they wanted to celebrate, I thought maybe they wanted to get a cake or something. Instead, with my multiple casts, I sat at a table with expensive champagne I wasn't going to drink on pain medication, being stared at by beautiful people, a lot of whom were our associates. I still looked beat up. It had only been weeks since I'd been rescued.

"Can we go home now?" I shouted to Javier, who was on one side of me, while Francisco was on the other.

Across from us at the table sat Alejandro. They'd been very particular about how they wanted us to sit.

"She wants to go home," he said to Alejandro.

"Why? You look so pretty in that dress."

My mouth fell open. Had he actually complimented me? That was a change. "Thank you. But yes, I want to go home."

"Sure, we can do that," Francisco answered. The entire situation felt orchestrated, like the email from my university. What were these three up to?

I'd no sooner wondered about it when Francisco leaned over and kissed me, hard. Tongue and everything. *We are in public*. What was he doing? I pushed back. "What are you thinking? People are staring."

"Yes." Javier turned me around and then repeated his brother's actions. "We know."

Alejandro grinned at me, leaning over the table to add his own kiss to the stack. "You see, we decided that there was no way we were going to live in secret anymore. You belong to all of us, and we want everyone to know it. We're in charge. They can take their cues from us, or they can die. It's really that simple. So do you still want to go home, or do you want to stay here and make a scene that everyone will be talking about for a very long time?"

I grinned. I couldn't believe that I was going to say this, but I was. "Let's make a scene."

"That's what I thought." Javier kissed me again. "Let them talk and talk."

This was how they were making me safe. If I was too well-known to kill, too infamous to be taken, then I'd always be okay wherever I was.

Drawing attention to me seemed counterintuitive, but it was just what Alejo had done with the fires. He'd made it impossible to ignore until something had to be done. No one was going to mess with me if I was all of their woman.

And we made a very big scene. I kissed and *kissed* them.

The next morning, when I woke up between Francisco and Alejandro, with the sounds of Javier in the kitchen, I saw my phone was blinking. I grabbed it to see what it said.

*What the fuck is going on down there in Mexico?* Armani wanted to know. *I've had five calls this morning.*

What the fuck, indeed? So much stuff. Where would I even begin? I grinned. In the arms of my men, that was where everything began, and where I wanted my happily ever after for the rest of our lives.

Thank you for reading Gunmetal Lilly. I hope you enjoy the next book in the series.
Ruining Dahlia by C.R. Jane.

# ABOUT THE AUTHOR

As a teenager, I would hide in my room to read my favorite romance novels when I was supposed to be doing my homework.

I am the mother of three adorable boys and I am fortunate to be married to my best friend. I live in Austin Texas where I am determined to eat all the barbecue in town.

I am in love with science fiction, fantasy, and the paranormal and try to use all of these elements in my writing. I've been told I'm a little bloodthirsty so I hope that when you read my work you'll enjoy the action packed ride that always ends in romance. I love to write series because I love to see characters develop over time and it always makes me happy to see my favorite characters make guest appearances in other books.

In my world anything is possible, anything can happen, and you should suspect that it will.

I'd love to hear from you! Please visit my website at www.rebeccaroyce.com to sign up for my newsletter and learn about my books!

Here's where you can find me online:

Rebecca's Randomness Reading Group https://www.facebook.com/groups/RebeccasRandomness/

https://www.rebeccaroyce.com

https://www.facebook.com/authorrebeccaroyce/

www.twitter.com/rebeccaroyce

Instagram: rebeccaroyce79

Cheers!!

Rebecca

# BOOKS BY REBECCA ROYCE

**Contemporary Romance**

**Redheads:**

Redhead on the Run

Redheaded Redemption

Real Men Love Redheads (coming soon)

**Reverse Harem Story (completed series)**

Unconventional

Unexpected

Undeniable

**Kiss Her Goodbye (completed series)**

Hard Truths

Dark Truths

Deadly Truths

**Stupid Boys** (writing with C.R. Jane)

Stupid Boys

Dumb Girl

Crazy Love (coming soon)

**Science Fiction Romance:**

**Wings of Artemis (completed series)**

Kidnapped By Her Husbands

Rescued by Their Wife

Crashing Into Destiny

Meeting Them

Reclaiming Their Love

Loving Them

Ship Called Malice

Saving Them

Dark Demise

Light Unfolding

Still Waters

Rising Tides

Lost Star

Pointed Arrow

**Illicit Minds**

Illicit Senses

Illicit Connections

Illicit Alliance (coming soon)

**Shifter World**

Planet Bear

Planet Cat

Planet Wolf (coming soon)

**Heart of the Nebula** (writing with Heather Long) **completed series**

Queenmaker

Deal Breaker

Throne Taker

**Stranded Hearts** (writing with Vivien Jackson)

The Girl Who Fell From The Sky

The Girl Who Crossed The Stars (coming soon)

**Through the Gates** (writing with Skye MacKinnon)

Purgatory City

Infernal Land (coming soon)

**Paranormal Romance:**

**Last Hope (completed series)**

Tradition Be Damned

Past Be Damned

Destiny Be Damned

Compassion Be Damned

Future Be Damned

**Dragon Wars (completed series)**

Forever

Eternal

Always

Evermore

Endless

**Wards and Wands (completed series)**

Hexed and Vexed

Curse Reversed

Meow, Baby (novella, co-written with Ripley Proserpina)

Tragic Magic

**Safe Haven**

Everywhere and Nowhere

Dimension X (coming soon)

More coming soon….

**Soul Bound**

Prisoner of the Dragons

More coming soon….

**Shadow Promised**

Strange Days

Weird Nights

Haunted Years

More coming soon…

**The Westervelt Wolves (completed series)**

Her Wolf

Summer's Wolf

Wolf Reborn

Wolf's Valentine

Wolf's Magic

Alpha Wolf

Angel's Wolf

Darkest Wolf

Lone Wolf

**Fallen Alpha**

Alpha Rising

Alpha's Strength

Alpha's Sacrifice

Alpha's Truth

Alpha Enticing

Hidden Alpha (coming soon)

**Cascade (completed series)**

Haunted Redemption

Phoenix Everlasting

Fragility Unearthed

Persuasion Enraptured

**The Swamp (completed series)**

Hidden

Pursued

Caught

**The Coveted** (writing with Ripley Proserpina)

Eyes in the Darkness

Voices in the Darkness

Return to the Darkness

**Prison Princess** (part of the Prison Princess world, writing with CoraLee June)

**Young Adult/New Adult Urban Fantasy/Post-Apocalyptic:**

**The Warrior (completed series)**

Initiation

Driven

Subversive

Redemption

Justice

**Warrior World (spin off of The Warrior, completed series)**

Deacon

Micah

Jason

**Fantasy Romance:**

**The Outsiders**

Love Beyond Time

Love Beyond Sanity

Love Beyond Loyalty

Love Beyond Sight

Love Beyond Expectations

Love Beyond Oceans

Love Beyond Flames

Love Beyond Lies

Love Beyond Death (coming soon)

**The Storm** (writing with Ripley Proserpina) **completed series.**

Lightning Strikes

Thunder Rolling

The Deluge

**Stand Alone Titles**

Under The Lights

No Quitting Allowed

Mr. Wrong

Bite Marks

Bitten Surrender

The Vampire and The Virgin

Demon Within

Crimson Lust

Call Me Crazy

The Men of Elite Metal

Gunmetal Lily

Made in United States
Orlando, FL
17 February 2024

43819584R00139